D0592662

Asleep
At The
Wheel

ASLEEP AT THE WHEEL

JOHN R. HANNY

Rutledge Books, Inc. RB Danbury, CT

Cover design by Frank J. Russom

Interior design by Sharon Gelfand

Rutledge Books, Inc.
107 Mill Plain Road, Danbury, CT 06811
1-800-278-8533
www.rutledgebooks.com

Manufactured in the United States of America

Cataloging in Publication Data
Hanny, John R.

Asleep at the Wheel

ISBN: 1-58244-220-7

1. Fiction

Library of Congress Control Number: 2001127227

Dedication

To all the good people of this world who desire peace
and the willingness to live together,
let it happen.

Out of courtesy to the United States Secret Service
and their ability to protect the president,
certain facts pertaining to the layout of the White House
have been altered or omitted.

* * * * *

The garden of the world near the new city
in the road of the hollow mountains.
It will be plunged in the tank, forced to drink
water poisoned with sulpher (CXQ49)
—Nostradamus

Acknowledgments

A very special thank you must go to my brothers Jim and Bud; everyone should be as blessed.

To Marilyn Smith and Kim Phipps of Rutledge Books for taking those steps to help a novice; that extra mile is appreciated.

To my children: Michelle, Lisa, Jane, Jennifer, Kristen and Jason. I love you.

To Frank Russom for his artistic expertise and extra-special effort with the book cover.

To Dee Dee Sandy and Judi Ziegler for all your work on this manuscript.

To Kelley Culmer, the world's best agent, many hugs for all your hard work.

To my dearest friends who are more than any man deserves: Bill Derrick, Paul Cleary and Bonnie Ann Powell. Life is so much better knowing you.

To Joe Gonzales for his photography.

And last of all, to my beautiful cocker spaniels, Wilma and LuLu, who never left my side during this whole project.

You all have one thing in common—YOU HAVE NO PEERS.

Be well always,

Jack

PREFACE

ON TUESDAY, SEPTEMBER 11, 2001, UNDER A CLOUD OF EVIL, AN ACT OF war was brought upon the United States of America.

I, as well as all Americans and decent people on Earth, witnessed an unprovoked attack on Washington, D.C. and New York City.

These madmen are the common enemy of the civilized world.

Three and one-half years ago, I woke from a horrible nightmare. At 4:00 a.m., visibly shaken, I went to my desk and immediately journalized what I dreamt, hence this novel.

This book, although a work of fiction, clearly shows what some of the world thinks of us. They call us the "Great Satan" and despise us. They are willing to die to bring us down. We must take serious precautions to prevent this from ever happening again. We must never allow a repeat performance.

Days, dates, and times are figments of my imagination. However, after consulting with some retired army generals and admirals, as well as some of the world's best profilers, plus other experts on terrorism, this work is as factual as it can get.

All scientific data are real, as are some of the characters— and you know who you are.

While researching this book, someone turned me in to the federal authorities. Three agents showed themselves at my door questioning my interest in weapons of mass destruction. I told them I was writing a book on terrorism and offered my research papers as proof. At that point they left, and the agency or someone else put a monitor on my phone. I could tell because of the different sound the phone made. It was on for a month or so and then it was removed.

I only wish for the benefit of the world these cowardly acts would cease.

Until then, a warning to all—never, never again let our government fall asleep at the wheel.

I would like to donate one-half of my royalty, as well as one-half of all speaking fees, to an education fund for the children of those lost at the World Trade Center and the Pentagon.

John R. Hanny
September 11, 2001

PROLOGUE

THE AIR UNDER THE HEAVY BLACK HOOD WAS STALE AND THICK WITH incense, tobacco smoke and the smell of sweat. Warren Dunn had lost track of how long he had been standing in the same place, hands at his sides, the world lost to the blackness under the hood. He strained to hear any sound that would give him a clue to what was happening around him, but found only silence.

He wasn't afraid of the threat of physical pain. Nor was he afraid of the uncertainty of the situation. He was very afraid of who might be assessing him while he stood, naked, hooded, alone, and somewhere he could not identify. Who would be making this decision about him and why wouldn't they allow him to speak for himself, sell himself, show his powers of persuasion and quick thinking to their best effect? He had no control over the situation, and that frightened him.

When the members of the Bohemian Club initially approached him, he had been stunned by their proposal. They wanted him to apply for membership. The handsome, dignified, forty-something senator had invited him for cigars and brandy after the inauguration of the new governor of Oklahoma. He had complimented Warren on his quick rise through the ranks of young executives at OILCO. As a member of the Bohemian Club, the senator told Dunn that it sought men with his potential, and offered to be his sponsor. Dunn only briefly questioned their motives. He was quickly assured that his ambition, his lust for power, and his greed were just what they were looking for.

That was three months ago. Since then, Warren Dunn had been scrutinized, interviewed, checked and cross-checked, and, he suspected, tested. Temptations were placed in his path to challenge his commitment. Warren must have passed, because now he stood waiting for the next step in the hazing process and his entry into the secret world of the Bohemian Club. His mind raced with the many possibilities that the situation presented, knowing that none could be as exciting as the reality.

Rumors about the Bohemian Club were rampant. Most of them seemed rather far-fetched to Warren. The sex parties and junkets to prime vacation spots, the drug use and gambling were exciting as far as rumor went, but he was far more interested in the wealth and the power.

Warren Dunn kept replaying in his mind the last conversation he'd had with his sponsor, hearing the self-satisfied tones of the senator's voice as Dunn was told that the club had great plans for him, and that he was going to "go places."

"My boy," the gentleman said placing his cold, skeletal hand on the young Dunn's shoulder, "there are so many things wrong with the way the world is being run right now. Our members have all dedicated themselves to solving those problems, and to making the world a better place, under one government."

"One government?" Dunn was confused, he'd never considered that before.

"Yes, Warren. One government would mean one currency, one economic system. What is the single greatest cause of war on this planet?"

"Religion," Dunn answered simply.

The gentleman laughed, "Religious zealots have seen their day. They are no longer a threat to total power. No, now the biggest threat is differing economies. People are inherently greedy. If we can unite the world under one system it will end the threat of war."

Dunn was impressed. It was a clean, simple solution, and he liked that.

"One nice side effect of our efforts is an increase in power and power equals money." The man fixed Dunn with a deep probing look. "And there's nothing wrong with that, is there? If we do the work of uniting the world, everyone benefits, as do we."

Dunn grinned broadly. He was going to like it here.

One

Executive Offices, OILCO
Oklahoma City, Oklahoma

WARREN DUNN, CEO OF OILCO, PRESIDED AT THE HEAD OF THE LONG cherry wood table that stretched the full length of OILCO's massive main conference room. The table was ringed by various associates of the billionaire, but the guests of honor—Oklahoma governor and presidential candidate David Walsh, and his chief of staff Ian Tuttle—held the places to Dunn's right and left. The room was heavy and still as all faces turned to Dunn, breaths held in anticipation.

Dunn addressed Walsh, "Governor, there is no doubt that you will be our next president." David Walsh raised an eyebrow and looked at Dunn, his face otherwise expressionless. Warren continued, a sly smile spreading his lips, "Money is no problem—just tell me how much—thirty million, thirty-five million? Just name it." Those assembled around the table stirred as one, shifting uncomfortably in their seats. Dunn glanced around warningly before turning his attention back to the governor.

"Thank you, Warren, but don't you think that such an offer may be seen as, well, inappropriate?"

"If not in direct violation of campaign finance law," Ian Tuttle murmured just loud enough for Walsh to hear.

Dunn grinned wider, "No need to worry, gentlemen. While I understand how touchy such contributions could be, we have resources to divert the funds through channels that will make it legal." Warren's expression clouded momentarily, his look an obvious warning to anyone in attendance who might be willing to risk a career by pointing out the fallacy of his last statement.

"Thank you, Warren, you know that I appreciate your offer. Ian, arrange with Mr. Dunn for a modest contribution—we don't want to violate any financing regulations." Walsh grinned as he favored the room with a look that was pure politician. Tuttle thought that if there had been a baby present, David Walsh would have kissed it repeatedly. Walsh turned his attention back to his benefactor. "When it's all over, Warren, I wish you would reconsider the ambassadorship. I can promise you your pick of posts," Walsh glanced at Tuttle who managed to keep his own face emotionless, "perhaps to the court of St. James, or France, or how about Russia?"

"Just think of it, Warren," Tuttle smiled up at him, "all that Siberian oil!" Polite laughter echoed around the room.

"No thank you, governor," Dunn said graciously with a small bow. "My job is right here." He gestured expansively around the mahogany paneled room. "All I ask is a little help lining up the countries my OILCO needs to kick OPEC in the ass." He grinned widely, and was rewarded with the head bobbing-laughter of a room full of yes-men.

"As you know, governor," he continued, "the price of crude is at a twelve-year low, and consolidations such as PE/Amoco and Exxon/Mobil are a concern. The customer base is shrinking, not to mention the increase in natural gas production here in Oklahoma."

Dunn stepped around the table to face one wall covered by an intricately detailed map of the world. He carried himself like a man who planned to rule that world. "The industry overheated a couple of years ago and we're facing a global downturn. Just look at what it costs to lift the oil out of the ground. It's almost impossible to make any serious money." He fixed the governor with a hard gaze, driving his point home with his look as well as his words.

"We all know that one must spend money to make money, and our investment is in you. You alone can be trusted, governor." Warren continued his circuit of the room. Ian Tuttle watched with interest as each of Dunn's staff seated around the table noticeably stiffened when the man stepped behind his chair. The atmosphere grew thick, and the smell of nervous sweat began to taint the cooled air. "At this moment, we're drilling dick shit, David. With all of the mergers and what have you, OILCO's salvation is in the control of Middle East oil production. We need to have it firmly in our grasp and then we can tell our competition, and OPEC, to fuck off." Dunn spun around to face Walsh directly.

"Imagine the benefit to the United States, David—cheaper fuel oil and gasoline, more tourism, more disposable income, the trickle-down will be enormous!" Warren Dunn smiled while imagining his real intent—increased prices and control of supply—to inflate his own fortune and to line his own pockets.

David Walsh stood, sliding the huge leather chair back before stepping around it. "Warren, you won't be disappointed." Walsh strode across the room to where Dunn stood before the huge plate-glass window overlooking downtown Oklahoma City. He extended his hand. "I'm going to leave you in Ian's capable hands. Ian, work with Warren and his people to get the details solidified. The sooner we get moving, the sooner we will see results." The governor pumped Dunn's hand vigorously. "Warren, I'll see you next week."

Dunn watched Walsh stride from the room, shaking hands and slapping backs on his way out. The governor was a seasoned politician; his public approval ratings were high; and there was no doubt that he could do the job. Warren smiled a tight smile before turning back to Ian Tuttle. "Ian, let's go talk this out over a cigar." He gestured toward the door that led to his private study.

Tuttle dropped into an overstuffed leather chair and helped himself to a Havana Dunn kept in an inlaid ebony box on the side table. Dunn poured them each a single-malt scotch before joining him.

"Are you sure that we can count on him, Ian?"

"Not to worry," he replied, puffing smoke into a cloud around his head. "Walsh can't afford the kind of campaign that will guarantee a waltz into the White House. You can provide that. Our boy has expensive tastes. The more we feed that and his ego, the more control we'll have. We can funnel all donations through your channels, and he won't even know how much money you've provided."

"Then tell me, just what the hell was that crap about campaign finance law?" Dunn's voice was quiet but held a threatening edge that usually brought his opponents to their knees. Tuttle just waved the smoke away from his eyes and smiled.

"Warren, David has to believe I have his best interests at heart. I have to watch out for him. If I look too eager, he'll get suspicious." Ian Tuttle grinned as the other man's expression softened slightly.

Dunn fixed Tuttle with a warning look. "Don't you ever forget who you really work for, Ian. You may report to him, but I am the one who controls those reports—don't ever forget that." A quiet menace underlined every word. Tuttle wasn't stupid enough to forget who held the purse strings. He'd worked too hard to get this deep into Dunn's organization to ever forget that.

"Warren, I am not very likely to forget that." Ian's tone was soothing, not quite conciliatory. "I know which side my bread is buttered on, and with what. Twenty to thirty million barrels a day plus what you're already producing will put you over the top. And when people are paying $3.00 to $4.00 per gallon for gas, I anticipate my butter getting sweeter with every barrel."

"Save the flowery imagery for Congress. Profit isn't a four letter word, but fuck is. And fucked is what we'll be if we don't all have a nice profitable wet dream. Do you follow me, Ian?"

Ian smiled, rolling the fat cigar between his long, well-manicured fingers. "Like a bull moose in rut, Warren."

"Your butter is in that case. Get to work; I have another meeting."

Tuttle drained his scotch, knocked the ashes off the cigar and hefted the case before saluting Dunn with a wave of his hand and striding, a little too self-confidently, out of the room.

Dunn watched the door where Tuttle had disappeared for a moment, then reached for the telephone. The line rang only once before the familiar, self-satisfied voice answered, "Yes, Warren, do we have our president?"

Dunn smiled, "Yes, I believe we do."

* * *

Ian rode the elevator the thirty-five floors down to the parking garage, all the while smiling at the small security camera in the ceiling. He pulled his sports car out of the garage into the brilliant sunshine of the Oklahoma afternoon. He only made it as far as a small park, a few blocks from OILCO, before he couldn't resist pulling over and snapping open the suitcase. Inside he found stacks of old hundred dollar bills, ten thousand of them in all. A cool million just for putting a deal together and baby-sitting the next president of the United States. He riffled a stack of bills before stuffing them in his wallet. He had a few vices to satisfy before he headed back to the governor's office. "It might be good to be king," he said aloud to the empty car, "but it's a hell of a lot better to be the kingmaker."

Two

Inauguration Day
Washington, D.C.

DAVID WALSH SAT AT THE BREAKFAST TABLE, THE MORNING PAPERS spread out before him. The headlines screamed his name and articles repeated the extent of his victory. Self-satisfaction practically oozed from his pores. He had won hands down, barely a contest from his rival who had slunk back to whatever backwater he had come from. Walsh stopped himself in mid-thought. What was he doing? Was he slipping into the same slimy behavior he had loathed in other politicians all his life? He had won, he suspected, due to the help he had managed to secure for himself from certain parties in Oklahoma. The point was the people had elected him and now it was up to him to make sure he lived up to the expectations of the American public. In short, he was determined to be the best damned president who had ever occupied the White House.

Walsh chuckled to himself while he folded up the papers and cleared some room for his coffee cup. These were probably the same thoughts of every man who ever faced Inauguration Day in Washington, D.C. He was no different, but he would be. There was no doubt about that.

"Time to leave, sir." Ian Tuttle slid into the room, his crisp Armani suit hardly making a whisper as he moved. Walsh looked up at the almost too well-kept man he had appointed his chief of staff. "Mrs. Walsh is waiting for you downstairs." Tuttle stepped to the side and gestured obsequiously toward the door. Walsh drew a deep breath, forced his nerves into check and stood. He fought to keep his own nervous excitement from showing, fought to keep from dashing to the door like a six year old. Tuttle reached out and brushed off the shoulders of Walsh's suit as he passed. Walsh shivered slightly at the man's touch. Startled by the reaction he managed not to flinch, but glanced back at his chief of staff, who smiled tightly.

"Well, let's get on with it!" Walsh marched out of the room.

* * *

The opening speeches that accompanied the transfer of power seemed to drag on forever. Walsh allowed his attention to wander over the assembled politicos, dignitaries and tycoons who filled the bleachers surrounding the podium. He could pick out many faces he recognized, supporters and opponents alike. Then he saw Warren Dunn himself, sitting like a king in the front row seat, a huge smile wrapped around the unlit cigar he clenched in his teeth. Dunn raised one hand to his forehead in a small salute and grinned even wider. Walsh returned the grin with a small, inconspicuous smile, then returned his attention to the podium.

The air was crisp that day, but comfortable. Next to him, his wife, Sarah, an environmental issues attorney, sat straight and tall in her tailored blue suit and crisp white blouse, the blue topaz pendant he had given her for their twenty-fifth anniversary sparkling at her throat. "Jesus, she's beautiful," Walsh thought smiling. "She will make an amazing First Lady."

David Walsh was pulled back into the moment when he heard his vice president, Harry Dent, reciting the oath of office. The crowd broke into applause and Walsh braced himself—the moment he had been waiting for most of his life was finally here. Right on cue, he stood and walked to the podium. Sarah stepped beside him, his mother's Bible cradled in her arms. The outgoing president stood to the side with his own First Lady. Walsh studied his face, now worn and haggard after two long, difficult terms in the seat of power. His once thick, dark hair was almost entirely white and the lines in his face were accentuated by his recent weight loss, the result of a nearly successful impeachment attempt. Even his wife showed signs of wear. Her once youthful, pretty face was now more mature, more handsome than pretty. Her own troubles showed in the lines around her eyes. Walsh wondered how much longer the couple would be able to keep their marriage together. Allegations of infidelity and the First Lady's own congressional aspirations were sure to bring more strain to their already tenuous relationship.

Precisely at 11:59 the chief justice began, "Governor Walsh, are you ready to take the oath of president of the United States?"

"I am," Walsh responded, his voice loud and echoing over the crowd. He placed his hand on the Bible Sarah held out to him.

"Please repeat after me, 'I, David Walsh . . .'"

"I, David Walsh . . ." Try as hard as he might, Walsh would never be able to remember speaking the words of the oath, only the sudden booming of the twenty-one-gun salute and the marine band belting out "Ruffles and Flourishes—Hail to the Chief."

Walsh shook hands with the chief justice and Harry Dent, then kissed his wife before turning to greet the former president and First Lady. The former president grabbed his hand warmly and leaned close to his ear. "Remember one thing if you remember nothing else," he whispered, "the man does not make the office, the office makes the man." He held onto the grip for a moment longer before releasing Walsh into what he was soon to find was the unknown.

* * *

The day was a blur, and Walsh found himself saying the same things repeatedly, possibly thousands of times. He was whisked from the congressional luncheon to the inaugural parade to one closed-door congratulatory toast after another before he and Sarah were finally dropped off at the doors of their new home, the White House. They only had an hour to change before they would begin whirlwind appearances at the eight inaugural balls being held across the nation's capital that evening. David steeled himself for the dreaded monkey suit and concentrated on the moment, long hours from now, when he would be able to slip between the sheets and lay his head down in his new bed.

"Sarah, c'mon darling, we don't have much time," he called into the dressing room. "Can you help me with this damned tie?"

Sarah flowed out of the dressing room in a full-length green satin cocktail dress that accentuated the curves of her figure and reminded him of Jackie Kennedy at the height of Camelot. She took the bow tie firmly in her elegant fingers and jerked it to and fro in a knotting ritual that David could never quite master. He smiled at her.

"David," she began, yanking rather viciously at the silk ribbon, "I think you should know that I have no intention of living here after this week."

Walsh laughed, "Ha, ha, very funny." He kissed the tip of her nose.

"David, damnit! Would you take me seriously just once in our marriage!" She was furious and Walsh was stunned. "I am not going to live in this monstrosity. I am not going to follow you about like some sort of well-dressed lapdog! And I am certainly not going to do whatever I have to do to make your political cronies happy!"

She spun away from him, her face red with an anger that had been building for a lot longer than David had realized. He stood, stunned into silence and inaction by this woman he thought he knew, but apparently did not.

"I'm sorry, David. When you first started this campaign, I specifically told you that I would support you through it. Just through it, David. I never said anything about if you won. Now I've done my share . . . "

"But, Sarah . . . " Walsh tried to stop her.

"No, David! No! I am sick and tired of every move we make, every move we've made since college, being about you and your political career. When I agreed to marry you I never agreed to give up my own life to live in your shadow. You only wanted kids because it would make you look good. Even when I wanted a dog, only a pedigree was good enough for you!" She was beginning to cry but fought hard to keep it inside. "We lived in Oklahoma City so that you could chase down the governorship even though you knew that my law practice was better off in Washington. I could not spend the time in Alaska when the *Valdez* went aground because it interfered with your agenda! Well, you've got what you wanted. You're in the White House with your purebred and your political goals. You don't need me anymore. I've done my bit, and now I'm out of here." Sarah was suddenly overwhelmed by the tears and they spilled down her face, ruining her perfect makeup and leaving tiny dark green circles on the bodice of her dress. David stood looking at her, his eyes wide and his mouth hanging open. He watched her cry for a moment before he reached out and enfolded her in his arms.

"I'm sorry, darling, so sorry. I didn't know . . ." Sarah pulled out of his embrace, swiping at her tear-stained face with her fists.

"That's just the point, David, you never know. You never pay attention. You didn't even notice yesterday at lunch with senator what's-his-name when I asked you to pass the arsenic. No, you just slid the salt shaker over to me without batting an eye! That's our marriage, David! That's all there is." She wept harder and ran into the dressing room, slamming the door on him.

Walsh was more than stunned, more than shocked. He was devastated by all the things of which he had been accused. David had tried all those years to take her into account in every decision he made. He thought he had made those decisions for her, not against her. But now that was no longer the case. All his carefully groomed illusions—and that's all they were apparently, illusions—were shattered. The joy of the day was forever ripped away from him. He needed to think. He needed to take Sarah and get away, maybe to the mountains or to that house on the lake in Wisconsin where they had vacationed. But no, he couldn't do that. He was starting his new job tomorrow and there would be no time for vacations, no time for Sarah, no time for anything but work. Walsh stared at his reflection in the mirror, half expecting Rod Serling to step out of the dressing room to let him and the unseen audience know that everything would be resolved in a thirty-minute television program, with commercials. But that wasn't the case. There was only his own hollow-eyed, empty expression and the complete silence of the empty room.

A few minutes later, the dressing room door opened slowly and Sarah stepped out. Her face was clean and perfectly made up. Her long auburn hair was swept into an elegant French twist, and her dress was neat and straight. She was the picture of cool and collected, while Walsh felt like he was wearing someone else's skin.

"I'll see you downstairs. I have to check something with Shirley before we go." And she swept out of the room again, leaving an almost palpable void where she had stood. Walsh shook himself like a dog and tried to make his tie and jacket look neat and presentable, but the glamour was gone and all he saw in the mirror was the guy he was at heart, hopelessly in love with a woman he didn't even know.

* * *

The limo ride to the first ball was tense and completely silent. The Secret Service agents, aware of the tension between their new charges, were jittery and on edge. Walsh caught the driver watching them both in the rearview mirror and finally raised the privacy window in annoyance. He watched Sarah, who only stared out the window at the passing city, her face an impassive mask. He wanted to hold her, to tell her he could change things if she would only give him the chance. She didn't have to give up her law practice. She could use her new position to promote the environmental issues on which she worked so hard, and being First Lady could further boost her goals. But he didn't dare say a word. He knew when Sarah got into this mood she had to come out of it on her own before he could talk to her reasonably. All he could do was wait.

The ring of the car phone jolted David out of his thoughts. Sarah didn't even flinch.

"Yes, what?" he said into the receiver, more harshly than he had intended.

"Mr. President," it was Ian Tuttle on the other end, "we were expecting you to arrive twenty minutes ago. I just wanted to make sure everything was all right."

"Yes, Tuttle, everything's fine," Walsh glanced at his wife. "We just had a last-minute hitch with my tie." He tried to laugh but the sound was hollow, phony.

"Is everything else all right, sir?" Tuttle put a little too much emphasis on the "else", as if he sensed something was amiss.

"Yes, Tuttle, we're in the limo now and should be there any minute." Walsh clicked off the phone and dropped it back into the carriage. "Sarah, people are going to know there's something wrong. This isn't a good time for either of us. You don't want to be caught scowling in some photo do you?" He took her hand and squeezed it gently, trying to draw her attention back into the car.

"Oh, don't worry, David, I made you a promise and I intend to keep that promise, for one more night at least." She didn't even look at him.

Sarah always kept her promises. They climbed out of the limo onto the red carpet outside of the Hay Adams Hotel and were met by a cluster of hulking Secret Service men and a mob of reporters and supporters. The camera flashes alone were enough to blind the new president, but when he looked at his wife she was the picture of contentment. She graced everyone with her beautiful smile, and Walsh could swear she looked at him with nothing but adoration. He was amazed and adoring himself. The woman was marvelous; he couldn't allow her to leave him, not after all this.

Inside the hotel they were marched down a receiving line of the wealthy and powerful, many of whom Walsh didn't recognize. He shook a thousand hands just getting into the gorgeously decorated ballroom. Inside they were escorted to their seats at the front where they had a clear view of the speakers' dais.

Tuttle slid into an empty seat beside the president.

"Congratulations again, Mr. President!" He beamed, the grin making his eyes crinkle and disappear into his face. "Mrs. Walsh, you look absolutely ravishing this evening!" Sarah nodded, not favoring Tuttle with her smile. Walsh knew there was some tension between his right-hand man and his wife. Granted, Tuttle was a bit much, maybe too ambitious, too pretentious, but he was good at his job and Sarah really had very little contact with the man.

"Mr. President, there are a couple of people here tonight who would like to see you before the speeches get started. You know you won't have much time after that." Tuttle waved to a waiter who approached timidly, eyeing the Secret Service agents surrounding the table. "Bring the First Lady a glass of champagne, would you? And Mrs. Walsh, do you mind if I borrow your husband for just a minute or two?"

Without waiting for her reply, Tuttle pulled the president out of his seat, and pointed him across the room toward a small oak door. Half of the Secret Service agents moved to surround the two men, the other half tightened their circle around Sarah, who sat looking around the room, smiling pleasantly at anyone who looked back.

"Tuttle, really, is this necessary? I don't want to leave Sarah . . . "

"Mr. Dunn would like a word or two with you, sir." Tuttle ushered him through the door into a small receiving room. One agent stood guard outside the door. The others covered the door from the inside.

"Mr. President!" Warren Dunn rose slowly as Walsh entered. He was an exceptionally tall man, made all the more apparent as he unfolded himself from the chair in the low-ceilinged room.

"Warren," Walsh shook his hand, "thank you for coming."

"I wouldn't miss this for anything!" Dunn's smile was obviously predatory, but David was too involved in his own turmoil to notice it.

"I won't keep you long. I know you have an adoring public waiting for you." Dunn motioned to a chair. "I just wanted to tell you again how happy and thrilled I am about your victory."

"Well, thank you, Warren. I couldn't have managed it without your support and that of the others." Walsh found the words, repeated for the millionth time that day, stale and dry in his mouth.

"If there is anything, anything at all I can do for you, all you need do is call. I am at your service." Dunn smiled coldly, and there was no warmth in his words.

"Again, Warren, thank you for all your support." Walsh rose.

"Now if you'll excuse me, I have to be getting back to Sarah." David stepped out of the room tailed by his Secret Service. Wrapped up in his own thoughts, he didn't notice that Tuttle had stayed behind.

"Well, well, well, what has our dear Mr. President so preoccupied, Mr. Tuttle?" Dunn asked after the door had clicked shut.

"Good question," Tuttle replied, brushing some imaginary speck of lint from the collar of his suit jacket. "Mr. and Mrs. First Family were late arriving, and I hear tell that there were raised voices in the presidential bedchamber when they were supposed to be getting dressed."

"Ah, the lovely Mrs. Walsh is causing some trouble?" Dunn turned on Ian, his voice dropping, but the menace of his tone increasing with each word. "Do not, let me repeat that, DO NOT, allow anything, not the new First Lady, or their dumb mutt, or anyone else to interfere in this plan, Tuttle. Do you understand?"

Tuttle hid his anxiety well, locking his gaze firmly on Dunn. "Of course, sir. Nothing is to interfere. I understand completely."

Dunn waved his hand impatiently at the chief of staff and turned his back as the man scuttled out the door.

Three

Warren Dunn's Private Office
Executive Offices, OILCO
Oklahoma City, Oklahoma

The motors of Warren Dunn's private elevator hummed smoothly behind the darkly paneled walls of his private office. He arranged himself in the oversized leather chair behind the hand-polished walnut desk and relit his cigar. This office was his sanctuary. Nobody was invited past its doors, or even dared to disturb him when he was locked inside. The main door leading into the front office didn't even have a doorknob. How he loved making dramatic exits from meetings by hitting the concealed switch under his desk, popping open the disguised door and disappearing into his sanctum.

But now Dunn was preparing to entertain an invited guest. This was risky, he knew, but he also trusted his own preparations more than he would have trusted security at the White House. Moments ago, a long black limousine, one of several identical cars in the OILCO fleet, had pulled up to the locked private elevator that led only to this office. Vinnie Speraza—the only member of his own security staff allowed access to the private rooms, elevators and passageways of Dunn's empire—climbed out of the front seat and unlocked the elevator, calling it down from its resting position midway between the garage and penthouse.

Dunn made a mental note to make sure Speraza's checking account showed an extra bonus this month. The man did what he was told, unquestioningly and without hesitation, and all he asked was that his baby daughter and her mother be protected. Dunn smiled, this was one of the best deals he'd ever made with the mob. Speraza had, until a few months before, been the mob's top hit man. But when the don discovered Speraza's indiscretions with the don's daughter, his life was worthless.

Dunn had heard about the man's problem and had intervened, buying the contract and taking Speraza's girlfriend and their daughter into his protection. Since then, Speraza had proven to be invaluable to Dunn's plans. He paid Speraza well, ensuring that the baby and her mother had a secure, comfortable home, and seeing to their every need. In return, Speraza stayed at Dunn's beck and call, followed orders and kept his mouth shut.

Dunn watched on closed-circuit television as Speraza held the door open while his guest, covered in long, flowing robes that completely shrouded the person's identity, climbed out of the limo and boarded the elevator.

Dunn composed himself as the elevator climbed the thirty-five stories to the penthouse. The monitor, sunk into the top of the desk, showed the interior of the elevator car, Speraza was standing, hands behind his back, to one side; Dunn's guest stood motionless in the center. Speraza glanced at the hidden camera, his apparently empty expression letting Dunn know that everything had gone smoothly to that point. Dunn smiled. He was playing with fire; no, with nuclear holocaust—he liked that mental image much better—and he could hardly wait for the next explosion.

The inlaid wood elevator doors in the office slid open silently and Speraza stepped away from the opening to let the guest pass. A flutter of black robes, softly rustling fabric and the crunching sound of something stiffer, accompanied the figure to where it stopped in the center of the room. Dunn stood, settling his expensive Italian suit with a slight shift of his shoulders. He laid the cigar in a crystal ashtray and regarded his guest with an open, predatory smile.

"Welcome! I trust your journey was uneventful?" Dunn knew not to proffer a hand, so he rested both, open fingered, on the surface of the desk, keeping them in sight and, therefore, himself trustworthy.

The robed figure reached up to the elaborately wound headdress and pulled a length of fabric free from one side revealing the biggest, darkest eyes Dunn had ever seen.

"Thank you, Mr. Dunn," the woman said in well-cultivated Oxford English, her Arabic accent softly echoing through the words. "I bring you greetings from his excellency, Osama bin Laden."

Dunn's breath caught in his chest. This was it, the moment he had been planning for. Speraza stepped back against the wall as Dunn gestured to one of the velvet chairs.

"Please sit, we have much to discuss." Dunn smiled.

* * *

It had been a long time in the making. Dunn had planned carefully, adjusting and readjusting for every new development, intent on ensuring his complete control over the situation. And now his would-be "partners" had sent him a negotiator who knocked him sideways. The woman sat in the chair across the desk with a regal composure and a gaze that could melt the hardest misogynist. But she was all business. She had pulled the concealing veil down so that now Dunn could see the fine cut of her nose and high cheekbones. But it was the eyes—her eyes held him, distracted him and unnerved him. He couldn't help but wonder what was hidden beneath all that fabric.

Speraza busied himself pouring small cups of thick, strong,

Turkish coffee for the two of them, while they casually discussed the weather in Oklahoma, the problems of commercial airline travel and the furnishings of Dunn's office. Formalities behind them, Dunn turned the conversation to the business at hand.

"Basically, Mr. Dunn," the woman, who identified herself only as Najla, began, "my masters are interested in what you can offer them in exchange for this assistance you've suggested."

She was good, this one. Dunn marveled at the sheer control she was able to exert over the conversation. She masterfully avoided any specifics without sacrificing a shred of her meaning. Oh, how he could use her! He wondered how much it would cost to get her into his employ.

"That's very simple. If we can force the American government's hand, show them the necessity of reconsidering their position when it comes to OPEC and the powers controlling the oil fields—and that certainly includes changing their misconceptions of Saddam—and once the OPEC nations have been undermined and their control of the oil fields usurped, your people can easily slide into a position of power." Dunn flashed his best smile, sure she would be awed by the sheer genius of the plan.

"Excuse me, Mr. Dunn, if I seem a little, how do you say it, slow? I am but a mere woman and need to understand so that I can communicate your intentions more fully to my masters."

Dunn smiled again. She was certainly anything but a mere woman.

"You are saying that you will assist my masters in gaining full control of the oil output of the Middle East in exchange for what?" Najla flashed her thick black lashes and broke eye contact with Dunn, almost modestly, although Dunn didn't believe it for a minute. She was certain of his intentions but needed him to say it outright before it could constitute an agreement. It was no surprise to her that bin Laden had trusted her with this assignment.

Mata Hari, he had called her, his little jewel, and she was proud of the honor. But this disgusting brute of a man made her wish for a dagger. Wouldn't it be better to remove the problem rather than negotiate with it? This Warren Dunn embodied everything she had been taught to despise about Americans. Their conspicuous wealth and inflated self-importance revolted her, but she smiled and allowed the smile to play into her eyes. She just had to ignore the feeling that he seemed to be looking through her clothing.

"Once we have full control over oil output," Dunn was saying, "we can control the prices paid in foreign markets and, at the very least, double our profits. Double or triple profits, split equally, will amount to several large fortunes, enough money to finance the overthrow of governments and the takeover of financial systems worldwide."

The greed of the man was unbelievable. Najla smiled again. "And for this you are willing to sacrifice your own government?" she asked innocently.

"Well, no, not quite. What I'm saying is that I will ensure that my government follows through with actions to benefit your, ah, masters. In exchange we will all become so rich there will be no need for the campaign against this country. Your associates will leave us alone and we will leave you alone. And as an added benefit, this will strike a blow, possibly a killing blow, to Israel in the process."

"It is a very ambitious plan, Mr. Dunn," Najla bowed her head before looking back into the loathsome oaf's eyes, "and you do come highly recommended by Adalla Marchia."

Dunn smiled, remembering his old college roommate. All those years ago at Harvard Law, he never would have guessed that his old pal would achieve such a high position in a terrorist organization. It only proved his own assertion that the people you least expect will be the ones you need to pay attention to.

"I will present it to my masters with all haste," Najla was saying. "I believe you will find them very receptive to it." She rose gracefully from her chair and readjusted her veil. "If I may impose upon your driver, I should like to retire to my hotel. It's been a long day." Najla made a short bow to Dunn before sweeping back to the elevator.

"Please convey my best wishes to . . . your masters," Dunn said, sliding out from behind the desk to follow her to the elevator. Speraza held the door open for her as she flowed into the car.

"I shall, Mr. Dunn," she said. "I shall."

Dunn watched the door close and listened for the whine of the motor lowering the car to the basement before he turned to the bar to pour himself a drink. The events were set in motion and all he had to do was sit back and steer.

FOUR

The White House
Washington, D.C.

"NEVER LET IT BE SAID THAT IAN TUTTLE DOESN'T KNOW HOW TO ENJOY the fruits of his labors!" Tuttle muttered to himself after his secretary announced the arrival of his staff. Tuttle stood behind the magnificent mahogany desk in the corner office adjacent to the Oval Office. Offices in the White House were assigned by rank, and Tuttle was feeling every ounce of his as his colleagues filed into the office to take their places at seats spaced around the room.

Tuttle had one thing and one thing only on his agenda for this little get-together. He wanted these people to know who held the power now, and who owned the president's ear. Over the course of the next hour, Tuttle had to impress upon these men and women, all powerful in their own right, that nothing, absolutely nothing, was to be brought to the president's attention by anyone but his most trusted chief of staff.

"Friends," Tuttle addressed the room, wishing for all the world that Warren Dunn could see him now.

* * *

In another part of the White House, James Sercu, Walsh's national security adviser, was meeting with the new president and Vice President Harry Dent to bring them up to speed on events throughout the world.

"Mr. President, I'm sorry to say that you have not inherited many friendships in the Mideast," Sercu said, thoughtfully tapping a pencil on the polished tabletop.

The vice president, midway through spooning sugar into a cup of coffee, laughed. "That's an understatement if I've ever heard one. Saddam Hussein hates this country. Osama bin Laden is out to get anybody who doesn't agree with him—that puts us at the top of the list—and there must be a few hundred other terrorists out there who are just waiting for their shot at bringing down the satanic U.S. of A!" Although Dent managed to maintain the appearance of a good-natured, easygoing fellow, Walsh knew he had deep misgivings about the role the United States had played in foreign affairs in the past. Walsh smiled at him before turning his attention to Sercu.

"So we have to keep *Air Force One* gassed up and ready to go," he laughed.

"Really, sir, it's more serious than that. There are hundreds of threats against the president every week, and those are just from our constituency. Uncounted more are made by foreign powers and terrorists, and sometimes I think they're the ones we should be most concerned about."

"I'm sorry, Jim." Walsh's tone became instantly serious and he shot Dent a look warning him to drop the jokes. "Harry and I both take this very seriously; you know that. We're just a little, I don't know, still giddy from the past few days."

Sercu nodded; he understood, but he also understood that there were threats looming in the world that none of them had a clue about. "Well, gentlemen," he said, as he settled into his chair, "we've got a lot to talk about."

FIVE

Khartoum, The Sudan

ADALLA MARCHIA LOOKED AROUND HIS CLEAN, WHITE HOUSE AND SAID a quiet prayer thanking Allah for the wealth and prosperity that surrounded him. He was a lucky man and he knew it. A successful medical supplies import business, his home, his family, a good wife, and now to be made Osama bin Laden's lieutenant. Surely he must be blessed.

"Maneda!" he called to his housekeeper. "Come here, woman!"

Maneda, a stooped, hefty woman who kept her face hidden behind a *niqaab*, the traditional veil of a Muslim woman, scurried into the room bowing rapidly as she walked, an affectation that Marchia secretly enjoyed. "Yes, sir?"

"I will be entertaining some, eh, business associates this afternoon," he said, pacing about the room. "Please prepare some refreshments and air out my study. We will be meeting there."

"Yes, sir." Maneda backed toward the door, dipping her little bows all the way.

"Once you have served, I want to you to stay in the kitchen. Find something to keep yourself busy there until you are called." Marchia dismissed her with a wave.

"Yes, sir." Out in the hall, Maneda straightened up and rubbed the sore spot in the small of her back. "Asshole," she whispered as she shuffled off toward Marchia's study. Inside the small room, she flipped on the ceiling fan and pulled back the soft drapes that blocked the morning sun. She was startled when the phone on the desk rang but watched to see when the red light stopped blinking, a sign that Marchia had picked up the extension in the living room. Slowly and carefully she held down the mute and speaker buttons on the phone and pressed the button next to the red light.

"Hello, my old friend!" She heard Marchia's voice over the speaker.

"Is everything set?" She didn't recognize the other man's voice, but had a feeling she could guess who it was.

"Of course! Would I ever let you down?" Marchia practically sang. Maneda's eyes strayed over the desktop and she spotted a red folder tucked under the blotter.

"So the timetables are set. Do you have access to the necessary supplies? Are the other members of our group ready to commence with our plans?"

Maneda carefully pulled the folder out and flipped through the contents, trying not to disturb the position of any documents.

"Everything is set. We're having a meeting here this afternoon to finalize the arrangements, and then we will be ready to begin."

Maneda smiled when she saw the detailed plans outlined on the papers in the folder. This was what she had been waiting for; now she had to figure out how to get the information out of Marchia's study.

"Good, good, keep me informed."

The phone clicked and Maneda scrambled to slip the folder back into place and take the extension off speaker before Marchia noticed.

"Maneda!" Marchia's voice echoed down the hallway and Maneda forced herself to breathe normally. Slipping into her stooped posture she opened the door and came face-to-face with her master.

"Sir, I was airing . . ."

"Yes, yes, get those refreshments going. I am going to change my clothes before my guests arrive." With that, Marchia stomped to the back of the house and slammed his bedroom door. Maneda drew a deep breath, gathering herself for her next move. When she heard the shower in the master bedroom, she quietly slipped back into the study. She stopped for a moment, thinking seriously about simply taking the original documents and getting out of the house as fast as she could. But that would mean less time to escape safely. And with Marchia's "guests" arriving any minute, she did not want to have to worry about all of them searching for her.

Maneda nodded to herself and grabbed the folder. She shoved the pile of papers into the copying machine Marchia had installed in the closet. She hit the start key and the machine jumped to life, sucking the first document in and spitting it back out once it was copied. Maneda smiled to herself as she hurried back to the hallway to listen for the shower. No sooner had she stepped out of the room than the copier beeped at her. Her heart leapt and she raced back to the machine. Out of paper. Maneda cursed herself for never having learned about these machines and struggled to find the opening where the paper would go in.

"Maneda!" Marchia's voice echoed down the hallway sending the woman flying out of the small closet, her heart trying to beat its way out of her chest. "Maneda! Where is my good linen suit?" Maneda flew down the hallway to the bedroom door where she struggled not to sound as out of breath as she was.

"It is hanging on the back of your closet door, sir . . . "

"Yes, yes, I see it, in the plastic bag."

Maneda stopped for only a moment to make sure she heard the rustle of the plastic cleaning bag before she raced as quietly as possible back to the study. Once she had the paper in the machine and had started it back up again, she went back to the hallway to listen for Marchia. She could hear him singing softly to himself as he dressed. By the time the copier had finished with the sheaf of documents, Maneda was certain she was going to drop dead, her heart burst through her chest, right there on the hall floor. When the machine's whirring had ceased, she gathered up the original documents in their folder and slipped them back under the desk blotter. She rolled the copies and stuffed them down the front of her loose robe before hurrying to the kitchen.

* * *

Four long black cars slipped through the narrow streets of Marchia's neighborhood, past houses that looked very much like his—low, whitewashed, and gleaming in the midday sun. All four cars stopped before Adalla Marchia's home, the drivers climbed out and followed one another up to the front door where Marchia himself welcomed them. Inside, he led the two Iraqis and the two Yemenites down the long central hallway of his home to the study, where he motioned for them to take seats in the plush overstuffed chairs. All four men were dressed simply, but expensively, and all four carried black brief cases and wore the same, serious expressions. Maneda hustled into the room with a coffee service and poured cups for each of them before Marchia dismissed her with a sharp command and a wave of his hand.

"Now, my friends," he addressed the four, "we have much to discuss."

Maneda lingered in the hall only long enough to hear the beginning of Marchia's speech. As quietly as possible she slipped down the hallway to the kitchen where she gathered her personal belongings, took one last look around the room and quietly went out the back door. She would not be returning here again.

* * *

Maneda hurried through the back alley of Adalla Marchia's neighborhood, afraid to look up or to straighten from her stoop until she was blocks away from her former employer's home. Once safely in the market square, she straightened to her full height and walked determinedly through the crowded streets, weaving her way through the quarter on the most roundabout route she could, just in case she'd been followed. When she found herself well into the heart of Khartoum, she headed directly for the British Embassy. There was no time to waste. Outside the embassy stood four British military guards, looking stern and immovable. Maneda walked up to the ranking guard, leaned close, and whispered what she now thought of as the magic words. The guard looked her up and down, taking in her shabby clothing and the heavy black veil draped over her face, before stepping into the guardhouse and making a phone call. A moment later he emerged, took her by the arm, and led her through the gates to the safety of British soil. Maneda allowed herself a minute of relief before reminding herself that she wasn't safe yet. She wouldn't be truly safe until she was back in Israel.

Maneda and the guard were met at the entrance by a man in the standard business suit of a diplomat. "It's a pleasure to meet you," he reached out for Maneda's hand. "We were informed by Mossad that you would be bringing in the documents we've been waiting for."

The diplomat took Maneda's arm and lead her into the security of the building. The guard watched them walk away before turning back to his post. "Bloody hell," he thought, "she was a member of the Israeli secret service!"

Six

President's Private Study
The White House
Washington, D.C.

President David Walsh paced the floor of his private study nervously. His wife, Sarah, had left the White House the night before without a word to him about where she was going or why. She had managed to lose her secret service agents in Georgetown Park Mall, and they hadn't been able to pick up her trail since. If this got out to the papers, who knew what kind of scandal the press would turn it into. There was a sharp rap at the door and Walsh ran a hand through his hair trying to regain his composure.

"Come in."

Ian Tuttle's perfectly groomed head appeared through the open door. "May I come in, sir?"

"Ian, when it's just you and me, you can drop the 'sir' crap. I think we've known each other long enough."

"Well, that may be true, David, but we do need to maintain a sense of propriety. This isn't a bar in Arlington, you know!" Ian chuckled at his own humor, but his expression turned serious when he saw the look in Walsh's eyes. "No news yet, I take it."

"No, not yet. I just don't get it. Where could she have disappeared?" Walsh dropped into one of the chairs, not caring about propriety anymore.

"More to the point, I think the question is why?" Tuttle took the seat across from the president. "Did you two have a disagreement?"

Walsh looked at Tuttle through the fingers covering his eyes. "Why? If we did have a fight, it's our business, not the staff's."

"Excuse me, Mr. President," Tuttle emphasized the words as much to bring the conversation around to an official one as to make a point about the nature of their relationship. "We have to consider spin control. If there is a personal problem between you and the First Lady, then we need to be aware of it so we can keep it out of the press."

David took several deep breaths. He knew Ian was right, but to have to go into the reasons why Sarah had bolted would just reinforce those reasons. Even their marriage could no longer be a personal thing.

"Yes, Ian, we had a disagreement. Mrs. Walsh does not want to take up residence in the White House."

"What?" Tuttle almost spat out the word . He had to work to control his own rising anger.

"You heard me." Walsh rose and stomped across the room to look out the window. Maybe she'd be there, walking the dog around the grounds, or sitting on the steps pouting like a child. She did that sometimes when they fought. It always softened David and he was more likely to give in to her. But never enough, he realized now. "Sarah doesn't want the position of First Lady; she wants to live her own life and pursue her own career." David sighed and looked back at Tuttle, expecting to see sympathy on the younger man's face. But he didn't find it there. He was startled to see what looked, for a moment, like seething hatred. Then it was gone.

"How can she not want to be First Lady? I just don't understand, sir." Tuttle was back to his old self again.

"You have to understand, Ian, that she gave up a lot for my career. More than I ever realized. Now that I've achieved my dream, she wants to go off and find her own. I can hardly blame . . ."

"No," Tuttle interrupted him. "No, she has no right to do this. It's not just your dream that she's walking away from. She campaigned for you. Part of the reason any man gets elected to the presidency is because he has a good woman behind him. When has the First Lady not been liked by the general public?" Tuttle punctuated his speech with waving arms.

"Well . . ."

"No, the simple fact of the matter is that she has made a promise to the American people and she has no right to go back on that promise." The anger was rising in Tuttle's face and he fought to keep it in check. "This could be the biggest scandal in decades. It will overshadow the last administration's problems and you'll have made your mark on your presidency before it's even begun. She must be brought back here and shown the error of her decision."

Walsh stared at Tuttle, a little taken aback by the man's sudden fury and pre-Victorian attitude.

"Ian, I hardly think it will be that much of a problem." Walsh laid a hand on his chief of staff's shoulder, but Tuttle jerked away from his touch.

"I'm sorry, sir, but we have to get a handle on this immediately. We'll need to call a meeting of your press secretary, the head of Secret Service, and the First Lady's personal secretary. We'll bring in the FBI if necessary."

"Tuttle! I think you're overreacting a little bit!" Walsh tried to stop Tuttle from racing out the door, but both men were brought up short by a loud knock. The door swung open and in walked Sarah, a brace of Secret Service agents behind her. Walsh knew with one glance that she was furious. He took a deep breath and readied himself for a fight.

* * *

"This had better be good, Tuttle," Warren Dunn's voice drifted through the phone, soft and menacing.

"Well, I wish I could say it was, but we've got a problem. Can you talk?" Tuttle managed to keep his own voice from shaking, knowing the reaction his news was bound to bring.

"I'll call you back in two hours. Be there." The phone clicked and the line went dead. Two hours, thought Tuttle. Two whole hours to rehearse telling this very dangerous man that one woman may be the undoing of all their carefully laid plans. He poured himself a strong drink, carefully hung up his suit coat and slid into his favorite velvet smoking jacket before settling down to wait for Dunn's call.

The couple had been locked in David's private office for an hour before anyone else was allowed to speak with them. When they came out, anger was still on Sarah's face, but David seemed calmer and more in control. Tuttle desperately wanted to know what had happened in that room, every intimate detail, but Walsh said only that as long as the press hadn't gotten hold of the story, there was still time for Sarah and him to work things out.

Tuttle was appalled by the woman's gall. How dare she think she could refuse the important position of First Lady—who did she think she was anyway? They would have to work fast to find something to use that could keep her in control. But what?

Tuttle was startled out of his thoughts by the jangling of the telephone. "Tuttle, this had better be worth my leaving that party." Dunn's voice was calm but cold. Tuttle explained the events of the day as quickly and succinctly as possible without sparing his own outrage at Sarah Walsh's behavior.

"Well, it's not unexpected, is it?" Dunn said at last.

"What do you mean, not unexpected?" Tuttle demanded.

"This bitch could have toppled everything we've worked the past three years to build and she could still do it!"

"Well, we'll just have to see what we can do about our dear First Lady."

SEVEN

Home of the National Security Adviser
Washington, D.C.

THE DISTINCTIVE ELECTRONIC BLARE OF JAMES SERCU'S DIRECT telephone line to the White House startled the security adviser out of his last few minutes of sleep. His wife, beside him in their bed, nudged him with her foot before going back to sleep. He grumbled at her, knowing full well that there was absolutely no reason for her to get up; she couldn't answer that phone no matter what was happening.

The phone rang again, sounding more insistent with each wail, more like a siren with each step Sercu took toward his study. If this phone rang, no matter what the hour, the news was never good. He wished for the thousandth time that he could simply ignore it and return to his warm bed and his wife's cold feet.

Sercu drew a deep breath and snatched up the receiver, "Sercu," he grumbled.

"Sir, we have a code yellow call from MI7." The woman's voice on the other end of the phone was businesslike and crisp, as though she had calls from the highest ranking office of British intelligence with breakfast every morning. Come to think of it, Sercu thought, she probably does.

"Patch it through, please."

There was a moment of silence before MI7's voice broke through the morning fog in Sercu's brain. "James, sorry to wake you at such an ungodly hour, old man."

"Quite all right, Richard. How is foggy old London anyway?"

"Same as always, but I'm afraid that I didn't call for a chat. We have some intelligence that you're going to want to pass along to your president without delay."

Sercu dropped into his leather desk chair. "Why do I think I'm going to regret getting out of bed for this?" he asked.

"Let's just put it this way, you'll feel better about getting out of bed when this is all over and done with."

"So tell me," Sercu felt his muscles tensing in anticipation of what MI7 had to say.

* * *

"How much anthrax did you say?" David Walsh slumped in his chair in the Situation Room of the White House.

"To put it simply, more than enough to wipe out the entire eastern seaboard," Bill Cassidy, the newly appointed secretary of defense, replied, the pencil clutched in his right hand jiggling noticeably. Walsh hoped the man would get his nerves under control before his shaking spread around the room. He looked across the table to where his vice president and friend, Harry Dent, sat. All the blood had drained out of Dent's face and his skin glowed a sickly white in the fluorescent glare. He was thinking about his two kids, away at college in Boston and New York.

"Is the source reliable?" Walsh asked, knowing the question was ridiculous, but needing time to collect his thoughts and not wanting to face the silence of the heavily insulated room.

"Yes, absolutely," Sercu said. "Mossad agents are incorruptible and frighteningly efficient. This one has been working as Marchia's housekeeper for the past two years."

"Two years, Jesus," Dent mumbled.

"Did they get her out of the country?" Walsh asked.

"Yes," Sercu said, giving the president a sideways glance. He wasn't sure why Walsh was stalling but was willing to give him the few minutes he seemed to want. "Not that it would matter. Mossad will die for their missions without a second thought. But MI7 said they shipped her back to Israel almost immediately."

"Okay," Walsh sat forward in his chair and looked around the table at the same pale faces and stunned expressions. "How long ago did this Mossad agent get the report to the embassy?"

"Four hours ago, sir," the secretary of defense answered.

"And did she give them any idea how long we have until she's missed?"

"She told them that she stole some household money and a few pieces of the wife's jewelry to cover her exit. If Marchia thinks she was just a thief, we'll have a few more hours," Sercu replied.

"So she didn't take the original documents?"

"No, she actually managed to make copies." Sercu couldn't help but smile.

"Well, Mossad must get some interesting training!" Walsh tried to get a chuckle from his advisers, but the attempt was cut short by the beep of the secure document fax. His aide jumped to the machine and retrieved the pages of plans the Mossad agent had managed to get to the British Embassy. Walsh leafed through the translated documents before handing them to Sercu.

"MI7 says that these plans specify entry points of Boston, New York City, Washington, and Atlanta," Sercu said. "Which means that someone, or several people, will try to get a sizable amount of anthrax-infected material through customs in each city. Once we get these analyzed we'll have a better idea how they'll try to do that and how to stop them."

"Okay, that defines our first maneuver," Walsh said, feeling more in control when he had specific orders to give. "Let's get security beefed up at the entry points. Whatever we need to do the job, get it moving. And, above all, let's keep this as quiet as possible; we don't need public panic if we can help it." Walsh looked around the table. His first official emergency meeting and it had to be a life-and-death situation. Trial by fire, he thought, what a way to start!

"There's one more thing, sir," Sercu said. "It seems that this is no ordinary strain of anthrax. Normally, symptoms take two weeks after infection to manifest. The documentation, according to MI7, indicates that this viral strain has been genetically engineered to take effect almost immediately, making this the most dangerous biological weapon ever seen."

Walsh thought the news couldn't get any worse. "What about the vaccine? Will the current inoculations still work?"

"There's not enough information on that yet, sir. Preliminarily, the British think that an increased dosage might be all that's needed, but we need more information before we can make that determination."

"What about the terrorists themselves? We know who their ring leader is. Perhaps we can nip this in the bud," Barbara Howe, the secretary of state, offered. She had been quiet throughout the entire briefing, but Walsh knew her well enough to realize that when she did speak it would be a good idea to listen carefully. "These people are so involved in what they see as their mission that the only way to stop them is to stop their leaders."

Walsh nodded, "Jim, can we pick up this guy?"

"Why not just pick him off?" Ian Tuttle said quietly, probably echoing the sentiments of the secretaries of the armed forces, all of whom nodded slightly at the suggestion.

"Well, I suppose that is an option," Walsh mused. "But you

can't get information from a dead man. Besides, it's illegal to order an assassination."

"We could have the police in Khartoum pick him up for us," Cassidy said, knowing what Walsh's response would be.

Sercu jumped in before Walsh opened his mouth, "No, they'd refuse flat out. We don't have the clout there."

"No, it's too obvious anyway. It would give too much away." Walsh's face clouded. "Besides, the last time we did that, too many innocents were caught in the cross fire."

Sercu could only nod. Heads had rolled after that blunder. He wondered how Walsh had found out about it.

"Send in your best," Walsh said, his voice suddenly hard. "Pick him up, take him someplace safe, and see what you can get out of him."

Sercu signaled to his aide, who stepped out of the room.

"Okay," Walsh addressed the rest of the table. "Once we get those documents translated, let's get to work on identifying the terrorists and get them picked up. And fast."

General Ned Seiffert, chairman of the Joint Chiefs of Staff, spoke up suddenly, "We could avoid all of this if we simply ceased all aid to Israel," he said so matter-of-factly that Walsh took a minute to let the full impact of the statement seep in. Seiffert was a no-nonsense sort of man who had worked his way up through the ranks. He erred on the side of caution in all of his decisions, and his skill was valued by his peers in NATO. The occasional comparison to George C. Marshall helped to reinforce that opinion.

"What?" Walsh and Dent said in unison, sharing the same stunned expression. Tuttle smiled behind a hand held to his chin.

"I'm only suggesting that if the terrorists want to negotiate, then we have a card to play." Seiffert knew that some of his strategies would prove unpopular with the new president, and he played his hand carefully.

"We do not negotiate with terrorists, general." Walsh regained a grip on his emotions with great effort. "We will do whatever we have to do to prevent any innocent lives from being lost, but it will be the continuing policy of this government not to negotiate with terrorists. We might as well just give in to their blackmail!"

"If they succeed in this, there will be no way to protect those people," Sercu interjected, "not to mention the effect it will have on the economy. Public reaction will be nothing but panic and our foreign affairs policies won't be worth the paper they're printed on."

Not to mention popularity ratings, Tuttle thought. He stifled another smile.

"All right, we have a rough idea of what we're up against here. Let's get some plans rolling, get security going at those airports, and we'll meet back here in, say, six hours." Walsh stood, signaling the meeting was over for the moment.

In the elevator back up to the main offices, Dent looked long and hard at Walsh. "Do we stand a chance of stopping this, David?"

"We don't have a choice."

EIGHT

Khartoum, The Sudan

GENERAL LOUIS BLAINE SAT IN THE FRONT SEAT OF A CAR THAT LOOKED like it should have been retired ten years earlier at the top of a rise one-half mile from Adalla Marchia's neat little home in the suburbs of Khartoum. Throughout the afternoon, he and his attaché had watched the comings and goings of the family who were unaware of the surveillance.

"Let Red Two know that we will move in at dusk," Blaine muttered past his binoculars. "Remind them to stick to plan. Dead hostages aren't bargaining chips."

"Yes, sir." The young man in the seat beside Blaine reached for the field radio and quietly relayed the orders to the men stationed around the neighborhood. Blaine had worked out this plan down to the minutest detail on the long flight to the Sudan from Andrews Air Force Base. Walsh was only interested in Marchia, but Blaine knew that if they had the rest of Marchia's family there would be some bargaining room. Not much room, he knew. Terrorists, especially in the Mideast, held less stock in the lives of their families than, say, Americans. This had often made it difficult to break captured terrorists.

Blaine lowered the binoculars and scanned the quiet streets

surrounding the house. President Walsh had specifically ordered that no civilians were to be endangered in the operation. Blaine would do what he could to follow that order, but when it came right down to it, he would do whatever was necessary, the consequences be damned. That's what cleanup crews were for.

"Red Two reports ready. We have men in position ready for your go-ahead, sir," the young marine reported dourly. It was the major's first mission with Blaine and he was doing an impressive job of ignoring the oppressive heat.

"Very good, major. Now we wait."

* * *

Inside the low, whitewashed house, Marchia also waited. The sudden disappearance of his wife's favorite household servant disturbed him. Looking back on events of the past few months, he saw many clues that should have given him some warning that the woman might be trouble. She was simply too willing to do the work asked of her. Not like the household servants he had employed in the past, those who would rather eat you out of house and home than do a drachma's worth of work. Maneda had worked hard, too hard. Marchia now realized she had been too good to be true.

But Marchia had no concrete proof that the woman had done anything wrong except for running away in the middle of the day. Perhaps his guests had frightened her off. But that made no sense. She had been her usual efficient and attentive self every other time he had had similar visitors. Come to think of it, she was possibly too attentive.

All this second-guessing was getting him nowhere. If she had been a spy, then a spy for whom? His contacts had heard nothing about her in the leaks from the Israeli Mossad, and the Americans weren't smart enough to plant someone like that. Besides, his friend, Warren Dunn, would have warned him long before it became a problem. He had to stop speculating. There was too much work to be done.

Marchia sat in his study watching his children racing through the small garden behind the house. Their laughter, carried on the breeze, blew through the window like a warm wave. Allah would protect; Allah would provide. Marchia heard his wife softly calling their brood to the evening meal and rose stiffly from his chair to join them.

* * *

"Man, this bites!" Bobby Francazi muttered from inside the truck where he waited with fourteen other marines for the go-ahead from Blaine. "Why don't we just slam in there and grab the fucker? All this waiting around is a waste of time."

The other men sat quietly, each with his own thoughts. For the most part, the Red Team was a well-organized bunch who knew how to take orders and carry out missions without complaint. This Francazi guy was the newest addition to the team and apparently hadn't learned to keep his trap shut.

"Shut up, Francazi," the sergeant whispered loudly through the flap of canvas on the back of the truck. They had the hood of the truck up and were tinkering with the engine. Their Mossad escort muttered to each other in Arabic.

Francazi snorted and John Hait, squad leader and senior member of the team, swatted him with the butt of his Uzi. Francazi glared, sullen, but kept his mouth shut.

The flap of canvas was pulled back suddenly and the men inside squinted in the surprising brightness of the setting sun. Hawley Sheppard, their six-and-a-half-foot tall sergeant, hoisted his massive frame into the back of the truck and squatted in the middle of the bed, looking around at the faces peering at him in the dim light. Sheppard was a giant among the huge men who made up Red Team. As he climbed into the truck he unzipped the coveralls he wore. Like a wraith from the mist he suddenly appeared in the truck beside his men.

"That stuff still gives me the willies," Hait muttered, referring to the new camouflage gear they were using. Specially treated fabric was woven through with fiber optic cables as thin as thread. When a soldier held perfectly still, the fabric reflected the surrounding terrain and the man literally vanished into the background. In the dim light of the truck, Sheppard was absolutely invisible until he moved. He let the top of the coverall drop to his waist and pulled the hooded helmet off his head.

Hait remembered when he had first seen the stuff; it was so top secret that there weren't even any rumors about it floating around. He looked the general doing the briefing right in the eye and told him he thought he was crazy. He had never doubted any top-secret technology since then.

"Okay, guys," Hawley drawled in his Georgia low-country accent, "in a couple minutes we're gonna get the order from General Blaine to move in. I jus' wanna make it puffuctly clear, no shootin' unless absolutely necessary. We have to take this family alive, got it? Every one of 'em alive and kickin'. Now there're kids in there, five of 'em. The youngest is two and the oldest is thirteen. Two girls, three boys—the oldest is a boy. You can assume that the daddy has already been teachin' the boys, 'specially the oldest, about fightin'. No shootin' the kids! Got that?" Sheppard looked from man to man, waiting for a nod of understanding. Francazi just grinned.

"How the fuck are we gonna kill anything loaded with these damned rubber bullets?" one of the men muttered.

"Those rubber bullets will do enough damage without killing anybody; don't worry about that." Hait countered. The man snorted in the darkness.

There was a loud rap on the side of the flatbed and the hood slammed shut. "That's it, on with that camo, and let's move!" Sheppard pulled up his coverall and moved out into the fading light. He watched as his team dropped from the back of the truck and faded into the neighborhood. Even a well-trained bodyguard would have been at a loss to explain what was going on. Once the house was surrounded and secured, General Blaine would join Hait and Sheppard at the front door.

* * *

Adalla Marchia and his family sat at a Western-style kitchen table piled with vegetables and rice, spiced lamb, and huge slabs of flat bread. The children chattered almost nonstop while they ate, and Marchia's wife kept her husband's glass of mint tea filled. Marchia enjoyed these nontraditional family meals. He basked in the attention of his children, laughed at their jokes, and spoke to them seriously about the importance of their prayers and their schoolwork. The children enjoyed the time with their father, too, asking him incessant questions and competing for his attention while devouring the meal.

Marchia had eaten his fill and settled back in his chair to enjoy a cigarette and let the food digest when there was a loud banging on the front door. His eldest son, Abdullah, rose to answer it, but something made Marchia call him back and go to the door himself. As he threw the heavy, carved door open, the marines of Red Team simultaneously burst through the patio doors and the garage entry at the back of the house. A sharp bang and a flash of light stunned the family, while Abdullah slipped into his father's study unnoticed. At the front door a huge marine barreled into Marchia, Uzi pointed at his head, throwing him to the floor and screaming "Down, down, down, hands over your head, NOW!"

The Mossad escort snorted their derision while they pushed

past the marines and translated the bellowed order to the stunned man on the floor at their feet.

"I know what he said," Marchia choked the words out in rough, broken English. "Who are you, and what do you want?" One of the marines leveled a boot at Marchia's back and he sprawled flat on his face on the intricate tile floor.

"Adalla Marchia? Consider yourself and your family guests of the United States." General Blaine stepped into the hallway as a heavy black hood was yanked down over the man's head.

"Everything's secure, sir," Hawley Sheppard began when the report of a small handgun echoed through the house followed by the boom of automatic weapons fire. "What the . . . " Sheppard gestured for three of the men to stay behind with Marchia while Blaine and the rest trampled down the hallway toward the sound of the blast. In Marchia's study they found Hait standing over Marchia's eldest son who writhed on the floor, screaming; a small hole was ripped through the chest of his shirt where the rubber projectile had collided with the boy's rib, shattering it and cracking the one next to it. A pistol lay on the floor. On the other side of the room was Bobby Francazi sprawled on a shattered table, his blood pooling in a dark circle behind his head, a neat hole punched through his left eye.

"Holy shit!" Sheppard muttered, looking from Francazi's body to the slight young boy rolled in a fetal position on the floor. The boy screamed and sputtered, but Sheppard could only make out the word "Allah" every so often. Apparently, the marines were being cursed. Sheppard shook his head sadly and looked to General Blaine, who stood impassively in the doorway. "Take the pup to the front room and tie him up with the rest of them."

Hait grabbed the boy by the arm and hoisted him up. He had to drag him past the general, who reached out and cuffed the boy hard on the side of his head. "Shut up," Blaine growled.

Sheppard started to take a step forward and then got control of himself. No sense defending the boy—he had killed a U.S. Marine and was lucky to still be alive as it was. Blaine, noticing the look of reluctance flash across Sheppard's face, glared at him before spinning around to exit the room. Sheppard looked from Francazi's body to the two men who remained.

"Clean it up and get him to the truck." He took one last look at the dead soldier before stomping out of the room. "Some days I hate this fucking job!"

* * *

In the front room of the house, the marines had gathered the family together, all wearing similar heavy dark hoods, except for the two year old, who clung to her mother's arm, tears streaming down her food-stained face. Sheppard looked around the room. Seven marines trained machine guns on the family sprawled on the floor. Marchia had ceased struggling when he heard each of his children's voices. He had shushed them, murmuring quiet words of comfort and prayers to Allah, and had taken a combat boot to the side of the head for doing it. Sheppard felt the bile rising in his stomach. Where he was from, you just didn't treat women and kids like this. So their daddy was a terrorist; that wasn't their fault. But he kept his trap shut like he was supposed to. He had no choice.

Blaine addressed the hostages. One of the Israeli Mossad agents translated in rapid-fire Arabic. "We are going to move you out of here fast and quiet before the local authorities show up. You want to put up a struggle, we'll kill you; it's that simple. Same goes for your missus and the kiddies." Blaine's face was a mask of disgust as he surveyed the helpless forms huddled in the middle of the room. "Adalla Marchia, you put up a fight and we'll kill your kiddies, beginning with the littlest one." The Israeli translator barely finished the sentence before Marchia's wife began keening and wailing pleas to Allah to save her children.

"SHUT UP!" Blaine bellowed at the distraught woman. The translator didn't bother to put the sentiment into Arabic; there was no need.

"NOW!" Blaine screamed, then dropped his voice to a menacing tone. "Do I make myself crystal clear, sir?"

Marchia nodded his head, the hood flapping his assent. Two marines pulled the man to his feet and draped a camouflage cloak of the same material as their uniforms over his shoulders. They steered him toward the door while others gathered up the family and draped them as well.

"General?" Marchia asked, none of the self-assurance and faith missing from his tone. "May I at least say good-bye to my family?"

Blaine glared at the man's back as Sheppard held his breath and waited. "Yes, but remember, we do know what it is you're saying."

"Oh, sir, I do remember." The soldiers allowed Marchia to move back into the room where his children and wife crowded against him. Unable to touch or see one another, the contact of their bodies seemed to soothe them.

"*Ma'assalama,*" Marchia said quietly.

Behind him, Sheppard heard one of the Mossad agents translate for Blaine. "He says, 'Go in peace.'"

"*Fi aman Ma'assalam,*" Marchia's wife replied, leaning her head toward her husband's voice until she felt his lips against her forehead.

"She merely replied in kind," the Mossad agent whispered.

"*Ma'assalama, Papa,*" the children echoed to their father. Marchia returned the blessing to each of them, fighting back the tears he knew his captors could not see for the hood. The marines grabbed him roughly by the shoulders and hurried him into the waiting truck. The rest of his family were herded out the back door and through the garden to a truck that waited in the alley.

* * *

Sheppard and the men of Red Team escorted Adalla Marchia and his family onto the gutted United 747 for the long, uncomfortable ride back to Andrews Air Force Base. Once aboard the plane, Sheppard made sure the hostages were given water and strapped into the hard flight chairs that lined the walls of the huge hold. His men watched him suspiciously until he looked at them, grinned, and muttered, "Geneva Convention, gentlemen. Gotta honor the code!" The men laughed and Sheppard grunted to himself.

Marchia sat stiffly in his seat and prayed out loud under the watchful eyes of the Mossad agents who refused to allow him to kneel in the proper way. Sheppard put the canteen down on the seat and stood watching the terrorist straining against the belts in an attempt to bow.

"*Yu-Muzillu . . . Yu-Muzillu . . . Yu-Muzillu . . .*" Marchia repeated, leaning forward as far as he was able between each chant. He wished that he could place his forehead to the floor in proper obeisance while praying that Allah would forgive him and punish his captors accordingly.

Sheppard stepped up beside one of the Mossad agents. "What's he sayin'?" he asked in a whisper.

"He is praying," the agent answered quietly. "*Yu-Muzillu* is one of the ninety-nine names of God in Islamic tradition. It means 'The Dishonorer.' He who repeats the name seventy-five times will be freed from harm by those who wish to harm him. Allah is supposed to protect him." The agent shook his head and walked to the front of the plane, drawn by the smell of coffee brewing.

Sheppard watched Marchia repeat his prayer a dozen times, each utterance the same as the last, and wondered if Allah cared that the man was a terrorist.

NINE

Private Quarters of the President and First Lady
The White House
Washington, D.C.

DAVID AND SARAH WALSH HAD BEEN ENDURING AN ENDLESS DINNER alone together when there was a sharp rap on the door.

"Yeah, come in," Walsh snapped, giving his wife a look that pleaded with her to behave.

"Sir," Jim Sercu stepped hesitantly into the room and nodded at Sarah, "Ma'am. I'm sorry to interrupt your dinner, but you asked to be informed when our target was reached."

"Yes, Jim, what's happened?"

"The general has attained the target, or should I say targets, and will be returning to home soil with them."

"Casualties?" Walsh asked, pleased that the operation had apparently gone smoothly.

"Yes, sir, a fatality."

Sarah looked up and studied Sercu's face. "Who? What happened?" she asked.

"Sarah," Walsh warned. But she ignored him.

"What happened, Jim?" Sarah insisted.

Sercu looked from Sarah to David, his reluctance written across his expression.

"Go ahead," David gave in. He had long since given up arguing with Sarah. She had already proven she could cause him no end of trouble, but as long as he placated her, she seemed to be behaving herself.

"A commander in the Marine Corps was shot, sir, ma'am."

"By your target?" Sarah asked, staring intently at Secru.

"By one of the targets, ma'am."

Walsh was puzzled by the answer; the other targets were Marchia's children, to be taken more for their own safety than anything else. "You mean . . . ?"

"Yes, sir, the eldest son shot and killed one of our men," Sercu said as he pulled a much-worn handkerchief out of his pocket and swiped it across his face. "This isn't something that can ever be public knowledge, sir."

Sarah, having put two and two together and not liking the answer, suddenly flew out of her chair. "I thought you said that they were terrorists! Now you make it sound like a child has killed one of our soldiers! What are you talking about?!" She demanded, the anger rising like heat in her face.

"Sarah," David tried to calm her, "the terrorist's family were present and one of them apparently tried to defend the rest. You can hardly blame him, can you?"

"Not at all!" Sarah, practically screaming now, paced around the dining room. "Especially since you sent your thugs after children! David, how could you?"

"That has nothing to do with it," Walsh tried to stop her wild pacing, but Sarah bolted down a hallway, slamming the door behind her.

Walsh turned back to Sercu, "Where are they now?"

Sercu glanced at his watch, "The plane should have taken off from Khartoum forty-five minutes ago. They maintained radio silence until well under way."

"And where are they going?"

"They are scheduled to land at Andrews, and then General Blaine will be moving the prisoners to one of the safe houses in Virginia." Sercu stole occasional glances down the hallway where Sarah had disappeared.

"Which safe house, Jim?"

"Blaine is keeping mum on that one, sir, but I can make a good guess." He paused until the president gestured for him to go on. "There's one that he had fully soundproofed and fortified a couple of years back. I'd bet it's that one."

Walsh thanked him and Sercu made a hasty retreat from the president's private quarters. James Sercu was a top national security adviser. He could be as cool as ice in stressful situations, but when it came to other people's marriages, he would rather pound nails into his own hand than get involved. Walsh smiled as the man's back vanished through the door. He, on the other hand, had to deal with this marriage.

"Sarah!" he called out, heading down the hallway to the door of her private sitting room. It was locked. "Sarah, c'mon out of there and talk to me. This isn't going to solve anything."

"There's nothing left to solve, David," she said through the closed door. Walsh could hear the rustling of papers and heavy objects being slammed down. He was suddenly glad for the locked door.

"Sarah, honey, there are things going on that you don't know about. I've got a lot to deal with right now. Please don't do this."

The door flew open and his wife, fire in her eyes, stormed past him back down the hall.

"It's never the right time, David. But don't worry, you won't have to deal with it anymore." Her voice was high and strained. He had never heard this tone from her before.

"Sarah, I was only trying to save you from having to deal with things right off the bat. Sit down and let's talk about it."

"It's too late, David, and you won't have to worry about saving me from anything anymore. I'm filing for divorce."

The words shocked him into silence. He felt the blood drain out of his face as the enormity of what she said sank in. She could not do this to him, not now, not when he needed her here beside him.

Sarah stopped and stared at him. "Oh don't pull this again, David. It's not going to work. The poor little brand-new president will just have to cope on his own. Imagine your legacy! Instead of illicit affairs and arms deals you can go down in history as the first president divorced while serving his term in office!"

TEN

The Carlisle Hotel
New York, NY

"DUNN," WARREN DUNN ANSWERED THE PHONE IN HIS PENTHOUSE apartment in New York City. When he heard the voice on the other end, he quietly closed the bathroom door so that the young lady currently taking advantage of the shower could not overhear. "What is it, Tuttle?"

"Blaine has picked up Marchia and his family. They're on their way back to the States tonight." Tuttle's voice sounded strained and his whispering all too obvious. Dunn could picture him huddled over the telephone like a rat with a piece of food.

Shit! Dunn thought, but held the surprise out of his voice. The less Tuttle realized the intricacies of the web he was weaving the better. "Yes, and . . . ?"

"Come on, Warren, you know who Marchia is!"

"Yes, Ian," Dunn spat out Tuttle's name like it was a bitter pill. "I know who Marchia is. Now tell me why this is a problem. Someone like Adalla Marchia will not talk." Dunn carried the phone into the sitting room opposite the bedroom. The hotel had provided a basket of fruit and he snagged a bunch of grapes before comfortably seating himself in an arm chair.

"It seems his son killed a marine," Tuttle whispered.

Dunn had to hold back a chuckle. That would be Marchia all right. Any offspring of his would never hesitate to grab the bull by the horns, or the marines by the balls, in this case. "Oh, now that is interesting," Warren said, his voice level and calm. "Where is Marchia now?"

"They're taking him to one of the safe houses in Virginia."

"Which one?"

"Are you kidding? Blaine wouldn't let his grandmother know which one, let alone a member of the president's staff. Walsh probably doesn't even know!"

"Yes, yes, that would be just like Louis." Dunn sucked the flesh out of a grape and dropped the empty skin on the carpet. "All right, Tuttle, you keep your ears open and your nose clean. I'll get back in touch with you when I need you." He softly dropped the receiver back into the cradle as a leggy blonde, fresh from a shower, sauntered into the room eyeing him with a suggestive smile. "Get out!" he barked.

The blonde looked hurt, but gathered up her things before sticking her hand out to Dunn with a pout. Dunn dropped a few bills into her open palm and slapped her rump sharply as he pushed her toward the door. "Now get lost." He slammed the door behind her and pressed his back against it. "I've got some work to do. . . ."

ELEVEN

U.S. Government Safe House
Virginia Horse Country

BLAINE'S MEN HAD MOVED MARCHIA INTO THE SAFE HOUSE IN THE early hours of a dark morning. They had carefully kept Marchia separated from his family and brought them to the property in different vans. Marchia was now shackled and blindfolded in a soundproof room in the basement of the old mansion while his wife and children were locked in separate, windowless rooms in the adjacent carriage house. The nearest neighbor was miles away and any passersby would have seen only a group of the apparently young and privileged tending to their mounts on the wide paddocks of the estate. No one would have guessed that the burly riders cantering along the fence line wore flak jackets beneath their weekend wear and had small submachine guns strapped under the stirrups of their saddles.

Inside the house, Red Team continued to hold watch over the hostages, a fact that had Hawley Sheppard less than pleased.

Sheppard sat in the estate's huge kitchen hunched over a cup of black coffee. He couldn't hear the cries of the children or the wails of Marchia's wife—the buildings were too well soundproofed—but he could still hear them in his imagination.

Sheppard wasn't a family man, forgoing marriage and children for his career. But he came from a large family and a strict army background. His father had served for forty years before his death, and he and his seven brothers and sisters had been army brats in the truest sense of the word. Now he rarely saw his siblings or their children, a sacrifice to his career. He knew in his heart and mind that he was violating one of the prime directives of Red Team: Don't get emotionally involved. He sat in silence waiting for the next phase to begin.

In a control room in the basement of the house, Blaine watched Marchia on a closed-circuit TV monitor. There wasn't much to see. Marchia sat in a hard wooden chair, arms and legs shackled, and rocked back and forth muttering prayers under his breath.

In the small concrete cell, Marchia's world had shrunk to the blackness of the blindfold and the painful scrape of the shackles on his wrists and ankles. He continued softly to chant the ninety-nine names of God, concentrating hard to keep his place in the progression and to keep from thinking about what might be happening to his family.

He always knew that his own capture was a real possibility, and his family would probably also be taken. Saddam had warned him. He should not have been so proud as to believe he could protect them. At least their deaths would be in the service of Allah, which was only as it should be.

Regardless of the personal risks, he had a mission to carry out, a message to deliver to the heathen American president. Once that message was delivered and his destiny fulfilled, Allah would care for his children; Allah would provide.

Marchia smiled as he mouthed the prayer in a whisper, "Ya-Muhaymin, He who protects . . ." He couldn't see General Blaine peering at him through the tiny window in the heavy metal door. All Blaine saw was a grinning madman.

Blaine would have left Marchia sitting there all night long, but, as the White House continued to remind him, time was short. He had only a few precious hours to find out everything the man knew. A soft tread of feet on the stair announced the arrival of Colonel David Ziegelhofer, a six-foot-six-inch mountain of a man who dwarfed even Hawley Sheppard. He stopped in the doorway and saluted his superior officer.

"Colonel, I'm glad you're here," Blaine pumped the big man's hand, then gesturing to the TV monitor said, "That's our man."

"Doesn't seem like much." Ziegelhofer's bass baritone fit every inch of his massive frame.

"They never do, do they?" Blaine gestured to the door and the watch commander threw the locking control. "You've been briefed? Ready to get to work?"

Ziegelhofer nodded and the two men stepped into the cell.

Marchia cocked his head to one side, "Ah, is it time then, gentlemen?" he asked softly.

Blaine and Ziegelhofer exchanged glances.

"There's one surefire way to make this easy on everybody," Blaine said, his posture dropping into parade rest. "Just tell us what we want to know and it'll be all over. For you and for those two sweet girls of yours." Blaine stared at the blindfolded man, measuring every reaction, every droplet of sweat that beaded on his brow. Marchia said nothing.

"I can't believe a good father like you would stand by and let anything horrible happen to those two pretty little things. What are they? Fifteen? Sixteen?"

"They are innocent, General Blaine, that is all. They can do nothing to help you." Marchia kept his voice low and even, belying the unease he felt.

"Well now, sir, there isn't much we can do about that . . . and I don't know that it really matters whether or not they can help us, if you get my meaning," Blaine's voice was cold and menacing.

"Yes, sir, I believe I do get your meaning," Marchia kept his face pointed where Blaine's voice was coming from, but he listened carefully for the movement of the other man. Nothing but silence. "I won't insult you by trying to make a deal with you, general," he continued. "You're a smart man, that's obvious. To put it simply, I have a message to deliver. But by Allah's supreme order I must deliver it to only one man."

"Oh, divine order, huh?" Blaine scoffed. "And to whom are you supposed to deliver this message from Allah?"

Marchia detested the way the brute said the holy name of the savior. Najla had implied these bastards weren't worth talking to, and now he saw her point. "I have a message for Mr. David Walsh, the president of your United States."

Blaine and Ziegelhofer looked at one another and Blaine nodded slightly.

"How about you just tell me what that divine message is and I'll make sure it gets to the president safe and sound." Blaine knew his mocking tone would only inflame the situation, but he was itching to get his hands dirty, and he had Bobby Francazi's memory to think about.

"No," Marchia said simply.

"Okay, let's try this one on for size. Either you tell us what we want to know, or we'll just have some fun with those little girls of yours before we ship 'em back to Khartoum."

"Their deaths will only create martyrs, general. Is that what you really desire?" Marchia fought to hold his voice steady. He refused to give these bastards anything.

"Oh, sir!" Blaine shouted, stepping around the chair and laughing. "I have no intention of killing anyone! Just having a good long screw and then maybe letting my men have some fun, too!"

Marchia's face flamed red with anger and embarrassment. If these men so much as touched his daughters their lives would be over, worthless, and their souls damned to hell. He spat, hoping to hit Blaine's well-polished boot but did not know where the man now stood. "You and all your like are truly heathen bastards! May Allah rain fire and torment on all your kin!"

"Colonel," Blaine said turning to Ziegelhofer, "I think it's your turn to try some persuasion on our guest."

An hour later, Blaine and Ziegelhofer pulled the cell door shut behind them. Inside the cell, Marchia slumped in his chair, the shackles the only things keeping him from tumbling to the floor. In the control room, Hawley Sheppard had relieved the watch commander and had to hide his agitation forcibly.

"I'll get on the horn to the White House," Blaine was saying. "Go to the carriage house and bring one of those girls over here. We'll try again as soon as I've spoken to the president."

Ziegelhofer snapped a neat salute and about-faced to charge up the steps two at a time. Blaine, who was not completely oblivious to Sheppard's state of mind during the operation, turned on the man unexpectedly.

"Okay, sergeant, you've obviously got a complaint with me. Let's hear it!" he barked, sending Sheppard flying to his feet at full attention.

"Sir," Sheppard yelped, surprised by his own voice, but there was no going back now. The general had asked a direct question and would not settle for any less than a direct answer. "Sir, I understand there are reasons for what has happened here today, but I cannot hide my discomf . . . "

Blaine cut him off with one huge step forward that brought the two men nearly nose to nose, Blaine not the least bit cowed by having to look up at the sergeant. "No, Sheppard, you obviously do not understand a damned thing!" Blaine lowered his voice. "You do not understand that this man is a terrorist, responsible for who knows how many innocent deaths, and is now behind a conspiracy to bring enough anthrax-contaminated material onto U.S. shores to kill thousands. Do you have any idea what that means, mister?"

Sheppard said nothing, but kept his eyes forward and held perfectly still.

"It means that in one single afternoon those bastards could wipe out the entire East Coast of this country. Men, women, and children—all dead."

Sheppard stole a quick glance at his commanding officer's face, saw the truth in the man's eyes, and drew in a sharp breath. Blaine eased back a pace but kept his gaze locked on Sheppard's face.

"Do you think this son of a bitch's life is worth the lives of your nieces and nephews? Would you put his offspring before your own people?" Blaine let the words sink in. "Would you, sargent?"

"No, sir." The words barely made it out of Sheppard's mouth. He was frightened, ashamed, angry, and furious, all at the same time. "No, sir."

TWELVE

The Oval Office
The White House
Washington, D.C.

DAVID WALSH SHOOED HIS SOMETIMES OVERLY ATTENTIVE SECRETARY out of the Oval Office and asked her to make sure he had a few minutes to himself. Things had been so busy the last few days he hadn't had time to think, let alone try to figure out what to do about Sarah.

After her grand announcement that she wanted a divorce, Sarah moved into guest quarters adjoining the president's suite of rooms. The rooms were normally reserved for family members, so she was able to maintain the appearance of everything being normal even though it was far from it.

Walsh settled into the high-backed leather chair and took a moment to look around the Oval Office. It really was an impressive room. Just thinking about the history these walls had seen overawed Walsh and made him feel very small and insignificant in the scheme of things. Occupying this office had been his dream since he was a teenager. He had fought long and hard to get where he was at the moment, and yet he wasn't at all sure it had been worth the sacrifice. But time would prove that, right or wrong. One thing he did know was that this office meant he could no longer spend time pondering the day-to-day problems of his personal life—and yet he couldn't bring himself to concentrate on work alone and let Sarah slip away.

David knew that Ian was holding a meeting of his staff in the adjacent office, but the room in which he sat was perfectly silent. No sound penetrated the well-insulated walls. He knew that office contained the best of the best, each person handpicked, each one worthy of the appointment. He had put together a good administration with Tuttle's help, the finest available. Now all he had to do was make that administration work.

The blaring phone on the desk shattered the momentary peace. Walsh groaned and rubbed his hands over his face before flipping the receiver off the cradle and catching it in midair. On the other end his secretary let out a little gasp, surprised he had picked it up instead of just using the speaker.

"Oh, ah, sir. Mr. Sercu is here and he says it's important."

"It always is, Colleen, let him in." Walsh hurriedly shuffled the papers on the desk and grabbed a pen—not good to be caught goofing off so early.

Sercu burst through the door, not the least bit mindful of what the president had been doing a moment before. "Sir, General Blaine is on the videophone from the safe house. He's asked to speak with you personally."

* * *

Something in Sercu's manner had set Walsh's nerves on edge instantly. The ride down the security elevator to the Situation Room and Control Center seemed to take much longer than it had the day before. Sercu fidgeted with his cuff links the whole way down. Walsh stood, hands behind his back, forcing himself to be still, to be patient.

In the Situation Room, Blaine's face filled the large screen on one wall. He saluted the camera when Walsh appeared on the monitor at his end.

"Mr. President!"

"General Blaine." Walsh slid into one of the chairs, unbuttoned his jacket, and braced himself for what was to come. "How's it going with our guest?"

"I wish I had better news to report, sir, but this guy isn't willing to talk to us. Colonel Ziegelhofer and I have personally interrogated the guest and he's stuck to his convictions remarkably well."

Ziegelhofer, Walsh knew, had a reputation for getting to the root of any issue. Blaine's euphemisms didn't disguise the reality of what must be going on down there.

"Sir," Blaine continued, "this Marchia says that he has a divine message from Allah that he can only deliver to one man."

Walsh controlled his urge to smile slightly. Blaine didn't like having anyone withstand his form of persuasion. "And who is it he wants to talk to, general?" Walsh already knew the answer. It was written in Blaine's eyes and in the scowl on his face.

"You, sir. He says he can only give the message to you."

"That's impossible!" Sercu blurted out. "Sir, I cannot allow . . ."

Walsh held up a hand to quiet him, wanting to be touched by the concern, but knowing it was far more than his personal security that was at risk here. "General Blaine, has Mr. Marchia given you any indication of what this message might be about?"

"I think we can guess. . . ." Sercu began.

"Jim," Walsh said the name quietly, and Sercu dropped back into his seat.

"No, sir, he hasn't said a word. We've tried several methods to persuade him to talk, but he's kept his mouth shut. I still have a few more things to try."

Walsh didn't like the sound of that. He fully understood what was at stake, but didn't like that route to the solution. "General, what would be involved in giving this man what he wants? Couldn't you just set him up in front of the videophone and let him talk?"

"Well, that would be my choice, sir, but he claims it has to be a face-to-face meeting, something about the will of Allah. Sir, I don't recommend . . ."

"General," Walsh cut him off sharply, "we don't have much time left. If the information provided by the Israelis is correct, we may have a biological disaster sitting at our airports as we speak. If I have to meet with a terrorist face-to-face to get the answer, then that's what I will do."

"Mr. President, I advise you not to do this. Who knows what he might have in mind? He may have some way of assassinating you that none of us can even imagine." Sercu was pale; thoughts of losing the new president barely weeks into his administration terrified him, not to mention the risk his friend was willing to take.

"General Blaine, do you believe that this man could possibly be a fatal risk to me? Can you foresee any eventuality in this situation?" His voice was stern, leaving no room for anyone to question his decision. His mind was already made up.

"No, sir, I don't believe he could do anything that would put your life at risk. But I do not condone giving in to any terrorist demand, even one as important as this."

"Duly noted, general. Where should we do this?"

Sercu jumped in, "You can't go down there. You'd have to take an entourage of Secret Service men with you; the helicopter could be traced and a car could be followed. We can't risk the safe house."

"Mr. Sercu is correct, sir. We would have to bring Marchia to you, at the White House. There is a system of tunnels that runs beneath the White House and the grounds. We could bring him in through Marilyn."

"Marilyn?" Walsh asked, confused.

"The Marilyn Monroe tunnel, sir."

Walsh almost laughed, "I thought those tunnels were an urban legend."

"No, sir," Sercu interjected. "They're very real. General Blaine will be able to pull an armored transport into the basement parking garage of the Treasury Building and then walk Marchia through the Monroe tunnel to the bunkers under the White House."

Blaine was interrupted by the muffled screams of a young girl in the background. "Excuse me, sir," he stepped out of the field of the camera and returned a few seconds later. "I'm sorry, sir."

"What was that, general?" Walsh asked, cautiously.

"That was one of Marchia's daughters. We were demonstrating to him that we mean business."

Walsh shot Sercu a look that left no doubt about his feelings on the matter, but he said nothing.

"General," Sercu said, taking control of the situation while Walsh left the room, "make your arrangements."

"Yes, sir."

THIRTEEN

Office of Prime Minister Eli Mordachi
Tel Aviv, Israel

IT WAS NEARLY 11:00 P.M. IN TEL AVIV, AND ISRAELI PRIME MINISTER Eli Mordachi had been thinking long and hard about the problems his American allies were facing. It was hard enough controlling his own borders, but if a terrorist like bin Laden was willing to take on the only remaining superpower in the world, it would not be long before his tiny country had more than just the Palestinians to worry about.

His ruminations were interrupted by the high-pitched ring of the phone that directly connected his home study to the government offices. He snatched up the receiver impatiently.

"Mr. Prime Minister, I'm sorry to disturb you, sir," the operator said carefully, noting the tone of the minister's voice, "but you have a call from the U.S. president David Walsh. He says it is urgent, sir."

Mordachi thanked the operator and waited for the click of the connection. "Good afternoon, Mr. President," he said more cheerfully than he felt. "Or is it evening in your part of the world?"

"Mr. Prime Minister, nice to hear your voice again," Walsh's voice sounded very far away and very strained. "It is getting dark here, in more ways than one. And I'm afraid it's going to get a lot darker if I can't prevent certain things from happening."

"Yes, I heard. Our Mossad has kept me informed of the events in Khartoum," said the prime minister. "How can we help?"

"Frankly," said David Walsh, "I'm not sure. As you know, we have Adalla Marchia and his family in custody now. What bothers me is that our team had no problem with the extraction. No interference and, aside from one of Marchia's sons getting the better of one of our marines, they didn't even put up a fight. It was almost as though he had been planning to be taken."

The prime minister listened intently. An old freedom fighter from the days of Hagganah, he understood terrorism—especially the Arab kind. Every action, or lack of action, had a purpose.

"Given your experience, I was hoping that you might have some insight into what Marchia may be trying to do that isn't readily evident on the surface." Mordachi was momentarily surprised by the request. Usually such exchanges of information would be handled through intermediaries. He was intrigued by Walsh's hands-on approach to the situation.

"Mr. President," Mordachi began, but was interrupted.

"Call me David, please. This isn't the time to stick to formalities." Mordachi chuckled, Americans never stuck to formalities for very long.

"Then you must call me Eli. David, I believe the man you have in custody has a message, a message he believes is very, very important. Otherwise, your people would never have gotten him alive. Remember, these people are fanatics. They believe that Allah will reward those who give their lives to him. And vanquishing the heathens is the best way to serve their faith and get to heaven. You must understand that we in the Middle East have always lived by a different code than Western peoples. This is changing in many ways, but the fanatical followers of Islam hold very tightly to their traditions."

Mordachi heard what could only be a sigh. "So, what would

you advise? This man wants to meet with me and me alone, face-to-face, before he will deliver his message."

"Do you feel that this message could aid you in averting the threat to your people?" Mordachi knew the answer even before Walsh spoke.

"I have to assume it will, Eli. We don't have anything else to go on right now."

"David, I will put at your disposal three counterterrorist agents of the Mossad. These men are specialists in Arab terrorism. I will have them to you no later than 3:00 P.M. tomorrow, your time."

"That really isn't necessary, Eli. My men can handle the situation from here and you need your people there."

"Three men aren't going to lose my war, David. If I can speak freely, I think your men do need our help. Do you know what the word *kidon* means?" he paused, giving Walsh time to wonder where this was going.

"No, Eli, I don't."

"It is a Hebrew word that means bayonet. The Mossad has three *kidon* teams. Everything you have ever heard about the ruthlessness of the Mossad is true one hundred fold for the members of the *kidon*. Your men are good, David. The *kidon* are one hundred percent effective."

"All right, Eli, I'll have General Seiffert get in touch with your intelligence and they can arrange . . ."

"No, David, you do not understand. There is only one person who can release *kidon*, and that is me. I am already having the orders drawn up for my signature. My friend, I do not think I am giving you a choice." Mordachi's laughter echoed through the secure phone line, leaving David wondering what hidden agenda he might not be seeing in this situation. Certainly the Israelis had a stake in the outcome of the next few days.

"All right, Eli, we welcome the help of your men," Walsh

consented and immediately felt better for it.

"Good, good! The *kidon,* together with the expertise of your men, will give you a better chance of beating this Adalla Marchia. And for the sake of us all, I hope you do."

David Walsh replaced the receiver and looked around the Oval Office for the hundredth time. Suddenly the weight of the presidency had increased tenfold. He fought down his doubts and rang an aide to bring more coffee. He had more phone calls to make.

FOURTEEN

10 Downing Street
Prime Minister's Residence
London, England

JOHN LAUGHTON HAD BEEN LIVING AT 10 DOWNING STREET FOR ONLY nine months, and he already felt that it was the only place in London where he could escape the pressures of Parliament. The British prime minister fancied himself a New Age Margaret Thatcher. Tall, slim, and handsome, he was a forty-six-year-old bachelor, something his opponents had tried to use against him in the popular election. The entire political world thought he was full of himself—but he was unstoppable in Parliament. Lords and peers alike were careful when they had to cross him, and his reputation as a fair and honest leader was growing. And, next to His Royal Highness, he was one of the world's most eligible bachelors, a title he relished more than any other.

The quality that Laughton's detractors disliked more than any other was his admiration for the new American president. He had followed Walsh's campaign through the election and had watched the inauguration with a fanatical attention, even allowing himself the minor conceit that if he had had a woman like Sarah Walsh, he would have eagerly given up his bachelor status.

When Laughton's phone rang at 1:00 A.M., he snapped out of a doze, knocked a thick volume of philosophy to the floor and stared around the small living room in confusion. With the second ring, he shook his head to clear the cobwebs before grabbing the receiver.

"What? Who?" he demanded of the sergeant major on the other end. "David Walsh? Well, bloody hell, put the man through!" He straightened his smoking jacket and ran a hand through tousled blond hair.

"Good morning, John," Walsh said after the click, "I'm sorry to wake you, but I've got some things going on here that I really need to discuss."

"David, how nice to hear from you. No, you didn't wake me, just sitting here reading. You know you're always welcome to call. What can I do for you, old son?"

Walsh reminded Laughton of the events in Khartoum and the role of the British Embassy there before filling him in on the events leading to his phone call.

"Well, David," Laughton said after listening carefully, "you know you can count on every cooperation from this end of the pond. Whatever you need, I'll push it through our house as fast as I can. And if they argue, I'll just do it anyway." He laughed in a particularly British nasal way. Walsh couldn't help but smile.

"Thank you, John. I knew I could count on you. The terrorism is aimed at the United States right now, but there's no way to predict where they will aim next."

"Quite right, quite right. And while I have you on the phone, I had an idea I wanted to run by you the next time we talked, and this seems as good a time as any."

Walsh reached for the pot of coffee the aide had left on his desk. "Of course, John, you know I'm open to anything you might suggest."

"No need to give this any thought until you're in the clear. But once this is over— it will end in your favor, of course— I propose that we organize a governing body to oversee antiterrorism initiatives. If we all work together, we'll have a better chance of nipping this in the bud. But time enough for that after we get you out of this nasty situation. For now, my advice to you, David, is to proceed with the utmost caution; use Mordachi's men to the fullest; and find out what this bastard wants from you. Once you determine that, get back to Mordachi and me and let's see what we can do to help sort this all out. And, as always, Mother England will be at your flank."

"Thank you, John. I knew I could count on you. Now go back to bed."

Laughton laughed loudly, "If you think I can sleep now! Good night, old son."

Walsh hung up the phone, an uneasy smile playing on his face. He had the best people behind him, but he was still facing the hardest parts of this crisis alone.

Walsh took his cup of coffee and stood in the window of the Oval Office looking out at the lights of Washington, D.C. It all looked so peaceful in the darkness. He couldn't hear the rushing of the traffic or the inevitable noises of a busy city. A plane blinked in the far distance, probably out of Dulles Airport in Virginia, but no rumble of jet engines penetrated the room. Walsh suddenly knew what it would feel like to be the last man on Earth. The loneliness made him shudder.

His thoughts were broken by the insistent dinging of his intercom. Putting down his coffee cup, he slapped the button on the phone. "Yes, Colleen, what is it?" His tone was harder than he had intended.

"Sir, you asked me to let you know when Mrs. Walsh returned."

"Yes, Colleen, yes I did."

"Agent Savage just reported that the Secret Service dropped her at your quarters a moment ago."

"Thank you, Colleen. Where is Sercu?"

"He was in the Control Center. Would you like me to find him for you?"

"Yes, Colleen, have him come up here ASAP."

"Yes, sir."

The president sank into his chair. Sarah was another problem he had been putting off. His first impulse was to go to her, explain the situation, and have her inoculated against anthrax as he had been only that morning. But she had barely spoken to him since she had learned of the death of that marine in Khartoum. She behaved as though she hated him. He knew she felt like a prisoner. He had had little choice but to keep a tight rein on her and the Secret Service agents were getting their shins kicked trying to follow orders.

Walsh felt his gut tighten and a formless ache in his chest when he realized he probably couldn't trust her anymore. If he explained the situation to her he could imagine her refusing the shot and then going straight to the press with the story. She was not vindictive by nature, but she was passionate and she would see it as her duty. No, if the rest of the cabinet had to keep the secret from their families, then he had no right to violate that trust, president or not. Besides, they were still working out a way to have the families inoculated without their knowledge. The experts merely hadn't found a way to do so yet.

FIFTEEN

Capitol Hill
Washington, D.C.

IT WAS 8:00 A.M. AND IAN TUTTLE FOUND HIMSELF IN A BLACK Lincoln town car on his way to the Capitol. Walsh had given strict orders that Tuttle was to round up the cabinet members in person— not on the phone, no pages, and no messages. He was to track each of them down, one by one, and ensure their presence in the White House Situation Room no later than noon. Tuttle grumbled softly to himself as he fidgeted in the oversized leather seat. The car sped quietly through the morning streets of D.C., without even a second glance from the people beginning their day. It was ridiculous, he thought, to waste his valuable time on this errand. He threw himself into yet another position and rested his cheek against the window. He didn't notice the driver, a highly trained Secret Service agent, watching his temper tantrum in the rearview mirror.

Then a thought struck Tuttle and he fished his cell phone from a coat pocket, disregarding the specially shielded phone provided in the car, and punched in Warren Dunn's number.

When Dunn picked up his phone, Tuttle grinned. "Good morning, Warren."

"Tuttle," Dunn growled. One day he would knock Tuttle silly

for taking such liberties with him, but for now . . . "What is it?"

Ian filled in Dunn on the events of the last few hours.

"I assume Walsh has called his friends in Israel," Dunn muttered more to himself than to Tuttle.

"That I don't know for sure, but I do know they're bringing Marchia to the White House bunkers this afternoon. I wasn't privy to the logistics of the move, but I did hear that someone named Marilyn is involved. I assume it's a code name for an operative." Tuttle puffed importantly.

"Tuttle, you idiot! Marilyn is the Marilyn Monroe tunnel, not an operative!" Dunn snapped. "They're bringing him in through the Treasury Department Building. How in God's name did you ever graduate from Princeton?"

"Warren, I really think that this is uncalled for; the Marilyn Monroe tunnel is merely an urban leg . . ."

"Stop being a fucking asshole, Tuttle! It's real and it's the perfect way to move Marchia in without calling attention to him." Dunn's mind raced to the implications of the next few hours. "Interesting . . ."

"Everything is going our way," Tuttle hurried to try to distract Dunn from his error. "If the terrorists attack the United States with Anthrax, I would be very surprised if Walsh didn't retaliate with every bit of force at his command. It would leave oil fields all over the Mideast ripe for the picking."

"Well, fuck the conjecture, Ian," Dunn said quietly with a tone of voice Tuttle found more than a little frightening. "Find out what he is going to do and let me know immediately." The line clicked and then went dead. Tuttle drew in an anxious breath.

In the front of the car, two Secret Service agents glanced carefully at one another, each reading the thoughts of his partner with unerring exactness. Tuttle had not noticed that the clear Plexiglas privacy shield separating the backseat from the front remained down. The Secret Service agents, realizing what was happening in the back of the car had waited silently while the phone call played itself out. Now they had some decisions to make.

Pulling into the secure garage at the Capitol Building, the driver said softly, "We're here, sir."

Tuttle looked up at the man watching him in the rearview mirror as the realization slowly dawned on him that the screen was down. He stared back into the mirrored eyes as the color drained from his face, a fact the agent did not miss. Ian swallowed hard, straightened his tie and snapped, "It's about time, too!" He let himself out of the car and momentarily toyed with the idea of reminding the two hulks in the front seat of the seriousness of their duty.

"Wait for me," he ordered, mustering every ounce of superiority he could before charging off to the elevator bank.

The Secret Service is charged with minding their passengers not their passengers' business, Tuttle reassured himself. Besides, he thought, they could not have the slightest idea about what was being discussed. They had been briefed before leaving the White House that this trip was of the utmost importance, and secrecy had to be maintained. And if that wasn't enough, he was Ian Tuttle after all, chief of staff to the president of the United States—that should be enough to keep their mouths shut.

* * *

In the parking garage, agents Bomen and Poule leaned against the car and watched Tuttle board the elevator.

"Asshole," Bomen muttered.

"Hey, Dave, watch it! Remember, these walls have ears," Poule said softly. "I think we have some things to discuss."

Bomen glanced at his partner. The two had been together for ten years and hardly needed to speak their thoughts out loud. "So it wasn't my imagination?" he asked.

"Not unless it was mine, too," Poule shook his head. "The only problem is, what chance is there that it wasn't what it sounded like?"

"Every chance," Bomen said quietly. "So do we risk it or do we clam up?"

"If this shit is as bad as it sounds, can we afford to clam up about it?" Poule knew his partner was the more levelheaded and trusted his intuition one hundred percent. But if they spoke up and the conversation they overheard had been ordered by the president, they would both be out of jobs and probably brought up on charges.

Bomen thought for a long minute. "With everything we've heard over the past few days, do you think anyone would blame us for being too cautious?" Bomen felt like he was violating every commandment, the Golden Rule, and half of the laws of the universe.

"Anthrax! Man, that's scary shit," Poule spoke for both of them.

"Yeah, it sure is."

SIXTEEN

The White House Situation Room
Washington, D.C.

BY 12:15 P.M., PRESIDENT DAVID WALSH'S CABINET HAD ASSEMBLED IN the White House Situation Room where they waited anxiously for the arrival of the President and Jim Sercu. The entire assembly flinched noticeably when the secure door at one end of the room slid open and Vice president Harry Dent entered the room. He nodded gravely, and quickly took his seat to the right of the president's chair.

The next time the door slid open President Walsh marched purposefully into the room, Jim Sercu at his heels.

"Thank you all for making it," Walsh addressed his staff as he dropped heavily into his chair. "We've got a lot to do today and some of what we're about to tell you is going to shock the hell out of you, so brace yourselves."

Walsh allowed Sercu to brief everyone on the events leading up to that moment. They all sat quietly and listened, knowing their questions would be better left until the briefing was finished. All except the chairman of the Joint Chiefs, Ned Seiffert. Seiffert sat stiffly in his chair, his anger becoming more apparent the longer Sercu talked. By the time Walsh took the floor to explain the outcome of his late-night phone calls to London and Tel Aviv,

Seiffert was coiled so tightly he appeared to be leaping out of his chair even though he sat perfectly still.

"So that's where we stand, people. The promised Mossad agents will be landing at Andrews in about an hour. We need to decide on appropriate security for the meeting, and begin planning strategies for every possible outcome we can imagine." Walsh glanced quickly around the table, gauging the reactions of his advisers and pinpointing Seiffert as the first obstacle to be overcome. "Any questions?"

"No, sir," Seiffert snapped rising to his feet. "There is no question that this can't be allowed to happen! It is unthinkable that any member of this staff would ever condone a face-to-face meeting between yourself and a known terrorist. I will handle the meeting myself."

Walsh paused, allowing Seiffert to take a breath before he spoke, "Ned, I appreciate your concern . . . "

"Excuse me, sir." Seiffert was obviously having a hard time controlling his outrage at the situation. "This is not merely concern, sir. I must object to this whole insane plan!"

"Noted, general. Now sit down, please." Walsh stood and Seiffert took his chair slowly. "I understand your concern, all of you. Believe me, I wish I had another solution. I don't relish it, but the simple fact of the matter is that General Blaine's best efforts have not budged this man." He paused while a quiet assent traveled around the table. "And we all know that if the general can't get an answer, we may risk losing that answer." Seiffert nodded knowingly. Barbara Howe, secretary of state, shook her head and frowned.

"Marchia won't talk to anyone. And short of killing his entire family . . . "

"David?" Harry Dent interrupted quietly, his face pale.

"Not now, Harry. We'll talk in a bit." Walsh fixed a hard gaze on his friend and vice president. "Don't break on me now, Harry," he thought. Dent looked hard at the blank note pad on the table. Harry Dent was an uncommonly intelligent person, well versed in the function of government and a master politician, the perfect man for a vice president. But he had a soft side that Walsh was afraid would show itself at a time like this. He only hoped Harry could control his emotions and pay attention to the bigger picture.

"As I was saying," Walsh continued, hardening his voice to drive the point home and to quell any further objections, "Marchia has refused to speak to anyone but me. I have no choice. The risk is too great for me to put my life above anyone else's."

"What do you think this man will tell you, sir?" Bill Cassidy, Walsh's secretary of defense, asked.

"I'm hoping he'll reveal something that will lead us to a peaceful resolution of this crisis," Walsh said matter-of-factly. "He may say nothing useful, but then again, the Joker always gave away his plot before he tried to kill off Batman and Robin." Soft chuckles spread around the table and Walsh smiled.

"I know I can't take this lightly, and that's certainly not what I'm doing, but I also can't get myself worked into such a state of fear that I sabotage the whole thing." Walsh took a chance that showing a little weakness would bring these people, these friends and colleagues, back into a strict consideration of what they could do to make the whole event as safe as possible. He glanced at Sercu, who took the cue and stood.

"Okay, people, we need to discuss security, surveillance, and analysis. Thoughts?"

The meeting jumped into gear and suddenly the room was bustling with discussion, argument, and conjecture. Walsh breathed deeply; if these people couldn't protect him, there was not much that could.

* * *

At 3:20 P.M. an aide announced the arrival of three Mossad agents. Ned Seiffert took the task of briefing the agents, who were escorted to the bunker deep beneath the White House. Precautions were under way and Walsh's staff had summoned the best of the best antiterrorist experts, as well as experts on Islam, Arabic culture, and even assassination attempts. No possibility was ignored, even the smallest chance that Marchia could try something as remote as poison-filled false teeth and internally concealed explosives were explored. Marchia would be examined by a doctor before he was brought to the White House. He would be searched, x-rayed, scanned and sniffed by specially trained dogs.

An argument was raging around the table as to the necessity to conceal Walsh behind bullet-proof Plexiglas and allow conversation only through a microphone, a plan which Walsh himself vetoed, when Harry Dent gestured for Walsh to join him by the coffee service at the back of the room.

"Harry, I know what you're going to . . . " Walsh began.

"Yes, David, you probably do, but let me say it anyway." He fixed Walsh with a searching look. "First, tell me who died?"

Walsh took a deep breath knowing the question was going to come and dreading it anyway. "One of Marchia's daughters."

"How?"

"Harry, don't do this to yourself," Walsh pleaded.

"How?"

"Blaine's man was making a point, trying to get Marchia to cave. I guess the humiliation was too great for the girl. She threw herself down a flight of stairs when they were moving her back to her cell. Cracked her skull really good and died on the operating table."

"My God, David, and you condone this?"

"Harry, what do you want me to do? We have hundreds of thousands of lives at stake, maybe millions. These men have been doing this for years with great success. I may be the president, but I don't have a lot to say about it." Walsh struggled to keep his voice low, but the conversation around the table dropped noticeably.

"I am sorry, David. Maybe I'm being naive, but I honestly believed that that kind of tactic was for the barbarians, the terrorists, not us."

"Amazing what a man will do when so many lives are at stake, isn't it, Harry?"

SEVENTEEN

The Treasury Building
Washington, D.C.

"WHAT ARE WE LOOKING FOR, SIR?" VINNIE SPERAZA ASKED, SHUTTING off the car's headlights, but leaving the engine idling.

"We are looking for anything that looks like an armored van or truck. I doubt they'll try using a car," Warren answered from a cloud of cigar smoke in the backseat.

"Wouldn't it be better to leave this kind of thing to the guys?" Speraza was unsettled by this change in plans. His job was nerve-wracking enough without Dunn changing his plans in mid-step and doing something so out of character as staking out the back door of a government building.

"It probably would, Vinnie. Thank you for your concern." Dunn blew out a stream of smoke and smiled; he really did like this man. "Call it conceit, but I just have this overwhelming urge to see this for myself."

"Excuse me, sir. I realize I can be thick sometimes, but what is there to see if it's an armored car?"

Dunn chuckled. "Nothing, Vinnie, nothing but an armored car. But we were in town and I don't have to be at the club until 9:00, so why not?"

Speraza shook his head. He often felt his employer spoke a

foreign language, but he had too much at stake to question anything Dunn set him to do.

* * *

"David," Sarah's voice was high pitched and urgent, calling after him down the long hallway leading to their quarters. "David, damn it, stop and answer me!"

David stopped with his hand on the doorknob. Three Secret Service agents stood in the corridor looking anywhere but at the president and First Lady. "Not in the hallway, Sarah. If you want to talk, come in with me and talk while I change."

"Why are you changing, David?" Sarah stormed into the bedroom behind him.

"Sarah, you're getting shrill. Calm down, please." David braced himself for her barrage of questions. The one thing he did not need now was anyone, not even Sarah, breaking his concentration.

"David, there's something going on and I don't like the whispers I hear around here."

"Since when do you put stock in rumors?"

"Since you've been unavailable for the past five hours. I've got three times as many Secret Service goons on my heels and you're putting on a bullet-proof vest!" She had come around the door to the massive walk-in closet just in time to see him strapping the Kevlar vest on under his dress shirt.

"I wear this a lot, Sarah. I'm going out and the Service wants me to wear it."

"Where are you going, David?" Sarah adopted her quiet demanding tone which meant she was bracing for a fight. "There are no State functions, no dinners, no briefings, nothing on your calendar at all! In fact, your calendar for tonight is unusually empty. You haven't even told Colleen where you'll be."

"I asked you once before not to put the staff in the middle of this," Walsh pointed out, keeping his voice steady and reasonable.

"Damn it, David, stop avoiding my questions!"

He stopped with his tie half knotted and looked at his wife. The sudden realization that all he wanted was to be alone with her, in bed, startled him. It had been so long since they had been themselves.

"Sarah, I'm sorry. I really am very sorry," he reached out to her, but she pulled away. "There are going to be things that I can't discuss with you. You know that." He searched her eyes for some indication of understanding, but found nothing but coldness. She wasn't going to accept anything he said for an answer.

A knock on the door sent her flying to the window where she stood with her arms folded and her shoulders hunched.

"Come in," David called, and Jim Sercu stepped through the door. He looked from Sarah to David, and waited for instruction from the president. Walsh motioned for him to step to the closet where they spoke in whispers.

"Sarah has heard whisperings and wants to know what's going on. If I don't tell her, she'll feel betrayed and it won't help my cause any."

Sercu nodded, trying to buy himself time to think. "Can you trust her, sir?" he asked.

"I just don't know, Jim. She's changed a lot. I want to trust her."

"Then tell her an abbreviated version—a terrorist threat, emergency meetings, that sort of thing."

"Your whispering is very obvious, David," Sarah said from the window. She glared at them.

"Sarah, I am honestly not trying to hide anything from you. These situations aren't easy to deal with and I have to consider the consequences of everyone I talk to, even you."

"What situations, David?" Damn, she was persistent.

"We've had some terrorist threats and we're still working to figure out how to handle them." David joined her at the window, wanting to take her in his arms and not knowing what to do next.

"I'm sure there have been terrorist threats before. Why is this one so much more difficult?" she demanded.

Walsh turned and waved Sercu to the door. With a nod, Sercu quietly let himself out to wait in the corridor.

"Sarah, this is my first terrorist situation." He took a deep breath and cursed himself for having to tell only half-truths, but he felt he had no choice. "I'm terrified, Sarah. More frightened than I have ever been before."

Sarah looked into his eyes, her lip trembling and her own eyes filling with tears. "Oh God," David thought, "maybe I haven't lost her after all."

"David . . ."

"No, let me finish. I can't let anyone else see how uncertain I am. I have to keep up the appearance of strength and ability. Sarah, please try to understand."

"David," she said softly, "I wish I could believe you."

* * *

"Hey, boss, is that it?" Speraza broke the silence in the long black car.

"Ah, yes." Dunn swiped the fog from the back window with a black gloved hand. "I do believe that is it. Perfect." He powered down the window far enough to send the butt of his cigar flying in an orange arc into the road. "We can go on to the club now, Vinnie."

Dunn watched the taillights of the Ford Expedition disappear past the guard gate into the bowels of the Treasury Building and smiled.

EIGHTEEN

The Treasury Building
Washington, D.C.

THE HUGE BLACK FORD EXPEDITION PULLED PAST THE GUARDHOUSE, entered the basement parking garage of the Treasury Building, and descended to the farthest point of the lowest level. The truck backed into a parking spot in a corner and the rear door swung open. Three marines with automatic weapons slung over their broad shoulders hustled a draped figure out of the back of the van and through a panel concealed in the cinder-block wall.

Adalla Marchia was shackled at the ankles and wrists with a thick chain looped through a heavy leather and metal collar strapped tightly around his throat. He was barefoot and wore only a loose fitting, plain brown coverall, a thick black hood covered his face. Colonel David Ziegelhofer double-checked the shackles and shortened the chain connecting feet to throat until Marchia was forced to walk at a slow shuffle. The hooded figure was guided up onto the platform of a heavy-duty hand truck where his shackles were chained to the cross rails and heavy leather straps were buckled securely across his chest, arms, and legs. The handcart would be dragged backward down the tunnel between two armed marines. Marchia would be unable to memorize the route from this position half prone and traveling backward. Signaling one man to stay at the exit, Blaine led the way down a long cement tunnel. The marines moved at a quick pace, bouncing the hand truck over the cement with little care for their passenger.

Marchia had no way of knowing where he was, only that it smelled damp and a little musty and felt like they were underground. He had no idea he was on his way to the White House.

* * *

David Walsh and James Sercu, flanked by Secret Service agents, walked quickly down the hallway from the bank of elevators to the Situation Room.

"Is Mrs. Walsh satisfied with your answers?" Sercu asked, falling back on their friendship for a moment.

"I don't know for sure, Jim," Walsh sighed. "I don't know if any answer would satisfy her right now. I do know I wouldn't want to be in your shoes if this doesn't go according to plan!"

Sercu stopped and gaped at the president. "Don't even joke like that, sir!"

"Don't worry, Jim, I have the utmost faith in all of you." Walsh stepped through the door and into the bustle of the Situation Room. Ned Seiffert put down a telephone receiver as they entered and hurried over to the president.

"Sir, General Blaine and Colonel Ziegelhofer are bringing the prisoner through Marilyn and should be in the bunker in about five minutes."

"Very good." Walsh found he had to remind himself to keep breathing; his nerves were stretched tight. He glanced back at Jim Sercu, "I wonder how Ms. Monroe would feel knowing there was a tunnel named after her." He smiled tightly.

"I would hope she would be honored, sir," Sercu said.

"Somehow I doubt it," Walsh shook his head slowly.

"If I may, sir, I would like to give you a rundown on the security preparations," Seiffert said, pulling the president back to the gravity of the current situation.

"Of course, Ned, what have you got?" Walsh dropped into his chair and grabbed a pen that was lying on the table, anything to keep his hands from shaking.

As Seiffert talked, Walsh could not help but glance at the monitor mounted on the far wall. Closed-circuit cameras followed General Blaine and his charge through the tunnel that twisted under the city from the Treasury Building to the White House. Walsh studied the hooded and shackled form of Adalla Marchia, marveling at the small, husky stature of the man responsible for so much. He didn't seem so frightening strapped to a hand truck. Walsh knew better than to allow his guard to drop even for a moment. He knew Seiffert and Sercu would have his back, and he trusted his staff's preparations implicitly, but he couldn't rest on the others. He still had to stay sharp and pay close attention to every little move and breath. His country depended upon it.

* * *

Elsewhere in the White House, Sarah Walsh had had enough of fuming over her husband's evasions. She knew, deep in her gut, that there was something very serious happening around her and she knew, too, that she should be frightened. The look in David's eyes had been a mixture of fear and desire. She had only seen that look once before, after they had cracked up their car during a rain storm in Oklahoma. David had struggled to pull her unconscious body from the wreck and she had come to looking into that same expression in his eyes.

He loved her, she knew that, and sometimes she regretted the way she felt about his career, her inability to give herself over to it totally. It wasn't really fair to either of them, she knew. But she had to maintain some allegiance to herself.

Sarah finally moved away from the window and looked around the comfortably furnished apartment she was supposed to be sharing with the president of the United States. Why couldn't she come to like it, she wondered. Plenty of women had, and she was still young. There would be many years left, even if he was reelected to a second term.

Going into the bathroom, she splashed water on her face, ran her fingers through her hair, and decided she needed a cup of coffee. She hesitated for a moment with her hand on the intercom to ring someone to bring it to her, but decided she wanted to make it herself and maybe find something to eat.

In the small kitchen attached to the apartment, Sarah rummaged through the refrigerator, finding nothing very appealing. She thought of the huge kitchens downstairs and decided it was time to do some exploring. In the hallway outside the apartment a Secret Service agent fell into step behind her with the usual brisk efficiency.

"Do you have to follow me through the house, too?" she snapped over her shoulder, walking faster in her anger.

"Yes, ma'am, afraid so," the behemoth answered in a deep, gruff voice. Sarah stopped suddenly and spun around, catching the man off guard. He pulled up short, and just missed barreling into her.

"Then do you have to be obvious about it? Can't you lurk behind potted palms or something and let me think I'm not being followed?" The man just blinked at her. He's good, she thought, not a sign of surprise or emotion. She decided she could not be the only First Lady to make his job difficult.

"Fine," she finally said, "then stay far enough back so I don't feel like you're stepping on my heels." She spun back around and charged down the hall.

"Yes, ma'am," the agent barked, waited a beat, and then followed her at twice his usual distance. Sarah sighed loudly and continued on her way in search of the kitchen.

NINETEEN

The Bohemian Club Chapter House
Capitol Hill
Washington, D.C.

WARREN DUNN ALLOWED HIMSELF TO BE LED BY AN OBSEQUIOUS LITTLE man in tie and tails into one of the private lounges of the Chapterhouse. The dark-paneled room was filled with high wing-back leather chairs and dark antique furniture. Cigar smoke swirled thickly about the ceiling and the smell of brandy and cognac battled with the odors of twelve-year-old scotch and fine Tennessee whiskeys. Dunn stopped in the doorway and surveyed the sanctuary, allowing his presence to attract attention for a moment before he entered the room. He made directly for one particularly distinguished senator who held court in the center of the room, pontificating to an assemblage of businessmen and politicos.

"Gentlemen," Dunn rumbled, dipping his head briefly.

"Warren." The senator rose to his feet with some effort and extended an immaculately manicured hand. "Glad you could make it; I'm anxious to hear how things have been progressing." The senator glanced around his little audience, and one by one the men excused themselves.

Dunn settled into one of the vacated chairs and favored the senator with a smile.

"Havana?" The senator signaled for a box to be brought and offered to Dunn who accepted, silently noting that his own store of Havanas was of far better quality. He toyed for a moment with the idea of sending the senator a box just to point out the difference.

The senator smiled through a fresh haze of smoke. "Well, Warren, don't keep me waiting . . . what have you got?"

Dunn glanced around the room, "Marchia is on his way into the White House right now."

"Ah, I heard some rumors about a member of his family."

"Yes, unfortunately, our armed service sometimes gets carried away. A daughter chose a headlong trip down a flight of stairs."

"Poor child," the senator shook his head, the glint in his eyes belying any real sorrow. "So, where do we stand?"

"We'll know in a couple of hours when I hear from my man inside." Dunn plucked a cell phone from his jacket pocket and placed it gently on the table between the two men. "Until then, I suggest we have a drink and discuss a few details."

The senator grinned at Dunn, his thin lips pulling back from long yellowed teeth made his face look like nothing so much as a fleshless skull. Dunn smiled thinly.

Twenty

Marilyn Monroe Tunnel to the White House

"Do not touch the bars," a brawny Secret Service agent barked at Blaine and his party. Blaine shot the man a disgusted look. "Bunch of guys playing at soldiers," he thought, but kept his comments to himself. Marchia wouldn't know that this man wasn't one of his marines.

"If you touch the bars before the power is cut, you will be fried where you stand," the man continued in his overloud monotone. Blaine knew it was more for the prisoner's benefit than any real warning to his men. "Please wait until the door is completely open before entering."

The heavy iron barred gate slid into the wall with a shriek of metal on concrete. The Secret Service agent stepped back to allow the party to pass into the reinforced bunker below the White House basement, a bunker that would appear on no plans or blueprints.

"Gentlemen, please surrender all weapons." The agent motioned to an MP who stepped up to relieve the marines of their arms. Armed guards moved in to escort the group through an electromagnetic arch to an elevator that would drop them down another level into a shielded bunker where the meeting would take place. Blaine patted his pocket once to doublecheck that he had left his personal cell phone behind. The electromagnetic pulse generated by the arch would knock out the electronic components of any communications device, computer, or calculator.

The elevator dropped swiftly and deposited them in an identical concrete bunker. A shielded metal door stood solidly at the end of the short hallway. Blaine eyed the cameras along the passage that followed their movements to the door. When they approached, the door slid ponderously to one side revealing another iron gate.

"General Blaine, Colonel Ziegelhofer," another Secret Service agent, with a heavy automatic rifle slung over one shoulder, greeted them before engaging the gate and ushering them into the room.

The furnishings in this room seemed out of place amid all the concrete and high-tech security measures in the bunker. An Oriental carpet covered the floor setting up an area where a leather sofa and three armchairs stood around a low table. Closed-circuit cameras followed the movements of each man as he entered the room and Blaine's marines wheeled Marchia to the edge of the carpet and set him upright. Their armed escort waited outside.

"General, the Situation Room is on the line for you, sir." The Secret Service agent pointed to a phone that hung inside a metal box beside the door. Blaine picked up the receiver.

"General Blaine," James Sercu's voice greeted him from the other side, "everything proceeding according to plan?"

"Yes, sir." Blaine scanned the room again, checking that each player was in place. "The prisoner is secure and awaiting the president."

"Hold the fort, general. We'll be there shortly." The line went dead and Blaine returned his attention to his prisoner.

* * *

In the Situation Room, Sercu turned to the room and favored Walsh with a grim nod. "They're ready for you, sir," he said softly.

The room fell silent. Walsh stood and let his gaze wander over his staff, noting the worry and severity of each of their expressions. "Then let's get this over with so I can get some dinner," Walsh smiled, putting on his best brave face for the benefit of his staff.

They had decided to limit the members of staff who would be present for the meeting. Jim Sercu and Ian Tuttle followed Walsh into the elevator flanked by Secret Service. Ned Seiffert and the other members of his cabinet would watch on closed-circuit monitors from the Situation Room.

Walsh concentrated on the smooth drop of the elevator and the absence of any shake or rattle beneath their feet. It helped him place his trust totally in the security measures and technology that made the meeting possible in the first place. His chief of staff, on the other hand, seemed to be having a harder time placing his trust in the situation. Tuttle fidgeted, shifting from one foot to another and checking the pockets of his suit jacket repeatedly. Jim Sercu stood perfectly still, his eyes fixed on the seal of the elevator doors.

The elevator came to a halt with a slight jerk and the doors slid aside to reveal a passage and an imposing metal door. Walsh glanced up at the cameras that followed their progress and nodded, trying to reassure himself as much as those watching from the other end. The military guard stationed at the door snapped to attention as the president approached. Once again the door slid into the wall and the president of the United States stepped into the bunker.

TWENTY-ONE

The White House
Washington, D.C.

SARAH MADE HER WAY TOWARD THE MASSIVE KITCHENS THAT SERVED the White House, her Secret Service watchdog on her heels. She chose to ignore the man's presence and placed her trust in the discretion that she had been told was indelibly etched into the Secret Service personality. The hallways were largely empty, although she could hear the quiet sounds of cleaning coming from many rooms. The clattering of pots and pans could be heard from far down the passage.

Sarah strolled along, enjoying the illusion that she was on her own. She found she was genuinely surprised and a little pleased that her escort was capable of moving so quietly that she could ignore his presence. As she walked she caught bits and pieces of conversation from some of the rooms. Women talking about their children as they cleaned. Men discussing how to repair a light fixture. Even at eight o'clock at night, there was still a great deal of activity in the bowels of the White House.

Sarah was brought up suddenly when she heard a gruff voice say her husband's name. She stood just outside a door that led to a lounge which served as a break room for some of the staff. At that moment the room was occupied by two Secret Service agents who sat huddled in conversation.

"Okay, so do we talk to Bud about this or keep it to ourselves," one voice said.

"How do we know Tuttle was doing anything wrong?" his partner asked.

"You heard what he said. Did that sound kosher to you?"

"No, but what do I know? We could be out on our asses if we're wrong. One thing I do know is that I don't want to be drummed out of the Service."

"And could you live with yourself if there is something going on and you don't do anything about it?"

"C'mon, Frank, you know as well as I do that part of the code is minding our own business."

"If what I think is happening is happening, then isn't it my own business?" Frank was having a hard time keeping his voice level. Sarah, suddenly remembering her new best friend, glanced back to see that her watchdog had taken up a position to one side of the hallway and was pointedly not looking at her.

"So, you really believe that Tuttle's involved in some kind of conspiracy?" Sarah turned back to the conversation.

"You know as well as I do that the order was that none of this shit was to be discussed on the wire. Then Tuttle gets on the phone and tells somebody all about what's going down here, more than even we knew up to that point, right down to the details of them bringing that terrorist into the bunker."

Sarah's eyes grew wide and she stifled a gasp. A terrorist? That was why David wouldn't tell her what was happening. He really was frightened. But why would the staff allow a president to get so close to a terrorist? It didn't make sense.

"I don't like any of this and I'd rather someone knew and made me suffer for it than keep it to myself and risk the whole situation blowing up." Frank was adamant. His partner kept quiet.

Sarah, galvanized by her own fear for David and what she

had seen in his eyes, spun around and charged back up the hallway forgetting the coffee. She passed her guard with a huff.

"How much of that did you hear?" she snapped.

"Nothing, ma'am." He fell into step behind her.

"Liar!"

TWENTY-TWO

A Secure Bunker Beneath the White House
Washington, D.C.

DAVID WALSH STOOD BEFORE THE HOODED AND SHACKLED FIGURE OF the right hand to one of the most feared terrorists in the world. He knew he should be concerned if not frightened, but he amazed himself by remaining calm and very much in control. Jim Sercu watched him closely and was awed by the president's composure.

General Blaine stepped forward. "I would like to request that the prisoner remain blindfolded during your interrogation, sir."

Walsh considered for a moment before he answered. "No, general, I would like to look into his eyes while he delivers his message."

Blaine made no attempt to hide his disdain for the president's decision, but Sercu noticed that Marchia's head came up slightly at the president's words. Walsh knew he had the man's attention.

Blaine signaled to Ziegelhofer, who roughly snatched the hood off Marchia's head. A leather gag encircled the man's head, but he raised his eyes to regard Walsh coldly. Walsh saw sadness, determination, and rage in the man's expression, but amazingly no fear. Seiffert had been insistent that Walsh understand that he would not be able to intimidate this man, and Seiffert was right.

"General, the gag." Walsh fixed Blaine with a determined glare, trying to end any more discussion about procedure.

Blaine again nodded to Ziegelhofer, who unbuckled the gag and pulled a hard leather ball from between Marchia's lips. The man gasped slightly and took a deep breath.

"Now, Mr. Marchia. You asked for this meeting. I have granted it." Walsh would have to stay sharp to maintain the upper hand during this interview. "You claim to have a message for me from Osama bin Laden and Saddam Hussein. I'm listening—deliver your message."

Marchia's glare traveled around the room stopping on each of the men in turn. "My message is for your ears only, not for these disciples of Satan."

Walsh raised an eyebrow, but resisted looking to his men for their reactions. "These men are my advisers. They will remain."

Marchia regarded the president. He was more than Marchia had been briefed, much more.

"Perhaps you are afraid to be alone with me?" Marchia asked, consciously avoiding use of any form of address or title, knowing the insult would not be lost.

Walsh held his ground. He stared at the man for a moment before laughing. "I hardly think you're in a position to pose any sort of threat to me."

Marchia dipped his head briefly. Walsh was correct, of course, but Marchia had not come this distance for any reason but to deliver his message.

Colonel Ziegelhofer, apparently deciding that Marchia had been silent long enough, used a billy club to jab Marchia in the ribs. "Get on with it," he bellowed.

Marchia fixed him with a glare before returning his attention to the president. "I am here as a warrior, a warrior of Allah. I have been instructed to give you this message only. I know nothing beyond this message." He paused, considering Walsh's expression.

"I have been instructed to inform you before the end of this month, the populations of the heathen cities of Boston, New York, Baltimore, and Washington, D.C., will be destroyed."

The atmosphere in the room grew thick. Tuttle had backed himself against a wall and stood there, ashen and fighting down the tremors that threatened to give away his own fear.

"We are already aware of that," Sercu interjected.

"And you are?" Marchia asked disgustedly.

"National security adviser," Sercu answered brusquely. "You must be aware that we already know about your plan."

"It is not my plan," Marchia spat back at him. "It is the destiny of the entire Muslim world and our solemn duty to bring an end to the heathen domination of our people and return the land to Allah."

"This land was never Allah's," Tuttle snapped, his voice betraying his fragile state of mind.

"But all land is Allah's. It is only the policies and schemes of the Israeli bastards and their allies that prevent the followers of Islam from their birthright!"

Walsh wondered how the Mossad agents, watching from the Situation Room, were handling this. He had vetoed their being present at the meeting, thinking they would only inflame the issue, and was now glad he had.

"Okay, enough." Walsh grabbed for control again. "You haven't told us anything we don't already know. Is that why you came this distance and risked your family, to tell us old news?"

"Your arrogance and self-importance are even more astounding than I had been warned," Marchia's tone brought the armed guards to alert and they trained their weapons at the immobilized figure. "Yes, that is the answer to everything, isn't it?" he continued. "Bring your weapons to bear, murder women and children. But be warned, your atrocities will not prevent our ascension to our rightful place."

Ziegelhofer planted the business end of his club on Marchia's ear, momentarily stunning the man into silence. Marchia shook his head and forced his eyes to focus on the president.

"My leaders demand that you break all diplomatic ties, financial and military support to Israel. If you do not, Boston, New York, Baltimore and Washington, D.C., will be nothing more than tombs for the thousands of dead Americans who will pay for your mistake."

Walsh glared at him, controlling his urge to wrap his hands around the man's throat and silence him permanently.

"When we are finished," Marchia continued finding strength from the reactions of the men standing around him, "your cities will be uninhabitable and the disease will spread, slowly at first, but then faster as your people panic and try to flee the infection. Before you are able even to regret your mistake, your families, your friends, your country will be dying around you."

"When?" Tuttle gasped from the back of the room. Walsh wanted someone to gag his chief of staff, the fear in the man's voice was disturbing.

"Our warriors are already here, on your soil, the jihad, the holy war, has already begun!"

Ziegelhofer slammed his club across Marchia's throat blocking the airway. Blaine stepped up beside the gasping terrorist.

"Who are they? Where are they?" Blaine demanded.

Marchia only grinned and continued to struggle for breath. Ziegelhofer pushed harder.

"Tell us what we want to know, scum! Maybe we'll consider letting your family live."

"Colonel!" Walsh snapped from behind the huge man. Ziegelhofer hesitated for a moment before stepping back.

Marchia gasped for breath but never stopped grinning. "My

family is a small sacrifice for the glory of Allah. They will be martyred!"

Walsh spun around and headed for the door. "Get the information out of him, general. I'll send the Mossad agents down to help you." Walsh didn't look back to see Marchia pale slightly before he started laughing. A slam from Ziegelhofer's club stopped the laughter with a thud.

Sercu and Tuttle hurried after their president, who stopped suddenly in the hall and turned to face them. "They have until dawn to get what they can out of that bastard. You have until dawn to get as many options on the table as possible. I want a plan and I want it fast!"

Twenty-Three

The White House
Private Quarters of the President and First Lady
Washington, D.C.

A very shaken President Walsh quietly closed the door to his quarters behind him before letting himself droop under the weight of his own fears. Marchia's words echoed hollowly in his skull, quiet narration to every picture of plague and destruction he had ever seen, flashing through his memory like a twisted grammar school filmstrip. Some small part of Walsh's mind screamed for an escape, to sink into madness like a thick, warm, suffocating blanket. But he was stronger than that, and forced the panic down to a small blip in his subconscious. He had too much work to do to allow his own fears to take over.

Walsh pawed at the tie knotted impeccably around his neck, suddenly feeling choked by the strip of silk. He had to think. Stripping off his suit coat and dress shirt, he slid into a creamy Irish wool sweater hoping it would help smother the chills that rippled through his body.

How could a small group of terrorists obliterate the eastern seaboard of the United States, he wondered, overwhelmed by the implications. And how could they be stopped? Walsh stared at his haggard face in the mirror over his dresser. A few months in office and already his face showed the lines and creases his predecessors wore as badges of honor after years of service. He fingered the gray spreading from his temples before turning away. There had to be a solution. The only superpower left in the world could not be brought down by a handful of terrorists—a handful of terrorists who had no regard for their own lives. It put the problem on a whole new playing field.

* * *

In his office next door to the Oval Office, Ian Tuttle slumped in his chair and stared glassy-eyed at the wall. Dunn had never even hinted that this could happen. It was supposed to be a simple plan, an easy way to make Tuttle and Walsh richer than they had ever dreamed. All Tuttle was supposed to worry about was guiding Walsh in the right direction. Dunn had never mentioned biological warfare. Anthrax? Was Dunn insane? Tuttle wondered. Anthrax?

Tuttle fumbled his cell phone out of the desk drawer and punched in Dunn's number. The phone rang once before it clicked and Dunn's smooth voice oozed through the receiver.

"Yes, Tuttle, what have we got?" Tuttle could hear voices in the background that went suddenly silent. Where was Dunn?

"What have we got, Warren?" he screeched. "We've got a fucking plague! We've got the worst terrorist disaster you can possibly imagine!"

"Tuttle, calm down and tell me what happened at your little meeting." Dunn's voice stayed steady and commanding.

"Our little meeting? Marchia demanded the United States break all ties and all forms of aid with Israel. It's the 'or else' that has me worried, Warren," Tuttle's voice pitched higher on each sentence. "You didn't tell me the terrorist would be dealing in anthrax! Explosives are controllable. Even hostages can be released alive. But anthrax? This is insane!" A smooth sheen of sweat coated Tuttle's forehead and dripped down his collar.

"Ian, I told you we would be playing hardball with this. What did you expect?" Dunn didn't try to hide the disgusted edge in his voice. "It's your job to make sure the threat remains nothing but a threat."

"H-h-how am I supposed to do that?" Tuttle demanded.

"By guiding our pet president into making the right decisions."

"Warren, I . . ."

Dunn cut him off, "Ian, you knew there would be risks when I first presented this plan to you." His voice was low and menacing. "Do your job, do it well, and no harm will come to anyone." Dunn allowed himself momentary misgivings about his choice of a pawn, but shook it off; it was too late now.

"Oh," Tuttle sounded like a sudden realization had erased all his fears, "so there really isn't a threat?"

"Oh, there's a threat, Tuttle. Don't ever let yourself believe otherwise. You can't bargain with an empty threat." Dunn cleared his throat. "Just remember that if you fail, the anthrax won't be the only thing you'll have to worry about." The phone clicked and the line went dead. Tuttle let the receiver drop to his lap. Suddenly his warm paneled office was colder than hell.

* * *

Warren Dunn slid his cell phone into his coat pocket and looked up into the cold gray eyes of his sponsor.

"Well?" the senator asked, steepling his fingers under his chin and fixing Dunn in his glare.

"The message has been delivered and is being taken quite seriously. We may see some results even sooner than expected."

"And Tuttle?"

Dunn took a shallow breath but kept his voice even, "Tuttle will not be a problem; I assure you."

"Good, good. Let's have another drink."

TWENTY-FOUR

A Secure Bunker Beneath the White House
Washington, D.C.

ADALLA MARCHIA HAD BEEN GAGGED AGAIN, BUT HIS CAPTORS HAD left his hood off. He could only watch as they moved about the room following their demon president's hasty departure. Marchia would have chuckled to himself if he could, his message had certainly filled this President Walsh with the icy frost of fear. Everything was going just as bin Laden had planned. Marchia was proud of his role in the great plan.

The huge metal door that led into the room slid back quietly to reveal three dark-eyed men dressed in simple khaki work clothing standing at attention on the other side. These were not big men, each shorter than the Americans and slight in figure, but their size belied their wiry strength and their Mossad training meant they could take on men the size of Ziegelhofer and triumph easily. Their thick dark hair was crowned with black yarmulkes, and their sharp features were set in menacing expressions that Marchia knew were meant to intimidate him. He could not let fear overwhelm him and began to chant the ninety-nine names of God to himself.

The hood was pulled sharply down over his face and he felt the hand truck he was still strapped to tip and begin the long roll back down the tunnel to the waiting Expedition.

The trip gave Marchia a chance to think about the events that would be taking place very soon. He needed to concentrate on the plan to avoid thinking about the fate that surely awaited his family at the hands of these barbarians.

* * *

Louis Blaine walked silently ahead of the hooded figure and his guards. The three Mossad agents brought up the rear, their steely expressions fixed on the job ahead of them. Blaine didn't like the fact that Walsh had allowed the Mossad to have any part in this. It was an American matter and should be left to American interrogation. The reputation of the Mossad did not help his attitude. Sure they were highly trained and arguably masters of their craft, but so were Blaine's men. And no one could claim that Blaine and his team were the slightest bit squeamish about what they were required to do. Blaine understood what was sometimes required to ensure the safety of his country, and the things he had had to do in the past certainly didn't interfere with his sleep.

Refusing to turn and look at the prisoner or the Mossad agents, Blaine kept his gaze steadily ahead and listened to their footfalls and the small squeak of the hand truck's wheels. He would be glad when this was over and they could move on to finding the terrorists before any damage was done. But there was still a long night to face before he could hope to get back out in the field.

* * *

The three Mossad agents, Namir Uriel, Zeev Abir and Ariel Jamin, were secretly appalled by what they had seen so far. That the Americans would consider bringing a known terrorist so close to their leader, regardless of secret tunnels, security bunkers, and high-tech equipment, was simply unthinkable. These American military men should have already had all the answers they needed from Marchia and he should have been dead long ago. But Prime Minister Mordachi had warned each of them that the Americans chose a different approach in these matters, and they were not to act without the expressed consent of their hosts. Uriel, superior to his companions not only in rank but also in experience and skills, would lead the interrogation once the Americans could be convinced to turn over the terrorist pig to them.

Uriel was contemplating his options for the interrogations when the team reached the outer door of the tunnel. General Blaine turned to one of the cameras mounted at the ceiling and waved a hand. The gate sprung open and the men could hear the locks in the outer door sliding to. Blaine pushed the door open in time to see the two sentries he had left behind jump to attention.

They wasted no time loading Marchia into the Expedition and securing his shackles to the thick rings bolted to the floor. Marchia tested his bonds to find he still could not move more than a quarter-inch in any direction.

The Mossad agents settled in for a long drive and their first glimpse of Washington, D.C.

TWENTY-FIVE

First Lady's Private Office
The White House
Washington, D.C.

SARAH WALSH FELT TRAPPED BETWEEN A ROCK AND A HARD PLACE, AND not for the first time in her life. It was no secret to anyone in the White House, and least of all to her husband, that she disliked Ian Tuttle. If she went to David with what she had overheard and it turned out to be a false alarm, as the one agent had feared, then David would be more than merely angry with her—especially if this terrorist thing was as serious as it sounded.

But given the seriousness of the situation, if she didn't go to him and the Secret Service agents chose to keep their mouths shut, what kind of danger would she be putting David and all of them in? "Why couldn't he have been honest with me about what was happening," she thought? "Then at least I'd have an idea of what to do."

Sarah suddenly felt more alone than she had in years. She had retreated to her office in the First Lady's suite. The rooms were deserted except for her and the two Secret Service agents who were posted outside her door. Now she found the silence oppressive, just like the rest of this new life David had won for them.

There had been a time when she could have gone to David with anything, any little concern or petty fear. And he could do the same with her. But this campaign for president, the difficulties and the final victory, had driven a wedge between them that they couldn't seem to overcome. David was so involved with his career that he seldom really heard what she was saying anymore, and their plans for a family and the future beyond the presidency seemed to have been forgotten.

Sarah picked up a framed photo from the table under her window. A young couple, roughhousing during a picnic, had been frozen forever in time, their unlined and carefree faces bright and grinning, the happiness so obvious it was almost ridiculous. Sarah didn't think she recognized them. Things were so much different then. How far had they come and at what cost?

* * *

David Walsh sat in the Oval Office, a cup of coffee and a light dinner cooling at his elbow as he reviewed the initial reports of the specialists who had observed his meeting with Adalla Marchia. A secretary had taken down the Mossad agents' observations as they watched from the Situation Room and their comments surprised Walsh most of all.

Marchia had stated plainly that he knew little more than the message he had been sent to deliver. Namir Uriel, the commander of the Mossad team, insisted that the man was lying. Ariel Jamin said that Marchia expected to escape this ordeal alive, simply because Marchia had seemed to be memorizing as much detail as he could. The third agent, Zeev Abir, believed that Marchia was completely expendable, whether he realized it or not. Bin Laden had no intention of getting him back alive. Uriel had gone on to say that the Mossad techniques were sure to squeeze out all the information Marchia could provide and quickly. Walsh hoped so, although he avoided thinking about the techniques to which Uriel referred.

Midnight came and went and Walsh still poured over the preliminary reports. An aide interrupted to say that Sercu and Seiffert had alerted the FBI, who were handling coordinating security at the airports in Boston, New York, Baltimore and Washington, and that FBI director Jim Marshall and CIA director Dennis Murphy had been contacted and were being brought to the planning meeting at dawn. David knew Dennis had been in Palm Beach on a golf trip, a long-anticipated break from the day to day business of the CIA. Dennis wouldn't be happy, especially when he heard the reasons his vacation had been cut short.

David sat back and rubbed his eyes. The words were blurring together, but he knew he wouldn't sleep even if he tried. The meeting would begin in a couple of hours, so there was no time for sleeping pills. Walsh grabbed the cold coffeepot from the tray and went to the outer office. Spotting an aide sifting through papers in another office, David asked the man to see if he could find some fresh coffee.

"There's an urn in the reception room. They just brought it up," Sarah said from the doorway.

"Sarah, why aren't you in bed?" David smoothed his hair down and composed his face into a blank.

Sarah watched the aide duck out another door with the carafe before she spoke. "What's going on, David?"

"I told you, Sarah, it's just some business that has to be dealt with as soon as possible." David sighed.

"I know it's more than that, David; I know it has something to do with a terrorist. A terrorist you actually brought to the White House."

Walsh flinched before he was able to hide his surprise. He should have figured Sarah would get wind of something eventually; he just didn't have the energy to deal with it right now.

"Sarah, I really have . . ." David was cut off by a voice outside the door.

"Mr. President," Asa Roberts, Walsh's press secretary, charged into the outer office, "we really need to discuss how we're going to handle spin control. The press will be on this . . ." Roberts suddenly noticed Sarah staring at him and swallowed hard.

"You don't have time to deal with me. Yes, I know, David. Just like always." Sarah allowed her anger to take over and she spun around and charged out of the room, nearly bowling over the aide who was returning with the fresh pot of coffee.

"Ah, sir. I'm sorry," Roberts stuttered, taking the blame for Sarah's outburst.

"Asa, it's all right, we were at that point before you came in." Walsh paused to take a deep breath and center himself before facing another issue. "You said 'spin control'?"

"Yes, sir," Roberts seemed to shake himself like a wet dog and suddenly he was back to his efficient self. "The press is going to know something's going on the minute the sun comes up. We need something to tell them to keep them from catching on to what's really happening."

"You know I don't ever want to have to deceive the public or the press, Asa. We agreed on that during the campaign." Walsh knew he wouldn't win this one, but felt better for saying it.

"True, but we didn't exactly see this one coming, did we, sir?"

Twenty-Six

U.S. Government Safe House
Virginia Horse Country

The Ford Expedition pulled up to the gated entrance of the safe house. Security was on high alert, and General Blaine knew several infrared cameras and not a few infrared rifle sights were focused on the vehicle as an armed guard opened the gate to let them onto the estate. Special explosive-detecting sensors scanned the undercarriage as the truck lurched over the metal threshold buried beneath the pebbles of the driveway. Additional sensors embedded in the wrought-iron gates scanned the truck for homing devices and radio transmitters. When the green all-clear light flashed in the concealed guardhouse, they were waved through and crawled carefully along the winding driveway to the main house.

Marchia could tell by the smell of the breeze through the ventilation of the car that they had returned to the place where he had been held. He drew in several deep breaths trying to calm himself and brace for what he knew was to come. It would be a long night for both him and the Mossad agents.

The American soldiers moved Marchia, still hooded and shackled, from the van into the main house. As they dragged him stumbling down a corridor, one of the men said, "So why do we need their help?" His partner laughed sharply.

Marchia assumed the men spoke of the Mossad agents who must have entered a different part of the building.

"Supposedly these three are legendary for their interrogation methods. Sheppard said that they have never failed to get what they want out of a prisoner."

Marchia wondered if this conversation had been set up to intimidate him. Fools; these Americans were useless.

"Like we can't," the other said disgustedly.

"I don't know, but I'd like to see these guys work."

"Scrawny little shits."

"Sheppard said the terrorists refer to them as the leopard, the lion and the wolf."

Marchia felt his heart leap in his chest. If these idiots were correct, the Mossad agents not only had brutal reputations, they truly were legendary. It was generally believed that if you were captured by the leopard, the lion and the wolf, not only would you never again see the light of day, your plan was doomed to failure. Why did Allah suffer the presence of these brutes on his beautiful Earth? Marchia could only assume they were a test of the true and righteous. But the fear still kept reaching deeper and deeper into his heart.

* * *

General Blaine and the three Mossad agents watched on closed-circuit TV as the American soldiers moved Marchia into his cell and strapped him to the straight-backed chair in the center of the room. Blaine, eyeing the Mossad agents skeptically, gestured to a small stack of aluminum cases piled on a nearby table.

"My men moved your equipment in from the van; I assume you're going to want to get to work right away."

"Yes, general," Uriel answered softly, "it is best to strike while the prisoner is still slightly shaken by the events of the evening."

Blaine watched as one of his men cuffed Marchia sharply for no apparent cause. His men were pissed, and understandably so. Many of them felt it was an insult for the president to have called in Israelis to do the same job his men were perfectly capable of doing.

"Well, I have my orders and we will give you complete cooperation, but I would request that two of my men remain in the cell during the interrogation."

Uriel glanced at his men before turning to the general. Blaine watched the exchange carefully. Like any team of soldiers who were a well-integrated unit, more was said with that one glance than was said with any words. Blaine couldn't reconcile these small wiry men with their legendary reputation. When he heard exactly who it was the Israeli prime minister was sending, he had envisioned large, obviously strong men, much like his own team. These men, except for their dark, cold gazes, were not intimidating and he wondered at the truth to the rumors of their effectiveness.

"That is acceptable, general," Uriel finally answered. "We would like to get started now."

Blaine gestured to the door and each man picked up a case as he passed the table. Blaine ordered two of his best to remain in the room before leaving the Mossad to their work.

* * *

Three hours had passed before Blaine was summoned back to the holding cell. The Mossad had finished their work.

"Well?" he demanded, marching into the control room. One of his men stood with his back to the door, fumbling with the coffeepot in the corner. The other stood back against the wall, his face drawn. He was slow to snap to attention. The other man sloshed coffee onto the floor as he spun around.

"Sir," the man by the door snapped, "the interrogation is over.

The Mossad agents have gone to clean up before the debriefing." The man sounded short of breath.

Blaine turned to the image on the closed-circuit camera. Marchia sat slumped in the chair, his shackles the only thing keeping him upright. Blood dripped from his downturned face, soaking his coveralls. Blaine saw blood puddled around the man's feet, where small objects seemed to be floating. What were they? Fingers?

"Is he alive?" Blaine asked indifferently.

"Yes, sir," one of the men answered, "but he probably needs medical attention if you want to keep him alive."

Blaine considered letting the man bleed to death, but thought maybe they should keep him alive in case the Mossad failed. "Get a medic in there to patch him up."

"Sir?" The man sounded confused.

"You heard me. Get moving." Blaine turned to the remaining guard. "Did the Israelis get any information out of him?"

"Yes, we did, General Blaine."

Blaine spun around to see Uriel standing in the doorway, his men directly behind him. Their hands and faces were clean but their uniforms were splotched with blood, soaked through at the cuffs and their dark eyes sparkled in an unsettling way.

"Yes, we did, and you're probably not going to like it. I have already asked that General Seiffert be summoned."

Twenty-Seven

The White House Situation Room
Washington, D.C.

President Walsh's cabinet waited uneasily in the Situation Room of the White House. The emergency meeting had been classified top secret, not a comforting thing given the state of matters.

Shortly, the doors at the end of the room opened and all stood as the president entered, flanked by generals Seiffert and Blaine. Walsh nodded a greeting as he took his seat. When everyone was settled, Walsh allowed his gaze to sweep over the taut, exhausted faces of the most trusted people in his administration.

"Ladies and gentlemen," he began, keeping his voice steady and even, "it seems our last gamble has paid off. General Blaine has informed me that the Mossad agents successfully helped his men to convince our guest to share the terrorist plans with us."

There was a shifting of bodies in seats but not a single eye left Walsh's face. "General Blaine," Walsh turned to the man standing at attention to his right, "please give us a brief rundown of where we stand and what we can expect to happen next."

"Yes, sir," Blaine snapped a salute and settled to parade rest before he began to speak. "After several hours of discussions with the prisoner, we have discovered that their plan, the work of Osama bin Laden and Saddam Hussein among others, is not a simple terrorist action, but what they call a *fatwah*." Blaine paused for effect, giving a lesser cabinet aide the chance to blurt out a question before he could control himself.

"What's a *fatwah*?" The man immediately sucked in a sharp breath and blushed furiously. "Uh, I'm sorry, sir!" he muttered to Walsh, dipping his head.

Walsh smiled tightly. "It's not the time to stand on formality. If someone doesn't understand something, go ahead and blurt it out. Correct me if I'm wrong, general, but a *fatwah* is the equivalent of a holy vendetta. We are, as far as these people are concerned, at war."

"That is basically it, sir. The term has other connotations to the sand nig . . . ah, Muslims, but for our purposes, that's a good definition."

Walsh shot Blaine a quick glance, "Thank you, general. Please go on."

Blaine cleared his throat. "According to the prisoner, this *fatwah* will begin February 28. Which means they are probably bringing terrorists into this country as we speak."

"That's only five days from now! How do we stop them, sir?" Barbara Howe asked in a small voice from the far end of the table. "They won't be declaring infected material to customs."

"No," Walsh agreed, "I don't think we can count on that. Any ideas?"

Jim Sercu shifted in his chair. "The current trend in terrorism seems to be what some of the boys at the Pentagon have referred to as satchel terrorism. Basically they're finding ways to bring their arms, or whatever, in right under our noses . . . in satchels."

"So we need to upgrade the security at all the airports in and around the four target cities." Walsh looked thoughtful for a moment. "Do they train dogs to sniff for biologicals?"

Sercu smiled. "I don't know, sir. I'll check into it."

"Okay, step one, get security going at the airports. Other ideas?"

Bill Cassidy began to raise a hand then yanked it back down again. "What if they come in by water? Those cities all have pretty busy harbor systems. They could smuggle it in on a freighter or even a yacht ."

"Good, Bill. General, can we upgrade harbor security?"

Ned Seiffert cut off Blaine. "We can do you one better. Our spy satellite system can photograph all traffic; actually we do it routinely. Anything suspicious can be tagged and checked out."

Barbara Howe sniffed. "I realize your satellites are good, Ned, but how are they going to find terrorists and biological weapons?"

Seiffert chuckled. "I guess we've done a pretty damned good job of keeping our capabilities secret after all." He glanced at Blaine, who smiled a small smile. "Our current technology can pinpoint an individual standing on a ship's deck with enough detail to count the chicken pox scars on his cheek."

"But we have no way of knowing who these people will be, so what good will that do?" she persisted.

"We know they will have to be bringing in at least some equipment. If we target anything that looks suspicious and then check it out from the ground, we might have something."

"Good enough," Walsh said. "Do it. Now, there's been some informal discussion of anthrax vaccines. Jim?"

"We've been doing some discrete checking to see how much of the vaccine is stockpiled around the country. There's not a lot, but we need to consider getting you and your immediate staff inoculated and then working on the armed forces around the target cities."

"Get to work on the armed forces first; we can't afford to lose a man."

"Pardon me, sir, but without you the armed forces aren't

going to be much good now, are they?" Sercu's tone bordered on a father speaking to an irrational child and Walsh understood the message perfectly: Shut up, and take your medicine.

"Point taken, Jim. Get to work on that."

"But what about the rest of the people, the populace?" Harry Dent asked almost timidly. Walsh knew the first thing on most of their minds was their own families and he couldn't blame them for that. Sercu jumped in.

"Mr. Vice President, there's not a lot we can do for the populace at this point. As I said, there's not much vaccine available and we can't boost production without causing a widespread panic. We've got sources in the government working on that right now. But in the meantime, we'll be making arrangements to move our families out of the area. I would suggest, with your permission, sir," he nodded at Walsh who dipped his head slightly, "that you find a reason to send your wives and husbands and kids away for a while. Treat them to Disneyland in California for a week. Whatever, just try not to make a big fuss about it. The less attention we get right now, the better."

No one had paid attention to Ian Tuttle, who stood at the back of the room, his sweat-soaked back pressed up against the cold wall. He felt as though he was watching all his work and plans go spiraling down a drain. For all his fear of the disease and its consequences, Warren Dunn was far more frightening. Tuttle forced himself to think clearly.

"And what about the rest of us?" he asked, his voice louder in the silent room than he would have liked. Every face in the room turned toward him and he regretted even opening his mouth.

"What's the matter Tut? Gettin' nervous?" Bill Cassidy chided him.

"Asshole!" Tuttle thought, scowling at the man. "Useless waste of air! I can't wait to see his face when I'm the one on top!"

Sercu broke in. "Essential staff will be inoculated—cabinet members, Secret Service, you—and we'll see how much we have left after that."

"What about Sarah?" Walsh asked quietly, he couldn't not ask. Not now.

"The First Lady is right under your name at the top of the list, sir." Sercu fixed Walsh with a steady look. Walsh sighed. Of course, they couldn't have him worrying about her. "Okay, people, let's look at worst-case scenarios." The room went silent. "If, and I say if because we're not going to let this happen, but if the terrorists succeed, how do we keep the country together until we can get the problem under control? And how do we get the problem under control?"

"Is there a way to neutralize the anthrax?" Barbara Howe asked.

Sercu looked thoughtful. "You've got me there, Barb. I don't know."

"Something else to add to your list of priorities then, Jim," Walsh tapped the pad on the desk. "How about the people? What can we do to prevent this from becoming a widespread disaster?"

"Well, the first step is to activate our interior defense systems and mobilize the National Guard. You may have to declare a state of marshal law, if it comes to that." Ned Seiffert rattled off the procedures as if by rote. "And there's the Domestic Protection Service initiative that Madeleine Albright and Janet Reno put into place. We'll just have to clamp down on the security end of it."

"Good. I'll leave that up to you, Ned." Seiffert nodded his agreement.

"Now, sir," Sercu began before Walsh could say more, "worst-case scenario. We're going to have to get you and the cabinet out of D.C. and somewhere safe."

"Not an option, Jim," Walsh said. Sercu cocked his head at his friend.

"No, sir, not an option for you. You already know the options should we need to move you out of the city." Walsh smiled. It was a no-win battle and he knew it.

"Ideally, I'd like to get you to Colorado and into the mountain," Sercu said, referring to NORAD headquarters, an impenetrable fortress in the Rockies. He was playing his weakest card first, and Walsh knew it.

"My next choice is the bunker at Greenbrier in White Sulfur Springs, West Virginia."

"There's always the Doomsday Hotel in Berryville, Virginia," Bill Cassidy added.

"Jim, Bill, I know what you're doing, but they're all too far away. I don't want it to look like I'm running away and hiding."

"Or," Ned Seiffert interjected, "we get *Air Force One* and *Two* off the ground, the president on one, the vice president on the other. They can stay airborne and safe from the virus for six months, if necessary."

"I like that plan much better—stay mobile and I can be more effective."

"Stay airborne and there's always a chance you get shot down," Sercu said almost sarcastically. The day was wearing on all of them and Walsh could easily forgive the man's concern.

"They'd have to find me first," he smiled. "Now, everybody get on your assignments. I want reports in my hands before midnight. And somebody do some research on what we can do to protect the water supply, and the power and communications systems."

The assembly stirred and quiet conversations sprang up around the table. General Blaine caught Ned Seiffert's eye and they exchanged grim looks.

"Excuse me, sir," Seiffert said loudly enough to get everyone's attention. "We've discussed what we're going to do here, but what are we going to do about the people responsible for this?"

"Bombing 'em off the face of the Earth would be all right with me," Barbara Howe muttered, then was stunned when she realized she'd said it aloud. Walsh looked at her closely. The fear was evident on every face around the table. It was time to deal with the hardest decision of all.

"That's certainly an option," Walsh said quietly. "I don't believe we can justify no retaliation, but we have to look at the benefits versus the costs."

"In a bombing, we can't target the specific terrorists," Sercu said.

"But can we hold the entire country responsible?" Bill Cassidy asked.

"We can if they refuse to do anything about their terrorists," Seiffert said.

"You can't bomb them!" Tuttle blurted out angrily. Walsh glared at him a moment. "You're talking about wiping our oil sources off the planet. Where will that leave us next winter when there's no fuel oil or gasoline? You have to consider the consequences!"

Walsh was surprised by his chief of staff's sudden, violent outburst. The reactions of the others who wanted revenge surprised him less than Tuttle's ill-timed rant. But there were a lot of things about Tuttle that surprised him lately.

"So what do you suggest we do, Ian?" Walsh asked.

"Maybe it's time to cut our losses, sir." Tuttle pulled himself up straight and tried to address the president with a confidence he did not entirely feel. "We've helped the Israelis for years now. They're stronger than they've ever been. Do they really still need us? Maybe we'd be better off pulling our aid and stopping this crisis before it becomes a disaster."

"Politically not a wise move, Mr. Tuttle," Barbara Howe said firmly. "We've built our foreign policy on the strength of our alliances. To leave the Israelis stranded now would not be prudent."

"I tend to agree with Ms. Howe, Ian," Walsh said firmly. He didn't like the sudden direction of the conversation. "If we turn our back on Israel now, it will send the wrong message to both the terrorists and our allies."

"But sir," Tuttle continued emphatically, "would the Israelis hesitate to turn their backs on us if their population was at stake?"

Walsh was stunned. Where had this come from? Was Tuttle just frightened? They all were, but Tuttle appeared to have taken leave of his senses completely.

* * *

An hour later, after they had exhausted almost every scenario, Walsh called the meeting to an end and watched as his cabinet filed out of the Situation Room.

"Hang on a minute, Ian." Walsh stopped Tuttle as he tried to slip out unnoticed.

"Yes, sir." Tuttle stood, hands behind his back, drawn up to his full height.

"You seem very adamant about changing our course of action, Ian. Why is that?" Walsh studied the man's face, looking for something he wasn't sure he'd recognize if he found it.

"Well, sir, I'm just concerned that we consider every option. There will be many repercussions to the decision to simply bomb what we perceive as the offending countries. That could be a mistake. I just don't want you making the incorrect decision." Tuttle spoke carefully and purposefully. But Walsh still felt that his speech sounded rehearsed.

"I can appreciate that, Ian. But you have to admit that we cannot be seen as taking a soft stand on this. We claim not to tolerate terrorism under any circumstances, but you talk as though you want me to avoid taking a hard line with the situation."

"Well, sir, that certainly wasn't my intention. I was merely trying to approach the problem from another angle."

Walsh wasn't sure he completely believed Tuttle's explanation—something didn't sound right, and he couldn't quite identify it. "Okay, Ian, thank you." He turned away from Tuttle, who hesitated a moment before taking his leave. Walsh dropped into a chair and leaned his head into his hands. He was suddenly more tired than he thought possible. Why couldn't this crisis have held off for another six months? It would have given him a chance to settle into the job and learn as much as he could before he had to protect so many lives and be responsible for so many consequences.

Walsh was thankful for his cabinet. They were all good people, sharp and knowledgeable. He would have been lost without them. But Tuttle was still a concern. Perhaps it would be a good idea to keep him as far away from the decision-making process as possible.

TWENTY-EIGHT

Patapsco River, Maryland

THE SUN HAD JUST BEGUN ITS SLOW CLIMB INTO THE EASTERN SKY WHEN an ancient cargo freighter coughed and sputtered its way into the mouth of the Patapsco River from the Chesapeake Bay. *Will o' the Sea* was stenciled in grimy letters on her bow, and an equally grimy-looking crew moved through the early morning mists attending to the choking machinery that barely kept the ship moving forward.

The captain stood on a rusting bridge peering through a cracked windshield at the brightening landscape at the shoreline. The *Will o' the Sea* rolled past Sparrows Point, and the captain could see the dim lights at the Dundalk Marine Terminal a mile or so away. He held the ship to the shoremost lane on the northern side of the river, and watched for the buoy marking the Harbor Tunnel. He would guide the small ship up the channel into Baltimore Harbor, where he would be able to dock near an abandoned warehouse without much trouble.

It had been a long, nerve-racking night, not unlike most other nights aboard the *Will*. But, this one was different and that difference gave the captain chills. This time they had met a yacht twenty miles off the Maryland shore and taken aboard seven foreigners. Dark skinned and dark haired, the men had carried aboard one small satchel each, paid the agreed-upon fee, and then asked to be shown to a cabin where they would stay until they docked. The crew had looked to their captain, who just shrugged. The money was just as American and just as green as any of the drug runners who used their services, and this run seemed like a lot less trouble than hundreds of kilos of coke, so the captain had ordered one of his men to see the foreigners below and they had gotten under way.

The sun had risen fully and the heat of the day began to build up by the time the freighter was in sight of the city of Baltimore. From the northwest harbor, the captain could see the bulk of the Baltimore Aquarium jutting into the sky in the distance. A few small pleasure boats scooted out of the Inner Harbor heading for the river, and some larger freighters cruised along unaware of the little ship plowing its way slowly toward the docks.

The captain guided the ship up to an empty dock, waving off the help of a tug, not much smaller than the ship itself. He radioed the harbormaster who, as usual, cleared them in with his customary skepticism, but the captain knew from experience that a little lucre would soften up the fat old bastard.

Once the ship had come to a stop and the moorings were in place, the dark-skinned foreigners appeared on deck and looked around at the grim district surrounding the commercial harbor. The one the captain took to be the ringleader nodded once before clanging down their gangway and disappearing into the maze of access roads, train tracks, and warehouses.

The captain drew in a deep breath and felt his nerves begin to settle as they always did once their questionable cargoes were off-loaded and no longer his crew's responsibility. With a few last, curt instructions, he headed off toward the harbormaster's office to settle up before the local booze shack opened for lunch.

TWENTY–NINE

Hay Adams Hotel
Washington, D.C.

WARREN DUNN SAT IN THE ORNATE SITTING ROOM OF HIS SUITE AT THE Hay Adams sipping twelve-year-old McAllen scotch and watching coverage of the cabinet dinner the president had hosted the night before. A cabinet dinner, he had to laugh. Interesting the way the president's press secretary was able to disguise the activities in the White House. Footage of the various cabinet members leaving the White House after ten o'clock that night showed them all clutching what appeared to be souvenir menus. Strange that none of them smiled, and those notorious for imbibing a little too much didn't seem the least bit inebriated. Dunn wondered at the stupidity of the American press. No one seemed to notice the obvious absence of wives and husbands. Very clever, but not quite clever enough. He toyed with the idea of calling his friends at the *Washington Post* and dropping a few little hints, but there was no time for such diversions, not now.

There was a sharp rap at the door and Dunn snapped off the television as Ian Tuttle let himself into the room.

"Warren," Tuttle approached Dunn with a hand extended, "thank you for taking the time to see me. I'd rather not risk using the phones at the White House with so much going on."

Dunn didn't move to take Tuttle's hand, nor did he offer the man a seat. "So, why don't you tell me what all the fuss is about." Dunn gazed disinterestedly out the window totally ignoring Tuttle's discomfort.

"Well, there was a cabinet meeting yesterday to discuss the threats by the terrorists. It seems General Blaine was able to get your friend to give up some more of bin Laden's plan."

"Unfortunate," Dunn muttered. "Adalla was a good man, if expendable. Go on, Tuttle."

"We apparently have only five days to respond to the terrorists demands before they begin distributing the virus."

"Yes, yes, Tuttle, cut to the chase and tell me something I don't already know."

"The meeting was to discuss options and how to deal with the threat. When the topic of how to deal with the terrorists came up, the suggestion was made to bomb the countries that refuse to cooperate with us and expose the terrorists." Tuttle knew he was walking a fine line and any minute Dunn could turn on him. The sweat ran down the back of his neck and the room was suddenly too small and too hot.

"It's your job to keep that from happening, Tuttle. You promised us that you could control Walsh. 'Have him in the palm of my hand,' you said." Dunn's voice was quiet and menacing, Tuttle began to panic.

"Well, uh, I did say that, yes. But now I have to deal with the rest of the cabinet, and I don't know if I can control them all."

"Tell me exactly what happened, Tuttle."

"When no one else suggested that the best course of action would be just to pull our aid from Israel, I felt I had to make the suggestion. It wasn't received very well, Warren."

Dunn sat perfectly still, his breath measured and steady. Just when Tuttle thought he had taken the news well and would be willing to help him find a solution, Dunn exploded out of his chair, sending his scotch flying at the television. He came to a stop with his face almost touching Tuttle's. Tuttle gasped and tried to steady himself.

"You have more balls than I ever would have thought, Tuttle! Daring to come here to tell me that you cannot deliver what you've promised!" The commotion brought Vinnie in from another room, his hand tucked into his jacket where a specially modified handgun was snugged in his waistband. Dunn glanced at his henchman, who slipped back through the door without a sound.

"Now, Mister Tuttle," Dunn snapped out each syllable precisely, "I suggest you tell me that you can fix this problem, that you will fix this problem."

Tuttle fisted his hands so tightly that the nails bit deep into the soft flesh of his palms. He shook visibly as the possible manifestations of Dunn's rage flitted through his mind.

"I, uh, I . . . I just don't . . . okay, I'll . . ." Tuttle stuttered, his voice cracking and breaking.

"You will return to your job and you will make absolutely sure that nothing goes wrong from this moment on, won't you Tuttle?" Dunn's voice dropped low.

Tuttle nodded his head, afraid to take his eyes off of the big man.

"Then I suggest you go and get on with it."

* * *

After Tuttle had beat a hasty retreat, Dunn got himself another drink. He knew that what was happening wasn't all Tuttle's fault. In fact, some of what was happening even surprised Dunn. It was beginning to look like their friends in the Mideast were changing the plan and not letting anyone know.

THIRTY

The First Lady's Private Office
The White House
Washington, D.C.

SARAH SAT IN HER PRIVATE OFFICE STARING OUT THE WINDOW, LOST IN thought. Since she had confronted David about the terrorist, he had made sure that she knew some of what was going on. It did not help at all. She wrestled with herself over how to tell David about Tuttle. She toyed with the idea of going to Jim Sercu, who would listen to her, she knew, and tell her if she was being silly. But he might tell her that anyway. She couldn't be sure with whom he was allied. Were his loyalties really with David, or was he somehow linked to Tuttle? The possibilities banged around in her mind like a pinball.

Finally she forced the wild thoughts to quiet down. Her allegiances were to David and the country, first and foremost. Unlike the Secret Service agents, she wasn't going to get thrown out of the White House if she was wrong.

Sarah stood slowly, straightened her jacket and, with a deep breath, headed for the door. She was just going to have to talk to her husband.

* * *

David watched while Jim Sercu carried a draped cage into the Oval Office.

"Is this really necessary, Jim?" he waved at the cage.

"Maybe not, but it's the best way to detect the presence of the virus." Sercu set the cage down on an end table and tugged at the cover, revealing two pale yellow canaries. The birds flitted about the cage, twittering at their new surroundings.

"Canaries work in coal mines, Jim. This isn't a mine." Walsh dropped into his chair and watched the birds for a moment.

"It's a safe bet that the birds will succumb to the virus long before you would, which will give us a chance to treat you. We've positioned cages in your personal quarters and your private study. We'll deliver one to Mrs. Walsh's office also." Sercu studied his friend's face, realizing how silly the whole thing would sound on any other day of the year. "C'mon, David, humor an old man. A couple of little birds will make me feel better."

Walsh laughed, "Okay, Jim. I guess it won't hurt. Just don't let the press get wind of it, will ya. I'm supposed to have a big goofy dog or an adorable little cat, not a couple of canaries. Welcome to the Oval Office, George and Martha."

Sercu smiled tightly, "The press hearing about canaries is the least of our worries right now." He was interrupted by a sharp rap on the door leading to the president's private passageway. The only person who would come through that passage was the First Lady.

Walsh looked questioningly at Sercu, "C'mon in, Sarah," he called out. The door, normally camouflaged as part of the walls around it, swung open slowly and Sarah stepped into the room. She pushed the door closed and leaned her back against it.

David looked at his wife for the first time in a couple of days. Her face was pale and drawn. She was tired and it was obvious. He regretted not having the time to talk to her, to really explain what was going on and what the ramifications could be. He needed her and had a feeling that she needed him right then.

"What's up, honey?" he asked softly, stepping out from

behind the imposing mahogany desk.

"I need to talk to you, David. It's important. I know you're busy, but this is really important."

"Sarah, we have a lot . . ."

"David, I know, and I promised you that I would not disturb you if I didn't think it was important."

Walsh softened, he wanted to talk to her. "Okay, what's going on?"

"Alone, please." Sarah looked at Sercu, then back to her husband. "Please David," she wished.

"Jim, do you mind?" Walsh said, not taking his eyes off his wife.

"No, not at all." Sercu turned to the door and nodded at Sarah, "Mrs. Walsh."

After Sercu had left the room, David led Sarah to the couch and sat down beside her. She drew in a deep breath and composed herself before she launched into the story of her explorations and what she overheard in the break room.

"David, I think there's something more going on here, and I'm afraid for you." Sarah took his hand in hers, praying that he had actually listened to what she was saying.

"Wow," David dropped against the back of the couch and looked at the ceiling, "that's a pretty serious allegation, Sarah."

"I know that, David. Why do you think it's taken me so long to come and talk to you? With everything else that's going on right now, this is the last thing you need to hear. But if it's true, he could be a liability right now." The whole time she was telling the story, Sarah heard herself sounding whiny and juvenile. She hated feeling so incompetent and out of control. But David could do that to her. He always could.

"If these two agents were so concerned about it, why didn't they come to me, or at the very least go to their superiors?" Walsh didn't want Sarah to think he doubted her, but as she had said herself, he couldn't afford to risk jumping to conclusions.

"I don't know, David. Maybe they have and it just hasn't gotten to you yet. Maybe they were just too frightened to say anything. They were worried about losing their posts."

"Okay," Walsh sat up and took his wife's hands in his, "I'm going to have to think about this carefully before I can decide what to do. And I've got everything else going on right now. Shit!" He leaned his head against Sarah's shoulder. He wanted to let go and just collapse into her, let someone else deal with these crises.

"David, what's really going on?" Sarah asked quietly, hoping that in this moment of intimacy he might actually tell her.

Walsh composed himself and suddenly became the president again. The transformation startled Sarah.

"Actually I wanted to talk to you. I want you to go to Nebraska for a while. Visit your folks, see your sister, play with the kids. Just take a break for a week or two."

Sarah stared into his eyes in shock. "You're sending me away?"

"It's not like that." Walsh sighed, "Please don't argue with me. We're in a potentially dangerous situation and I don't know if I can prevent it from becoming deadly. I just want you to be somewhere safe, and D.C. isn't the place."

"What's going on, David. Tell me." Sarah fought to keep her voice down, but sounded shrill to her own ears.

"There've been terrorist threats." He paused. How much should he tell her? "We have information that a certain terrorist group is going to try to release anthrax into our population." Sarah gasped, her eyes wide in horror. "Anthrax? But that could wipe out the whole coast!"

"The whole country, if they're really serious about it." Walsh reached out and gathered Sarah in his arms. "I'm terrified and I just want to know that you're safe, so I don't have to worry about you."

"My place is here, David, not Nebraska." Sarah fought down her tears and pushed away from his chest.

"Please, Sarah, please just go see your folks." Walsh resigned himself to pleading if that's what it took.

"How soon would I have to go?"

"In the next day or two."

"I'll think about it, David. No promises, but I'll think about it."

Walsh wrapped his arms around her and held her tight. Now that he had finally said the words, the fear was welling up and threatening to take over. And he still had Tuttle to think about.

Thirty-One

The Oval Office
The White House
Washington, D.C.

David had taken a mere thirty minutes to conclude he needed Jim Sercu's help to decide what to do about Ian Tuttle. Jim sat quietly and listened as the president related Sarah's story, then pointed out a few things he had noticed himself.

When Walsh paused to give Sercu a chance to digest everything he'd said, Sercu sat quietly. David knew the wheels were turning in his old friend's head, and he waited patiently.

"I'm concerned that the Secret Service agents haven't come forward with this information. That's a problem right there," Sercu spoke softly. "And I see your point about the things you've noticed happening with Tuttle. But the question is, why? To what end?"

"What's he got to gain by whatever this is?" Walsh added.

"And who was on the other end of the phone?" Sercu asked. "David, can you think of anyone Tuttle might be connected with who could need that information?"

Walsh found it increasingly hard to concentrate. He was tired and his mind was jumbled. "I don't know, Jim. It'll come to me, but I just can't put a name to it right now."

Sercu nodded. "Why don't you go and get some rest. But I think we need to talk to Mr. Tuttle in the morning. See where he stands without giving away what we know."

"He seems so adamant against bombing, and that we should just dump the Israelis altogether." Walsh rubbed his stubbled chin. "Let's ask him what he thinks about asking the Israelis to do the bombing."

"Hmmm, that might give us an idea of which side he's coming from," Sercu said thoughtfully. "We just have to be very careful, David. We can't afford to have any dissension in the ranks right now, and if word gets out that we're targeting someone, it may bring out the sharks."

"Oh yeah, it sure will."

* * *

Sleep evaded the president of the United States. The big bed, the fine cotton sheets, the plump pillows just weren't enough to settle his mind and allow him to get some rest. Walsh sat on the side of the bed sipping a whiskey in spite of the pounding behind his temples. He wanted to drink until he passed out, but that wasn't an option anymore. Being on duty 24/7 didn't leave time for self-indulgence.

Sarah had stayed away from their bedroom that night. Walsh desperately wished she were there, just to hold her, to be awake with her. But she was coping in her own way, and David knew that included just being by herself. He had to give her space and just pray she'd make the right decision and head for Nebraska.

Morning found Walsh dozing fitfully, troubled by nightmares of disease and disaster. He snapped awake with a start and, seeing the light beginning to color the windows of the bedroom, dragged himself out of bed and into the shower. He would have to find Jim Sercu and get on with the events of the day, come what may.

Less than an hour later, Sercu found the president polishing off a bagel in the Oval Office, his desk piled with reports detailing the emergency management procedures quietly being implemented in the target cities.

"Morning, Jim," Walsh mumbled, hastily slurping down the last of his coffee. "Are we ready?"

"Ready as I'll ever be, sir." Sercu poured a cup of coffee from the service at the sideboard. "But I have to tell you I'm not looking forward to this."

"Me either. But let's get it over with." Walsh punched the intercom on his desk and asked his secretary to find Tuttle and have him come to the Oval Office. He smiled sadly at Sercu, and the two sat in uneasy silence waiting for Tuttle to arrive.

It took about five minutes before Tuttle tapped on the office door. When he entered the room, Walsh was struck by how the man had changed over the past few days. His normally impeccable Italian suit was rumpled, the tie knotted crookedly. He had let his manicure go and the nails looked bitten and raw.

Walsh gestured to a chair and composed himself before beginning.

"Okay, I wanted to talk to the two of you alone to get your ideas on something that has been brought to my attention as a solution to our retaliation problem." Walsh watched as Tuttle fidgeted, seemingly unable to get comfortable in his own clothing.

"We've discussed the possibility of a nuclear strike against the countries harboring known terrorists." Walsh glanced at Tuttle in time to see him stiffen and go pale. "We've heard the pros and the cons of that plan. It's been suggested that if we could persuade the Israelis to do the bombing themselves, then we could sit back and keep our hands clean."

Jim Sercu nodded slightly and held his tongue, waiting to see if there would be a reaction from Tuttle. Walsh looked from one man to the other, trying to keep his face a mask. He waited a few more beats, then said, "Okay, so it's not such a good idea."

"Actually, sir, the idea has merits, but needs to be more fully considered before it becomes a viable option." Sercu looked pointedly at Tuttle offering him the opportunity to express his own thoughts.

"Well, sir," Tuttle began, his voice hard, "it doesn't address the real problem, does it?"

"What's that, Ian?" Walsh turned to face his chief of staff.

"The terrorists have made their demand, and I think that serious consideration has to be given to meeting that demand in order to avoid a disaster." Tuttle found his voice as he grew more confident that he had the president's attention.

"We've already established the conviction that we will never give in to the terrorists' demands," Walsh said simply.

"But, sir, look at it from a realistic angle!" Tuttle was becoming more shrill.

"We are approaching this realistically, Mr. Tuttle." Sercu turned to face Tuttle. "If we begin to meet terrorist demands now, we will be forever at the mercy of any fanatic with a bomb."

"It's not an option," Walsh stated flatly.

"It has to be an option, sir!" Tuttle's voice rose with his panic. "Can you honestly say that relations with a small country like Israel, which you have to admit is really no power at all in the greater scheme of things, is worth risking the oil supplies to the United States?" Tuttle almost flew out of his chair before he reined himself in and forcibly settled back into the seat.

David stole a glance at Sercu and saw the same shocked awareness in Sercu's eyes. "No one mentioned oil, Tuttle."

"Well," Tuttle felt the stutter beginning again, "the real concern, of course, is for the safety of our people. But you have to admit that if we bomb, if anyone bombs, even if we can keep them from releasing the virus, we'll still lose access to oil reserves. The economy won't be able to recover, and we'll be facing a very cold winter next year!" Tuttle's argument was coming apart at the seams and he was beginning to realize it.

Walsh had had enough. "Okay, obviously we aren't at a point where we can really move on any option yet. They all require further research." Sercu nodded his agreement.

"So," Walsh stood stiffly, "I'm sure you both have things that need your attention. I know I do. That'll be it for now."

Both Sercu and Tuttle rose to their feet and headed for the door.

"Jim," Walsh called out, "I want to discuss this canary thing with you, if you have a minute."

Tuttle scampered out of the room, leaving Walsh and Sercu looking at one another with concern.

"Oil," Walsh said sadly. "There's your payoff. The damned fool handed it right to us."

"And the other party?" Sercu asked, knowing the answer already.

"Has to be Warren Dunn."

Thirty-Two

U.S. Government
Safe House
Virginia Horse Country

Adalla Marchia had been isolated for eighteen hours. No guard, no soldier, no one had entered the cinder-block cell where he sat, held upright in the chair by the shackles.

His mind had wandered madly during the long hours alone. He had long ago lost his ability to concentrate on his litany. Prayers to Allah seemed a thing long stripped from him. Now his imagination filled the time with hallucinations.

A low rumble signaled someone had entered the room outside his cell and he waited for what would come next.

General Blaine stood purposefully in the watch commander's post outside the prisoner's cell. He had resolved during the hour-long drive from the White House to break the son of a bitch no matter what it cost. It was up to him now to make the bastard tell when the attack would take place. Everything was in his hands.

Blaine saluted the watch and stood before the closed-circuit monitor watching his prisoner slumped in the chair in the next room. Blaine took long slow breaths, willing his heart to beat slowly and steadily, gathering his strength and fixing his goal firmly in his mind.

The heavy door behind Blaine swung open and his superior,

General Ned Seiffert, stepped into the room. The watch guard snapped to attention, sending his chair skidding back to the wall.

"At ease," Seiffert growled stepping up next to Blaine. "General."

"Sir!" Blaine snapped a salute.

"What more do you think he has to tell us?" Seiffert wagged his chin at the closed-circuit image of Marchia.

"Only he knows for sure, sir," Blaine said quietly. "But something about this doesn't add up. Why would they tell us their plans? Sir, they are arrogant, we know, but not stupid. It just does not make sense."

"So you believe that he's been feeding us false information?"

"Yes, sir, I do."

"And you believe this man knows the real plan?"

"I hope so, sir." Blaine's gaze never left his prisoner.

"Then get on with it. We haven't got much time left."

Blaine turned on his heel and snapped another salute. "Yes, sir! Commander, get Colonel Ziegelhofer down here."

* * *

Jim Sercu found David Walsh pacing around the Oval Office. Doing laps was more like it. The man moved with a steady long-legged stride, as though working off energy he couldn't control.

"Mr. President?" he asked almost cautiously as he stepped into the room.

"Jim, c'mon in." Walsh didn't lose a step. "What's up?"

"Are you all right, sir?" Sercu asked quickly closing the door behind him.

"As all right as can be expected, I guess." Walsh stopped dead. "I'm sorry. I just suddenly felt like I needed some physical activity."

"We could have a treadmill or exercycle moved into the office, sir." Sercu suggested.

"I don't need a clothes rack in here, Jim," Walsh smiled. Sercu cocked his head questioningly. "Never mind. Old joke of Sarah's. What can I do for you?"

"I've met with the head of Secret Service, Arthur Hite. He's going to talk to the two agents Mrs. Walsh overheard and see what's up."

"I don't want those men to feel like they're being punished one way or another." Walsh slid into the chair behind the huge mahogany desk. "It bothers me that they would even have a reason to feel they couldn't air their fears, grounded or not."

"And I made sure Director Hite understood that, sir. The agents won't be facing any consequences."

"Good. Let me know when we have some more information. Did you run that second background check on Tuttle?"

"I did, sir, and it showed exactly the same things we found the first time around, except for one thing."

Walsh looked at Sercu, wanting to see some indication of whether or not the news was good, "Do I want to hear this?" he asked.

"Probably not," Sercu shook his head. "It seems Mr. Tuttle has had a little more cash than usual lately. His bank records don't show any large deposits, but he has been spending more and in ways we hadn't found before. Mostly on entertainments." Sercu emphasized the last word carefully. Walsh nodded.

"So, the implication is that Mr. Tuttle has found a new source of funds."

"Apparently."

"What about Dunn?"

"His background check turned up the same things that we found back when he expressed interest in your candidacy. Some less-than-clean dealings, but nothing that could be classified as obviously illegal. I wanted to look a little deeper into his association with the Bohemian Club, but as usual with that particular organization it was like banging your head against a wall to see what's on the other side."

"The Bohemian Club?" Walsh asked, trying to remember where he had heard that name before.

"The club that invited you to join when you were governor of Oklahoma." Sercu prompted.

"Oh, that good old boys, leather chairs and cognac deal in Wisconsin. Now I remember."

"Well, it's a bit more than that, sir," Sercu said, flipping open a file folder he held on his lap. "The members of this club are the biggest movers and shakers in politics and business. Much of the membership is a big secret, and their dealings are an even bigger secret than the U.S. defense grid."

"Makes one wonder what they're hiding."

"Exactly. And Mr. Dunn is a member, a longtime member from what I can gather."

Walsh bit at a thumbnail and stared off at a far corner of the room. Sercu knew he was deep in thought and waited patiently.

"Okay," Walsh suddenly popped back to life, sitting up straight with a renewed sense of purpose. "We can't risk calling Tuttle on any of this right now. We need to find out what's going on and what, if anything, it might have to do with the current situation. I can't help but feel that there's a connection here somewhere."

"I agree, sir, but can we just allow Tuttle to carry on as though we suspect nothing?"

"Yes, we can. I'm not going to give him any hands-on involvement, but he can continue to function as chief of staff. I want a Secret Service escort assigned to him, the best men we have, and they're to be instructed to report back every move the man makes, every conversation he has, every place he goes. Put an escort on all our cabinet members. They should have them right now anyway."

Sercu nodded, "What about his phone? We can monitor the White House line, but what about his cell phone and his line at home?"

"Good idea. In fact, let's get Jim Marshall and Dennis Murphy in here. It's about time they're briefed on the situation and I want both of them involved in this. The FBI can handle monitoring Dunn."

"Yes, sir."

"Okay, did Blaine go back to the safe house?" Walsh opened the leather portfolio on the desk and riffled through the situation reports it contained.

"Yes, he and Ned Seiffert headed back out to Virginia after the meeting. Blaine believed that he could get more specific information out of Marchia, and Seiffert wanted to be present."

"I don't blame him. Sometimes you need to feel like you're doing more than reading reports." Walsh dropped the stack of papers back on the desk. "Let's hope they discover something useful this time."

Sercu nodded gravely.

Thirty-Three

U.S. Government
Safe House
Virginia Horse Country

MARCHIA HAD LONG SINCE STOPPED SCREAMING. BLAINE STOOD OVER him, a bloodied pair of cruel-looking snips in one hand. Marchia's hands were no longer shackled and he held the bloody stumps of ten fingers, clipped off at the joints, under his arms. The blood spurted endlessly, soaking his coveralls and dripping with a relentless, thick sound onto the concrete floor. The remnant of Marchia's left eye was swollen shut, his lip cracked open, and a strip of flesh hung limply on his stubbled chin.

Blaine stared down at the ruined gray face and saw nothing but the faces of countless children swollen and convulsing in the throes of deadly biochemical weapons. The image made the work much easier.

"Last chance, asshole," Blaine hissed. "You think this was bad? I've got some real doozies to show you yet."

"I cannot tell you what I do not know," Marchia croaked.

"Well, funny thing," Blaine slammed Marchia's left ear with the flat side of the snips, "I don't believe you."

Marchia's head snapped and he groaned. Blaine knew his prisoner was rapidly becoming numb to the pain and it would be increasingly harder to reach him. But he had a way around that, too. He tossed the snips to one side and pulled the long, lethal-looking cow prod out of his belt. He had ordered Marchia's bare feet placed in a tray of water and used the prod, cranked up to the fullest jolt, to soften him up for questioning. The prisoner's screams had been satisfying.

The heavy steel door of the cell ground open, and Ziegelhofer filled the door frame with Marchia's sixteen-year-old daughter and his wife cowering before him. Ziegelhofer shoved the two women into the room sending them sprawling against the far wall. Marchia's wife looked to her husband for help and an ear-piercing shriek echoed off the hard walls of the cell.

"Now, let's see about what you know and what you don't know." Blaine's voice would have frightened the strongest man as the blood lust dripped from every word. He had his goal clearly in mind and wasn't going to allow anything to get in the way of ending the threat to his country.

Outside the cell, General Ned Seiffert watched the interrogation on the closed-circuit screen. He had seen a great deal of this sort of interrogation during his career in the military, but unlike General Blaine, it had never gotten easier for Seiffert. There was no other way and he knew it. He watched dispassionately as Ziegelhofer dragged the two women into the cell and prayed that this would finally force Marchia to divulge the information they needed before Americans began to die.

"What a world," he thought, "that forces men to take these measures to protect their families."

Inside the cell, Blaine had dragged the girl away from her mother and held her, limp and sobbing, before her father.

"Look at her, Marchia. Look at your little girl and realize what you've done to her." Blaine's voice was low and menacing. "You've done this, Marchia, you and the rest of the sand niggers you call friends!"

Marchia dragged his eyes up to Blaine's face. "We live and die for the glory of Allah," his voice barely a whisper. "You cannot murder our souls."

"Oh, but I can." Blaine grabbed the loose fabric of the girl's flimsy dress and ripped it down off her shoulders, exposing her small soft breasts. "I'm not going to kill her. Oh no, I wouldn't do that! I think she might provide a bit of fun for my men before we ship her back home." Marchia's wife wailed when she saw her husband's one good eye grow wide in alarm.

"What do you think, Ziggy?" Blaine flung the girl back into Ziegelhofer's arms. "Had a virgin lately?" Blaine turned his attention back to Marchia. "I know full well what will happen to her once she gets home, 'defiled by the infidel'! Isn't that the phrase?"

Blaine watched Marchia's face carefully, looking for the sign that he had finally reached the place from where his prisoner could never come back. "And the other girls? They'll be fun, too, I'm sure. Oh, and the boys? Imagine what will happen to the boys when we send them back. Especially the oldest one, the one who killed my soldier!" Blaine's voice rose to a bellow. Marchia's breath was coming in gasps now. He probably would have been shedding tears if his eyes still worked correctly.

Blaine walked idly over to where Marchia's wife cowered against the wall, leveled a kick at her abdomen, and the woman screamed. Blaine nodded slightly to Ziegelhofer and the big man pulled the girl up to his wide chest and fondled her breast with one pawlike hand.

Seiffert could hear Marchia's scream through the thick armored door of the cell.

Thirty-Four

The Oval Office
The White House
Washington, D.C.

David Walsh watched the trim, blond woman seated on the couch across from him as she outlined her proposal. Barbara Howe was known as a barracuda among the White House staff and that was just fine with her. She understood that underneath the grumbling, complaints and sometimes fear, she was respected among the staff and her colleagues. She was tough, no nonsense and often difficult to work for, but she was effective and Walsh valued that over and above almost anything else.

"Sir, I think it's important that we exhaust as many options as we can before we take drastic action." She regarded him intently.

"I just don't like the idea of any member of my cabinet leaving the country right now. It isn't safe," Walsh's protest lacked enthusiasm. He knew she was right, but felt he had to speak his mind regardless.

"My safety is not the concern, sir. The safety of innocent people is the only concern. If I can convince some of the Arab heads of state to cooperate, we may be able to avert this crisis before it becomes a disaster."

"You realize you have your work cut out for you?" Walsh said, relinquishing his position.

"Yes, sir, I am well aware of Arab attitudes toward women, but I have been successful in talks with Middle Eastern powers before."

"Yes, you have, Barbara." Walsh sipped at his cold coffee, and grimaced. "Do you have any idea how you're going to approach this?"

"Well, I don't think the standard 'United States as world power' argument will work in this case." She smiled tightly. "So, I'll have to rely on appealing to their need for power and any sense of self-preservation that might remain. I'd like to believe that the world has changed enough that even they will see reason eventually."

Walsh shook his head sadly. "I wish I had as much faith as you do, Barbara. But what we've seen so far doesn't indicate that anything has changed."

"That may be, sir, but I have to try."

"Of course, see Jim for whatever plans you need to make and check back with me before you go."

Howe rose to her feet, her perfectly tailored skirt falling neatly to her knees. How she managed to always look unrumpled mystified Walsh.

"Thank you, sir." She spun about sharply and marched out of the room.

He was uncomfortable sending one of his best on what could easily turn into a suicide mission. He resisted the urge to think in terms of sending a woman on a suicide mission. That wasn't fair to Howe, who had worked hard to get the position she now held. But to try to convince a handful of power-hungry heads of states that had existed for centuries on their blood lust and fanaticism that they needed to band together with the infidel. Well, it was a fool's mission, but Barbara was right, she had to try at least. And in a way it would cover the U.S. government's collective ass. When the dust settled they could still say they had tried.

Walsh allowed a long sigh to slip past his lips as he sat unmoving on the couch. The Oval Office was getting bigger every day, proportionate to how heavy the role of president was beginning to feel. He listened to the quiet of the big room, savoring the stillness for the first time in days. He wished it would go on for another week, just to give him a rest before the next crisis reared its ugly head.

A rap on the door shattered that dream and his secretary poked her head in timidly. "Sir?" she called softly waiting to see if Walsh moved. He slowly turned to her and smiled. "Generals Seiffert and Blaine are on the videophone in the Situation Room. They've asked to speak with you."

Walsh sighed again, dreading whatever their news could be. It couldn't be good.

"Thanks, Colleen, I'll be right there."

After the door shut silently, Walsh pulled himself off of the couch listening to the pops and creaks of his tired joints. Even if there had been time, he was too exhausted to think about hitting the White House exercise room. He had to get used to the sounds of age in his body.

* * *

Ned Seiffert's face filled the screen in the Situation Room giving Walsh the creepy feeling of being a very small fish in a very small fish bowl. A hand suddenly appeared on the general's shoulder and he was gently urged to step back away from the camera.

"Damned things . . . why the hell we can't just use the secure telephone lines . . ."

"Maybe we should go back to carrier pigeons, huh, Ned?" Walsh asked smiling at the general's bluster.

"Sir! I'm, uh, sorry about that, sir." Seiffert snapped to attention catching Walsh's amused face on the screen at his end.

"It's okay, Ned. What have we found out?" Walsh slid carefully into a high-backed leather chair trying unsuccessfully to keep his knees from popping too loudly.

"Sir, General Blaine has broken the prisoner and obtained further information about their plans." Seiffert's face hardened and his voice dropped.

"What do we know, general?" Walsh asked again.

Seiffert stepped back and the screen was filled with Blaine's face. His hair was wet and slicked back.

"Sir, the prisoner has informed us of the extent of the terrorists' plans and has given us specifics of weapons. He has also confirmed for us the veracity of some his previous statements."

"The veracity, general?" Walsh felt the same chill creeping up his arms and into his hairline. He kept his voice steady.

"Yes, sir, he has confirmed the timing he already confessed. But more importantly, we now know what kind of armament we're up against. The terrorists have amassed . . ."

Walsh cut him off in mid-sentence, "Get back up here and present your findings to the cabinet. We're going to have a lot of planning to do."

"Yes, sir!" Walsh could see both men snap a quick salute as the line went dead. Seiffert looked as exhausted as Walsh felt.

Suddenly, jogging him out of his own thoughts, Jim Sercu was at his shoulder.

"Mr. President," he said softly. "I'm sorry, I didn't mean to startle you."

"That's okay, Jim, somebody had to before I dozed off." Walsh laughed, but it sounded empty.

"I've met with Barbara Howe and her arrangements are under way as you requested."

"Good. That was Seiffert and Blaine. They've managed to get Marchia to talk a bit more. I've asked them to get back up here and present what they've found to all of us at once."

"Very good. I'll call the meeting." Sercu glanced around the room at the handful of Secret Service and aides present before he went on. "David, I think you need to get some rest. Just a few minutes before Blaine and Seiffert get back."

"Yeah, you're probably right." Walsh leaned heavily on the table. "I have a bad feeling that there won't be much time for it after this."

THIRTY-FIVE

President's Private Study
The White House
Washington, D.C.

WARM SUN FILTERED THROUGH PALM LEAVES THE SIZE OF A FOOTBALL player. The sand held the heat, scalding the bottoms of feet and warming behinds sunk into the beach under slowly tanning bodies. The wind carried the sweet smell of tropical flowers and fruit down from the trees to compete with the coconut oil drenched sun bathers. There was no noise except the pounding of the surf as it crested over the reef and broke onshore. The drink was red and tasted fruity and heavy with rum. Then something blocked out the sun.

"Mr. President! Mr. President!" A female voice called David Walsh from a far distance and the beach shattered around him. As the memories of the present began to flood into his brain he could feel his heart rate building until it would have drowned out the sound of the surf in his ears.

"Mr. President!"

Walsh sat up suddenly almost bolting to his feet, his eyes wide and his breath in hitches and gasps.

"I'm sorry, Mr. President, but you asked me to wake you." Colleen stood before him wringing her hands. Her bright flower print dress looking crisp and clean in the darkly paneled room.

"Oh, no, Colleen, I'm sorry. I must've been dreaming." Walsh ran his hand through his disheveled hair. His head felt stuffed with cotton and his mouth was dry.

"Sir, Mr. Marshall and Mr. Murphy are here. You asked me to wake you when they arrived," Colleen said, calmer now.

"Yes, I did. Thank you. Um, I'll meet with them here. Show them in and bring some coffee would you? I'm just going to get cleaned up."

"Yes, sir." Colleen slipped silently out of the room before Walsh tried to get to his feet. He shook his head trying to clear the grogginess, then checked the clock. He'd been asleep an hour; he should have felt more refreshed than he did.

In the private bath off his study, Walsh drenched his face with cold water and scrubbed at it hard with a towel. As he struggled not to gag on the suddenly too minty toothpaste, he heard Colleen usher Marshall and Murphy into the office. The clink of a coffee service being set on the table was followed by the snick of the door and he knew he couldn't hide in the bathroom any longer.

Walsh looked at his haggard face in the mirror one last time before stepping through the door.

"Jim, Dennis, I'm glad you could make it." Walsh shook both men's hands warmly before gesturing to seats in the overstuffed chairs and the couch. "Coffee?"

Jim Marshall moved to the coffee service before Walsh could. "Why don't you sit down, sir. I'll get the coffee."

Walsh looked at Marshall, noting the concern in the older man's eyes. "They must both see how exhausted I am," he thought.

"Thanks, Jim." Walsh dropped into one of the chairs and took a deep breath. "I'm going to cut to the chase. You've both dropped other things to be here and I appreciate it, so I won't waste your time."

Dennis Murphy grinned, his bright blue eyes shaded in spite

of the smile. "Yeah, I was under par, too!" he laughed.

Walsh returned the smile. "Believe me, I wouldn't have dragged you away for just anything. Did Jim Sercu brief you both?"

"Oh, yes," Marshall said, handing a steaming cup to Walsh and one to Murphy before sitting down. "And I'd say that counts as not just anything."

"I'll second that," Murphy said. "We've already mobilized agents and specialists into position for possible attack, and you know whatever we have is at your disposal."

"So has the FBI," Marshall said. "We've got the airports at all three locations thoroughly covered and have replaced the usual airport and customs security with our own people. I'd like to see those terrorists sneak through now."

David looked at both men, sitting side by side on the couch. They were the best of the best, both chosen to head their respective services for their competency and their dependability. Walsh had to trust in that now.

"Actually, that's only part of the story," he said quietly. Murphy and Marshall exchanged looks before turning their attention back to their president.

"We'll be having an emergency meeting shortly, and I'd like both of you to sit in on that. But what I need to discuss with you now is something different but related, and I need to know how it's related."

Walsh recounted the events of the past day, telling the FBI and CIA directors everything he knew about Tuttle's background, his reactions to current situations and his attempt to sway Walsh's decisions. When he was finished, the three sat in silence while Murphy and Marshall tried to absorb everything they had just heard.

"We did all the requisite background checks on Tuttle when you appointed him," Marshall said. "We didn't find anything unusual."

"Mr. President, you sound like you have some idea about who

else might be involved in this," Murphy said gently, obviously stunned by what he had heard.

"Yes, yes, I do." Walsh paused. It was too late to go back now. He only hoped that his suspicions would be proved false. "I think Warren Dunn is behind the whole thing."

Both Marshall and Murphy showed no reaction to the news. They had slipped into their professional personae and were gathering information, not drawing conclusions. Not yet.

"Well, I can see possible motives for his involvement. But do you really think that this terrorist problem could stem from whatever he's up to?" Murphy asked.

"It all boils down to oil, doesn't it?" Walsh rose to refill his coffee cup. With his back to the two men, he continued. "The implications of their involvement in this are just too terrible to try to think through. That an American citizen might be responsible for what's happening out there is . . ."

"Terrifying," Murphy finished Walsh's sentence.

"Yes, terrifying. So we need to decide what to do about it." Walsh sat down again. He felt a mixed sense of relief and foreboding. He was taking positive action, but positive action against someone he considered a friend. Someone he trusted.

"Well, if we can prove this and we move on it immediately, there's no guarantee that it will resolve the terrorist problem," Marshall said. Walsh marveled; he could almost see the man's brain kick into gear.

"No," Murphy interjected, "it won't, no matter what happens to any one individual in any terrorist campaign. I've never heard of a single instance where it changed their plans."

"And there's always the chance it could accelerate the plan," Marshall said.

"True." Murphy tapped the rim of his coffee cup, keeping rhythm with the speed of his thoughts. "So, the first priority is derailing this plot and then turning our attention to Tuttle and Dunn."

"That's my take on it," Walsh said. "The only problem is keeping Tuttle uninvolved until we can handle the terrorists."

"True, you don't want to raise suspicions or we might lose any shot we have of cornering him or Dunn," Marshall said, staring off into space as though he were looking for an answer.

"How about Secret Service?" Murphy asked.

"We've already upped his escort and required reports as to anything suspicious he might be doing. At least that's some surveillance."

"And the phone lines? Faxes?"

"Jim's taking care of that. We're also tracing his private cell." Walsh allowed himself to feel the relief that came with turning a sticky problem over to someone else. He could now feel comfortable facing the other troubles he had to deal with.

A rap on the door preceded Colleen, who announced that Generals Blaine and Seiffert had returned and the cabinet were assembling in the Situation Room.

"Gentlemen," Walsh stood, "shall we?"

Thirty-Six

The White House Situation Room
Washington, D.C.

A sea of worried faces greeted Walsh as he entered the Situation Room, trailed by Jim Marshall and Dennis Murphy. Ned Seiffert was already seated at the table, stiff and serious; General Blaine stood behind him. Barbara Howe hustled in just as David was sitting down, making her own apologies, which sounded less like apologies and more like challenges to anyone who might question her lateness.

New tension filled the air, making the huge room seem very small. Walsh knew they were all exhausted, on edge, and worried about their families just like he was. But he had to show them a different face, one that wasn't succumbing to the stress, one that had full confidence in their ability to win this thing, and one that wasn't facing the betrayal of a friend. David forced himself to look where Ian Tuttle sat farther down the long table, forced himself to keep his face impassive, and then move on to regard each person present. He hesitated a few moments before beginning the meeting.

"Okay," he began, then cleared his throat, "let's skip over the formalities and jump right to the dirt. General Seiffert?"

"Mr. President," Seiffert said in a voice that betrayed none of his anxiety, "General Blaine has questioned the prisoner further and managed to uncover further details of the terrorists' plot."

Walsh eyed Blaine. "General?" he prompted.

"Well, sir, after further questioning . . ." a quiet, low murmur flowed around the table. Walsh looked up long enough to silence it.

"After further questioning," Blaine continued, "the prisoner has confessed to misleading us about the locations of the terrorist attacks." The room grew silent. The implications of what Blaine was about to reveal hung heavily over each person present. "They never had any intention of attacking Boston, New York, or Baltimore."

"That means . . ." Barbara Howe whispered.

"Yes, that means that they are focusing their attack on Washington," Blaine said ominously. "We have also discovered that our attempts to catch the terrorists on their way into the country were for naught. While we were monitoring for an influx of materials that could be identified as weapons, either artillery or biological, they had already assembled their armament somewhere in this country. The terrorists have been preparing for this for a very long time."

The silence in the room was becoming oppressive. David wished someone would gasp or scream or something, anything to break the silence.

"So," he would have to do it himself, "any thoughts on the implications of this?" Walsh let his gaze wander around the room, resting momentarily on each person at the table. He stopped on CIA director Dennis Murphy, who was studying Ian Tuttle's reaction to the news with interest. Tuttle sat, eyes downcast, face pale and a slight twitch vibrating his left eyelid. Murphy glanced at David, the director's expression confirming Walsh's deepest fears.

"Well, sir, it seems like we need to refocus our efforts on locking down the city and rooting out the terrorists. We need to recall all agents and forces in other cities to beef up our protection here."

Jim Marshall was first to speak. Walsh knew he was thinking about the agents he had sent to man the airports in Boston, New York and Baltimore.

"Yes, that would be the first step, Jim. Dennis, take care of your own agents, if you would." The two men nodded their agreement.

"Okay," Walsh tried to stall for time. He had to think but felt like his head was full of rice pudding. "If you'll allow me to change the subject for the moment, we need to get one thing out of the way so Ms. Howe can carry on with her plans. We've decided to send Barbara on a mission to the Middle East to talk to the Arab heads of state."

Bill Cassidy snorted his derision. "What good will that do," he sputtered, "if I may ask, Mr. President?"

Barbara Howe glanced at Walsh before taking up her own argument. "We have to try at least. If I'm successful, perhaps I can convince some of them to see reason and we may be able to head this off before it becomes even more serious than it already is. If not . . ."

David jumped in, giving the weight of his position to hers. "And if it's not, then we at least can say that we tried before we took more definitive action."

Cassidy looked thoughtful. "It just seems awfully dangerous."

"All part of my job, Bill." Howe's tone summed it all up: Don't give me grief about being a woman. You should know better.

Walsh favored her with a tight smile before turning to Sercu. "Jim, did you get me the information I asked for?"

Sercu pulled a thin folder out of his brief case and took a deep breath before looking at the president. "It's not good, sir."

"Sum it up for us, please, Jim." David sat back in his chair, forcing his muscles to relax and his expression to remain impassive. The cold knot of fear was tightening in his gut again, but he couldn't allow these people to see that.

Sercu cleared his throat before opening the folder and shaking his head ruefully. "We looked at the threat to the drinking water reserves. There are 324 reservoirs serving the four cities. They hold approximately 4.1 billion gallons of water among them, and cover an area roughly 12.5 million acre-feet. The northeast is fortunate to have such a bountiful water supply compared to some other areas of the country. But," Sercu paused and looked at the ashen faces staring back at him, "but, it only takes a couple of teaspoons of botulinina, the infectious agent created from the botulism strain, to infect the entire area and kill millions."

Walsh took several deep breaths, holding his face relaxed and belying the panic he felt in his gut. "But how easy would it be for a terrorist to infect that water supply to that degree?"

Sercu turned to Bill Cassidy, who shook his head gravely. "There are countless examples, sir. In 1985, plutonium was found in New York City's water supply after city hall received an anonymous letter threatening contamination. Someone had no problem pulling that off."

"With all the tightened security, how would someone be able to get anything into the country to infect the water?" the vice president asked, sounding too much as if he were grasping at straws.

"In 1988, trying to disrupt elections, followers of the Bhagwan Shree Ragneesh contaminated salad bars in Texas and Oregon with salmonella. Seven hundred and fifty people were hospitalized. In 1992, Senate investigators looked into fears that members of the Aum Shinrikyo cult went to Africa to bring back samples of Ebola virus. In '94, a man from Arkansas was arrested by Canadian customs agents with four guns, 20,000 rounds of ammo and enough ricin to kill 30 million people."

"Ricin?" Walsh heard someone in the back of the room ask, sounding bewildered.

"Ricin is an extremely dangerous toxin made from castor

beans," Cassidy answered offhandedly. "There are just too many examples, and those are only the ones we know about. Back in '97 two guys had enough time to paint ten-foot-high letters on the Kensico Dam in Valhalla before authorities caught them. That translates to more than enough time to plant a bomb or infect the outflow with something dangerous.

"The way it was explained to me by one of the brains over at NIH," Cassidy went on after taking a deep breath, "is that one small boat carrying just one-half pound of anthrax material can wipe out literally hundreds of thousands of people within hours, if the wind is blowing toward a city the size of, say, Boston or New York or D.C. The shit—excuse me, sir—is colorless, odorless and there's just no way to know it's there until people start to die." Cassidy's eyes had tightened to slits. His anger only partially masking the fear that they all felt.

"So, how do we prevent it from happening? Or, worst case scenario, how do we clean it up?" Walsh asked.

Sercu flipped through his papers. "It seems the greatest danger of contamination is at the point between the filtration process and the tap. The chlorination and filtration processes help to cut down any threats, but that's public knowledge. A little bit of research will tell you where you need to break into the system for the threat to be effective. And if any of them obtained access to the filtration plants, it's even worse."

"Okay, we need to lock down all the filtration plants and place regular checks on any points where a terrorist could break into water lines, pumping stations, that sort of thing. And let's do it for the whole eastern seaboard just to hedge our bets."

"Even with the filtration system, Mr. President, if the reservoir is contaminated, some of the toxin could still get through," Sercu said, reading from his report.

"How do we check for reservoir contamination?"

"Wildlife is the best indicator," Bill Cassidy interjected. "We just have to get the water authority to sweep for dead fish and birds."

"Okay, let's get a plan of action drawn up by yesterday and get this moving. Any other comments?" Walsh surveyed the table, but no one seemed to have much more to say, so he moved on.

"We need to reformulate our defense strategies in light of our new information. I need each of you to return to your original plans and rework everything to concentrate on Washington, except where it concerns the water supplies. We need to pull in whatever information we have about terrorist activities in the city, any local groups known for speaking against the government, any possible connection. Don't overlook anything no matter how trivial it may seem." Once again he tried to fix each person with a look that conveyed the seriousness of what was happening. Ian Tuttle avoided his gaze entirely.

Ned Seiffert cleared his throat and waited until he had the president's attention. "We have not yet finalized plans for retaliation. I think that in light of this news we need to decide our course of action as soon as possible." General Blaine nodded his agreement and the low murmur around the table rose once again.

"You're talking about the possibility of bombing, is that correct?" Walsh asked. He stole a quick glance at Tuttle, whose head snapped up, eyes wide.

"Yes, sir, I am. I don't believe we can limit ourselves to fighting this battle only on home soil."

David sat perfectly still for a few moments, thinking, or trying to think. The ramifications of a strategic strike on any of the Arab nations would be bigger than anything the United States had faced since World War II. "That will make the Gulf War look like a game of Risk," he said softly.

"Quite possibly, sir, but we cannot back down on our policy of zero tolerance. We cannot risk giving any terrorist group the notion that they can ride roughshod over this nation, sir."

Walsh only nodded. "Pull a plan together for me, Ned. Let me see your targets, potential damage, projected casualties, the usual stuff. And overall cost." He could feel the tension building back up again, but ignored it. "All right, everyone has their next step, so get going. I need some answers fast. And, Barbara, Godspeed!" Walsh stood up and took Howe's hand, squeezing it for moment. The rest of the room echoed his good wishes, and Howe hurried out of the room.

Papers rustled and chairs were pushed in as each cabinet member hustled off, aides and assistants in tow.

"Mr. President?" Ian Tuttle's voice jerked Walsh back to the room. "I really need to speak with you about this." The man's hands twisted together madly and a slight sheen of sweat shone on his forehead.

"Yes, yes, of course, Ian. One moment." Walsh turned to catch Murphy and Marshall as they trailed out behind the rest. "Jim, Dennis, I'd like to speak with you about your next move. Hang around for a minute, will you?" The two men assented and moved off toward the far side of the room. "Now, Ian, what is it?"

"It's this plan to bomb, sir. Have you really thought it through?"

"As much as I've been able to without more information, Ian. What's got you so upset?"

"It's just . . . it's just so early in your administration, sir; I'm concerned about the effect hasty decisions are going to have on your future."

David studied the twitch making Tuttle's left eyelid dance. He had to be careful not to ask questions that would reveal his suspicions. "Well, of course, that's part of my consideration, Ian, but don't you think the potential destruction that could come from this attack should be more of a concern?"

"But, sir, to be known as the president responsible for the deaths of so many innocents?"

"The Americans who will die if anthrax is released in Washington are innocents, also."

"Yes, yes, of course," Tuttle was becoming impatient, his tone harsh. "The damage to this country's reputation, not to mention the economy, I mean . . . the damage to our oil supplies alone could cripple us!"

Ah, there's the core of it again, Walsh thought. Over Tuttle's shoulder, David could see both Murphy and Marshall watching from the other side of the room. Walsh hoped Tuttle didn't make the connection.

"In that case, we would have to work harder on alternative fuel sources. In fact it might force technology to find cleaner solutions finally," Walsh said matter-of-factly.

"Well, that certainly works in theory, sir . . ." Tuttle grew quiet.

"It's all right, Ian." Walsh took Tuttle's arm and turned him toward the door. "You'll know when I've made any decision on this matter, and as always, I will welcome everyone's input." Tuttle looked beaten down, suddenly tired, as he allowed himself to be led to the door.

Once Tuttle was gone and the door slid shut again, Walsh turned to Murphy and Marshall, who looked at him gravely.

"Well, that was telling, sir." Murphy shook his head.

"He certainly isn't the Ian Tuttle I've dealt with in the past couple of months," Marshall said.

"No, he's not," Walsh dropped into a chair. "So you both think my fears have credence?"

"Definitely," Marshall murmured; Murphy nodded.

"Then you two do what you have to do."

The directors of the CIA and FBI headed off to begin assembling evidence against Ian Tuttle, leaving the president alone with his thoughts.

Thirty-Seven

Janey Elementary School
Washington, D.C.

The teachers didn't notice the long black car parked across the street from the school playground. Nor did the teachers notice the white ball with the big blue star on it that the children found under the monkey bars. But shortly after a group of third graders began an impromptu game of dodgeball, they knew something was very wrong.

The ball bounced wildly through the group of players, leaving a small puff of brown dust on hands and jackets as it moved along. A small, towheaded boy grabbed the ball out of midair and lobbed it to a pigtailed girl before rubbing his nose with one grubby fist. The men inside the black sedan watched as the action was repeated again and again across the playground. Small hands rubbed noses and eyes; small fingers carried unknown substances toward delicate membranes.

The towheaded boy was first to fall. The teachers took a moment to notice something was amiss, waiting for the boy to scramble back to his feet. When he didn't, a yell went up and several teachers ran to attend to the child.

In the car, the dark-skinned man in the passenger seat nodded to his driver and the car pulled away slowly as more children fell to the pavement on the playground.

* * *

At the White House, David sat in an aged leather armchair in his private study, listening closely to what FBI director Jim Marshall had found out about Ian Tuttle. Dennis Murphy, head of the CIA sat nearby.

"Well, sir, what we've uncovered so far is that Tuttle's background checks out pretty much the same as in the initial investigation. We did find a few, shall we say unusual, personal preferences, but nothing that has ever caused any trouble."

"So, my chief of staff has a kinky side?" Walsh asked, a sad smile on his lips.

"Well, uh, yes," Marshall seemed embarrassed to have to be sharing that information.

David nodded to Marshall. "Sir, I'm afraid the news I have isn't quite as reassuring."

A loud rap announced the opening of the door and an ashen-faced Sercu hustled into the room without waiting for a go-ahead from Walsh.

"Jim? What's the matter?" David put down his coffee cup, sitting forward in the deep chair.

Sercu ignored the question and moved to the large television screen set in the wall. Grabbing the remote he clicked it on and scanned to a locate network affiliate. A blond woman's troubled face filled the screen, and the scene behind her looked like something out a made-for-TV miniseries. Yards of yellow police tape encircled what appeared to be a playground, but the yard was filled with lumbering figures dressed completely in white, shiny silver shields where faces should have been in the squared-off hoods.

"What the hell?" Murphy's shock overcame any sense of formality. Sercu rolled up the sound on the television until the woman's quivering voice filled the room.

"So far, thirteen children and four teachers have died and a dozen more have been taken by medical helicopters to local hospitals where they are under quarantine until the source of this strange affliction can be found." The camera panned away from the reporter to the white-clad hazardous materials workers combing the school playground carefully taking samples of dirt, grass, and scrapings off the wood and metal equipment. One held a large white ball with a dusty blue star on it in a heavy plastic bag emblazoned with the biohazard symbol.

"The principal, with whom we spoke by phone just moments ago, states that the teachers saw nothing unusual when they accompanied the children outside for recess. Shortly, a friendly game of dodgeball turned into disaster as one child after another collapsed. Symptoms of infection have been sudden high fever, chills, sweating, nausea, and gastrointestinal bleeding. Police have cordoned off the area, and as you can see behind me, the Haz-Mat team is collecting evidence while awaiting the arrival of representatives from CDC momentarily."

Walsh was white. He could feel his knees trembling, and his fingers dug into the chair's soft leather in a vain effort to camouflage the shudder that threatened to shake his body apart. The other men in the room were just as pale and stared dumbly at the television screen.

Finally, Jim Sercu broke the silence. "CDC personnel are on their way and I've taken the liberty of calling out the military to enforce a quarantine. We need to pinpoint the source of the problem before the press takes this any further."

Walsh could only nod, waiting for the shock to subside and for his faculties to return. He felt like he was swimming in a pool of thick mud.

"Yeah, we're going to have to call a press conference." Walsh struggled to think of what to do next. The sheer force of the event pushed everything he knew right out of his head. Thirteen children? How could they have attacked children? Why? His mind reeled. Those parents—what they must be enduring right now was beyond his imagining. Not to mention the poor kids in the hospital enduring the torment of the poisoning. Once the press got wind of what this was, there would be total panic and no way to control the public. Walsh didn't need that now.

Walsh cleared his throat, but his voice still sounded weak and thin. "We need to give the press something that's not a lie, but might send them off on a different track for awhile until we sort this out."

"Sir, if I may," Dennis Murphy squawked, his own voice catching and failing him. Walsh thought of Dennis's two little girls at a similar school somewhere in nearby Virginia right at that moment. "That school is in Spring Valley, in Washington, D.C."

"That's right," Marshall said almost under his breath.

Walsh could only look at him. No connection was made in his brain. "I'm sorry, Dennis; I just can't get all the cylinders to fire."

"Spring Valley is the neighborhood that was built on top of a military facility, a biological weapons dumping ground. There's been a lot of noise about seepage into the groundwater and soil contamination," Sercu said, rubbing his chin thoughtfully. "I think Dennis might just have solved one of our problems."

"Okay, so we alert the greenies or the peacies or whatever they're calling themselves now and let them cover us for a little while until we can get our ducks in a row." David started to get some sensation back. He clamped onto the idea of Spring Valley, and held on while he forced his nerves under control.

"That might just do it," Sercu said, heading for the door. "I've already called everyone together for another emergency meeting."

"Emergencies are the norm now." Walsh wanted to laugh but it caught in his throat. "I think we need a new designation." He turned to the heads of the CIA and FBI. "I can use you at this meeting, gentlemen. Care to join us?"

Marshall nodded.

"I'd just like to make one quick phone call, sir," Murphy said. Walsh squeezed the man's shoulder as warmly as he could.

"Of course, Dennis, and give Bridget my reassurance that we'll get this under control."

* * *

In the hall Walsh gave his secretary what he hoped was a reassuring smile, and followed a brace of Secret Service agents toward the bank of elevators at the end of the hall. When the men stepped aside, he saw Sarah standing under the huge gilt mirror beside the door. She, too, was pale and stunned. Walsh went to her, wrapped his arms around her trembling frame and held her to him for a moment. Sarah pushed her face into her husband's neck, looking for the reassurance of his warm smell, and craving the feel of his arms blocking out the world.

"David, those children," she sobbed into his neck. "What are we going to do?"

Walsh tightened his grip on his wife, feeling more in love with her in that one desperate moment than he thought was still possible. "We can't bring them back, Sarah, but we can do everything possible to make the terrorists pay for this." He pulled away from her embrace to fish a handkerchief out of his pocket and dab gently at her tear-streaked face.

"Kill them, David, for those little babies. Just kill them—they don't deserve anything less."

Walsh was both surprised by her words and a little saddened. His gentle lady had found what it took to make her vengeful. This was going to be a long fight.

THIRTY-EIGHT

The White House Situation Room
Washington, D.C.

ONCE AGAIN THE PRESIDENT WAS GREETED BY NERVOUS AND DOWNright terrified faces as he entered the Situation Room flanked by Jim Marshall and Dennis Murphy. This was becoming a habit he could do without. But what was the answer? Short of declaring martial law and hoping to be able to root out the terrorists before all hell broke loose, he didn't have a clue. He only hoped someone in this group might.

Scanning the faces as he took his seat, he noticed Ian Tuttle, once again at the back of the room, his eyes downcast, his face pale and waxy looking. The strain was beginning to show, and soon Tuttle would make the fatal error that every person in his position eventually makes. David just hoped that it wouldn't be irreparable.

"Sir," Bill Cassidy's voice, husky now, either with strain, stress, or simple emotion, pulled Walsh back to the moment. "I've taken the liberty of setting our earlier emergency plans into motion. We are continuing the mandatory vaccinations of all personnel and whatever military that has yet to be inoculated. The National Guard is moving into Spring Valley to aid with the quarantine procedures, and we've notified the CDC that this operation is code red." Cassidy hesitated a moment to give Walsh a chance to speak.

David was suddenly struck by the fact that Cassidy specifically told them that he took a liberty. He had said he took a liberty to do something that they had already agreed was to be done immediately upon the occurrence of certain events; therefore, making it less a liberty than a direct order. "Strange," Walsh thought, "why did he do that?"

Cassidy, now uncomfortable with his chief's interminable silence, began again. "The Secret Service is preparing the bunkers under the White House, at Camp David and at Greenbrier. The only decision left is when to move you and Mrs. Walsh out of the city."

"The bunkers under the White House aren't secure enough for the president," Tuttle said matter-of-factly.

"Actually there is more to the system under this building than you know. Back during the Truman administration, the White House was totally renovated. The Cold War was hitting its peak, so it was decided that a series of additional bunkers would be built beneath the White House that were impervious to nuclear attack. During the Reagan administration, the bunkers were updated again. Then, in about '81, another bunker was added in basement three that is impervious to weapons of mass destruction. The whole system is locked down by special codes."

"Even I didn't know about that one!" David exclaimed, sending a quiet chuckle around the room. "But what use is it locking me away in the basement when there's a crisis on? I'm needed here."

"Now for the beauty part," Cassidy smiled like a little boy showing his father the fort he had built in the backyard. "The whole thing is set up for wireless computer access and communication grids with cabling buried so far beneath the White House that archaeologists a million years from now won't be able to find it."

"That's all well and good, but I'm not ready to be sequestered just yet," David said, hoping to bring that part of the discussion to an end.

"You don't have to be, sir," Cassidy continued. "The complex is accessible through a tunnel to basement number three, then a set of stairs to the bunker hatch that will hermetically seal after you've entered. Dry runs have made the trip from the Oval Office to the door in less than five minutes. Well, that is at a full run. The tunnel is accessed through a door next to the fireplace."

"There's no door next to the fireplace," Walsh said dryly.

"Actually, there is; I'll show it to you later," Cassidy was enjoying this. He rarely had so much inside information he could share. "And there also is the panic room in your quarters, sir."

"Panic room?" It was Sercu's turn to be surprised.

"Yeah, there's this little hole in the wall behind the closet in my bedroom," Walsh said before Cassidy could answer. "It's big enough to hold Sarah and me if we should need a quick escape."

"Interesting," Sercu nodded.

Cassidy continued. "That room is shielded exactly the same way the bunker is. Both will withstand chemical, biological and nuclear attack, and will do a damned good job at repelling a missile explosion, too, if it comes to that. The bunker will support ten people for three months with the same systems and supplies as those used on *Air Force One.*"

"Cassidy's jumping the gun," David thought, looking into the man's troubled eyes and trying to see what might be below the surface. His own sense of security was long gone, and he found himself looking for a traitor in every situation.

"Bill, I've been briefed on all the security precautions built into the White House and it doesn't seem to me that we have much to worry about. This place is a fortress." One of the first things the Secret Service did when he took office was to give him a crash course in all of the many systems designed to keep him from harm. The place was riddled with secret tunnels and bolt holes should he need to disappear instantly. All the windows and doors were bulletproof and soundproof, as were the outside walls. The air and water supplies, as well as the waste removal, were all closed systems. Nothing could get in through the baffles, filters, sensors and other gadgets. The place was stocked with provisions for a hundred people or more for three months. Just the scope of these precautions was mind blowing.

"How can a building be shielded from weapons of mass destruction?" Tuttle's whiny voice interrupted Walsh's thoughts. "That's the purpose of chemical and biological warfare, to get into the buildings."

Cassidy smiled again; one would think he was taking credit for designing these systems. "The technology is astounding," he said enthusiastically. "During the Reagan administration, a high-tech ventilation system was installed that, no matter what the weather—hot or cold—keeps the air pressure inside the White House just slightly higher than outside."

"So that's why my ears pop when I leave the building," Barbara Howe said suddenly.

"You're especially sensitive to it; most of us aren't," Cassidy never lost a beat. "But the higher pressure inside prevents anything from entering through cracked glass or chinks in the mortar. Any small faults are basically sealed by the air pressure. Any chemical weapon would have to be released inside the White House. The air and water systems are filtered through a top secret screening system that doesn't allow anything through."

"Top secret?" Walsh asked. When Cassidy confirmed this, he looked around the table. "Well, that's one system that can't remain top secret. Get on how we can apply it to the public water system ASAP." He snapped the order hoping to avoid any arguments.

The faces around the table regarded him with a mixture of stunned shock and fear. "You heard me."

Sercu jumped in to change the subject before anyone might be bold enough to try to challenge the president. "How about communications, Bill? How do we keep that going?"

"The Army Communications Corps installed their own special generator system that would keep the power going for at least three months after the national grid has gone down. The same with communications. We wouldn't be able to call the Denny's in Poughkeepsie, but we would be in touch with NORAD and bases around the country."

"Well, it sounds to me like we're perfectly safe right where we are," Walsh said, hoping to end discussion about what to do with him. It was making him decidedly uneasy.

"As good as they are, in this situation we can't afford to assume they're good enough." Cassidy was firm. Walsh sensed the Secret Service agents around the room stiffen. He silently willed everyone to remain calm; they didn't need interdepartmental squabbles now.

"Well, first, I think we need to discuss how to proceed now that the terrorists have shown their hand." Jim Sercu, ever vigilant to Walsh's state of mind, attempted to direct control of the meeting back to the president.

"Blow the damned terrorists right off the map," Ned Seiffert muttered, his own thoughts straying to his grandchildren. "My apologies, sir," he said loudly when he realized his comment was not exactly as quiet as he had intended. "But I do believe that we need to move in and dig these vermin out of their hidey-holes. We can't afford to wait for them to show themselves again." Seiffert's voice dripped hatred and sarcasm.

David drew in a deep breath and concentrated on centering himself in the moment. Wasn't that an eastern meditation technique? His mind strayed and he pulled himself back to the situation with more force than before. He gestured to one of the confidential assistants poised to one side to bring him a cup of coffee before speaking.

"It's obvious that the plan Marchia confessed to us was a ruse. Either that, or they've accelerated their plans because we broke Marchia."

Seiffert's face drooped ever so slightly. "But that would mean that they had some knowledge of what is happening at the safe house," he spoke the words very deliberately and slowly.

"Yes, I suppose that's a circumstance we need to keep an eye open to," Walsh said. He desperately wanted to look at Tuttle, but didn't dare give away too much.

"Okay, so the one thing we do know is that we have no time left. What we don't know is what they're going to do next." David sipped the hot coffee gratefully. One more simple thing he could give his attention to for a few second's respite from the firestorm in his head. The room waited expectantly until he set his cup down.

"Ned, is there any chance that Marchia could know any more than he's already told us?"

"Well, sir, there's always a chance. I wouldn't put any possibility past those bastards. Who knows what fanatical brainwashing they put their operatives through."

"All right then, get on the phone to Blaine and let him see what else he can find out."

"Sir, if I might?" Sercu interrupted. "From the medical reports I saw this morning, the prisoner is not in very stable condition. He might not survive further interrogation."

Walsh tried to focus on Sercu, but the red film that seemed to cover his eyes and color everything around him would not be blinked away. He felt the unfocused anger in his heart suddenly find a target, and like a SCUD missile fly directly into the heat of the emotion. "Jim," he said through gritted teeth, "thirteen children, THIRTEEN schoolkids, are dead because of these sons of bitches. I don't really care if we end up killing one of them or all of them if it means we're any closer to stopping this plague."

David's voice had risen to a roar, startling no one more than himself. He drew a deep breath and looked to his friend in apology. "Ned, see to it that Blaine does what's necessary. Jim, I'm sorry; I know you're doing your job." He turned to face the table. "For the moment we all know what we need to do. Let's get the situation under control in Spring Valley and then regroup."

David stood, forcing the others in the room to stumble to their feet respectfully. "I believe we have a press conference to organize." He spun about on his heel and, gesturing to Sercu to follow him, left the room.

Ian Tuttle, dark circles shadowing his eyes like a corpse, watched his president leave the room. A granite boulder had planted itself on his chest and the weight threatened to flatten him. They knew. Tuttle was certain they knew; and now it was too late to save anyone.

THIRTY–NINE

Hay Adams Hotel
Washington, D.C.

WARREN DUNN WATCHED THE NEWS BROADCASTS WITH SOME INTEREST. What were the bastards up to? None of this was part of the plan he had worked out with his contacts. But he admired their balls, attacking a school first. Not quite the cowardly act it might seem at first glance. Dunn was well aware that in the Middle East if one wanted to enrage one's enemies, the quickest and surest way was to hit them where they lived. He had to admire bin Laden's talent for strategy. But this deviation from the plan would drastically impact his profit margins.

Dunn snapped off the television and checked the time. His private jet was being readied at Ronald Reagan International Airport to take him back to Dallas and away from the possibility of anthrax infection. It was time to go.

He had just finished gathering his personal items and snapped the case closed when the shrill alarm of his cell phone broke the silence.

"Dunn."

"Warren, Tuttle. What the hell is going on?" Tuttle's shrill voice screeched over the high-tech receiver. The man was in a full-blown panic, and Dunn reacted immediately and angrily.

"Mister Tuttle!" Dunn hissed. "I thought you had learned your lesson the last time I warned you not to speak to me in that tone of voice!"

"Can it, Dunn!" Tuttle was beyond caring, and Dunn sensed he was losing control of his weakest link. "You swore that the anthrax was merely a threat! You never, never, never mentioned killing kids!"

"Tuttle, damn it, calm down." Dunn adopted a more fatherly tone of voice. "I appreciate your blind faith in me, but you have to understand that I cannot control our counterparts in the Mideast."

"Cut the crap, Dunn!" Tuttle screamed now. Dunn wanted nothing more than to silence the man permanently.

"Tuttle, where are you?"

"At the White House, where do you think I'd be?!" Tuttle was completely beyond control now. Dunn's mind raced with possible ways to cut their losses.

"Obviously, you idiot. Where are you in the White House?" Dunn kept his voice modulated and flat. He couldn't risk inflaming Tuttle any more.

"The washroom off my office, Dunn. What do you think I am, a complete retard?"

Dunn held his tongue for a moment, gathering his thoughts. "Listen to me, Tuttle—so a few measly kids died. Big deal. The benefit of this show of force is far greater than the collateral damages. If Walsh finally comes to his senses and does the right thing, then we're in the clear and it's smooth sailing from here to Kuwait!" Dunn's tone became playful as he carefully manipulated Tuttle. If you can't kill them, charm them. He wondered where he had heard that. But it didn't matter, it was his now.

"Warren, you don't understand," Tuttle's voice had dropped to almost a whisper. "Walsh isn't going to cave. He's just sent

Blaine back to Virginia to get as much as he can out of Marchia even if it kills him."

"Well, well. Our pet president is finally showing a nice set of brass ones, is he?" Dunn laughed.

"And that's only the beginning, Dunn." The panic was rising again in Tuttle's voice. "They're on to us."

"What do you mean 'on to us'?" Dunn demanded sharply.

"They know; they know you, me, we, that something's going on and there's someone inside working with the terrorists."

"But you're not working with the terrorists, Ian. You're working for me." Dunn stalled while he ran a list of possibilities through his mind.

"For Christ sake, Dunn! Listen to what I'm saying, not what you want to hear! I'm being followed. My Secret Service escort has changed, different guys, shifty-eyed guys who pay too close attention to what I'm doing." Tuttle was running out of steam and was rapidly approaching an emotional meltdown.

"Ian, Ian, your escort changed because there's a crisis and you're just imagining that someone's following you."

"Yeah? Yeah? Then how do you explain the tap on my phones? The fact that my mail is now opened before it reaches my desk, or the fact that my personal files have been riffled?"

Dunn considered a moment before responding. "There was, of course, nothing to be found in your personal files?"

"What do you take me for, a fool?"

"Okay, Ian. Here's what I need you to do. Try not to panic. Stay away from Walsh for a while, if you can, and concentrate on the tasks before you. Try, Tuttle, try to look as though there's nothing odd happening and I promise you that this will work out in the end. But don't do anything more until I contact you again."

There was silence from the other end of the line. Dunn could barely make out Tuttle's labored breathing. "Tuttle, do you hear me?"

"Yeah, yeah, I guess so." The phone clicked and the line went dead.

Dunn was hardly surprised Tuttle had broken down like this. He had anticipated it. What he hadn't anticipated were Walsh's suspicions. How could he have discovered any part of the plan? He should have been too busy with the crisis situation to notice anything else. Dunn was having doubts about his choice of Tuttle as an inside man, and Dunn hated doubting his decisions. He would have to give careful thought to just eliminating the cause of this doubt.

There was a sharp rap on the door and Vinnie's voice from the hallway announced that the plane was ready to go. Dunn smoothed his hair back, shook out his suit coat, and assumed his most winning smile.

FORTY

U. S. Government Safe House
Virginia Horse Country

GENERAL LOUIS BLAINE SAT IN HIS TEMPORARY OFFICE IN ONE OF THE bedrooms of the estate in the Virginia countryside that the U.S. government often used as a safe house. He stared thoughtfully into a cup of coffee his aide had placed before him on the empty desk some time before. He didn't have much time to waste, but he needed the few quiet moments to steel himself for the task ahead.

It had been a very long time since he had had such a difficult interrogation. Adalla Marchia was a tough one, amazingly enough. To look at the bastard, Blaine never would have thought he could be so strong. It took the physical assault of his daughters to make him shed some light on the terrorist's plans. "Son of a bitch! "Blaine thought to himself." The asshole thought so little of his own family's lives that he held out even in the face of his children's torture."

But at the same time Blaine had to admire it. He had encountered few men with that much force of will, and he was secretly impressed.

All of this would have to wait until the crisis was over, however. The order had come from General Seiffert, direct from the president. Blaine now had carte blanche to do what he had to do to get the information out of the prisoner. Death was not to be a concern.

Blaine rose from the chair, straightened his uniform shirt and brushed off his trousers. Assured that his boots were immaculate, he headed for the basement isolation cells where the prisoner waited.

* * *

Hawley Sheppard was on watch at the prisoner's cell. He snapped to attention when Blaine passed through the door and marched stiffly to the small window in the cell door.

"Sheppard!" he barked.

"Sir!" Sheppard snapped another clean salute.

"Get Ziegelhofer over here. I'll need his help."

"Yes, sir!" Sheppard reached for the shielded phone on the wall by the door.

"And Sheppard!"

"Yes, sir!"

"That box of equipment we dragged out of here yesterday?"

Sheppard stole a glance at his superior officer, remembering the bloody mess of implements they had pulled out of the cell the day before.

"Has that stuff been cleaned up?" Blaine asked, his voice getting softer and more menacing.

"Yes, sir!"

"Get that stuff back in here."

Blaine turned back to the small window and watched the prisoner, still slumped in the hard chair and unmoving. A medic had superficially treated Marchia's wounds and a few clean white bandages shone against the man's bruised and filthy skin. "Shouldn't have bothered," Blaine thought, "waste of medical supplies."

Forty-One

The Oval Office
The White House
Washington, D.C.

David Walsh, President of the United States of America, leader of the Free World, sat behind his desk in the Oval Office feeling like a four year old. Jim Sercu had taken the liberty—he was hearing that phrase a lot today—of ordering a meal for him and his secretary. Colleen now stood before him, hands on hips, insisting that he eat.

"Colleen, I will eat, but not right this minute," Walsh sighed, knowing he wouldn't convince her to leave until he'd taken at least one bite.

"Sir, I have strict instructions from Mr. Sercu and Mrs. Walsh to make sure you eat something." She had invoked the name and he knew he'd never get away from it now. His wife had laid down the law, and there was no way Colleen was going to violate that. Walsh picked up his fork and poked at the green salad and broiled fish on the plate. It wasn't much food, but with the images of thirteen dead children still fresh in his mind, it was the most unappetizing food he thought he'd ever seen. He broke off a piece of the fish and popped it in his mouth, grinning at Colleen around the mouthful.

Colleen smiled with satisfaction. "Now you make sure you

clean that plate! And I don't want to find greens in the waste basket." She spun on her heel and left the office.

"My God," thought Walsh, "she can be a smug bitch, can't she?" But he knew she acted only out of concern. And he knew he'd be lost without her simple efficiency and subtle prodding.

Walsh continued to poke at the food, his mind flashing over the problems he desperately needed to solve. Where were the answers?

The intercom beeped from the desk and he looked at it indifferently.

"Sir?" Colleen inquired.

"Yes . . ."

"Call for you from the Jordanian Embassy, sir. It's Secretary Howe."

"Please don't let this be bad news," Walsh prayed reaching for the receiver. "Thanks, Colleen."

The line crackled as he placed the receiver against his ear. It was a shielded call.

"Barbara? How's it going?"

"Mr. President," she sounded exhausted already; he didn't envy her the task she had set for herself. "I'm afraid it's not going as well as I might have hoped."

Walsh waited for her to continue.

"I've met with King Abdullah, who has promised to help us in negotiations with the other emirates. But I'm not sure how far that support will go. He expressed a desire to maintain good relations with the United States since his father's death, but I sensed something else going on beneath the surface."

"Well, King Hussein never had any problem with U.S. policies. He was always very supportive. If Abdullah intends to carry on his father's legacy, then I don't see what the problem would be." David knew it could never be so clearcut. There had been questions about Hussein's motivations. Luckily U.S. presidents had always chosen to take the ruler at face value. It had proven to be the right decision.

"Well, sir, Queen Noor requested a private meeting with me. She told me that Abdullah had briefed her on the events of the past week. She expressed sorrow for the recent deaths but went on to question me about my roll in this mission. Apparently there is great concern that you sent a woman to handle this. I think Abdullah was uncertain how I would take the news, and sent Noor to break it to me gently."

Walsh laughed, "Anyone who is the slightest bit familiar with you, Barbara, would be concerned about saying that." Howe remained quiet. "Okay, have you contacted the other leaders yet?"

"Yes, sir, I'm waiting for replies."

"And if they refuse to meet with you?"

"I'll have to try to persuade them," Howe's voice sounded tiny, but confident.

"And do you have a backup plan should your persuasion not work?" he asked, dreading one more problem to deal with.

"That is simply not an option, sir."

Forty-Two

U. S. Government Safe House
Virginia Horse Country

Adalla Marchia knew he was about to breathe his final breath. Fervently, he prayed to Allah to forgive his wife and daughters' disgrace at the hands of the infidel, to take their lives as he was about to take their father's for the glory of Allah. They had served well and resisted every attempt to ruin them; they deserved an honorable death.

Colonel Ziegelhofer held Marchia with his arms trapped behind his back and one of Ziegelhofer's huge arms crushing his chest. Marchia's face was a ruin of slashes and dangling flesh, his eyes swollen so he could barely make out the figure of General Blaine before him. The pain had subsided into a low throb long ago. He simply had to wait for his death, his release and the coming glory of heaven.

"C'mon, scum, you know you're not going to walk out of here alive. Tell me what I need to know and I'll end it now, quick and easy." Blaine spat the words with disgust. The prisoner had taken far more than Blaine would have guessed. By this time he should have given up everything he knew, and stopped trying to survive. But not this one, this one was holding on 'til the bitter end.

Blaine glanced at Ziegelhofer, who tightened his bear hug on Marchia until the man's breath could only come in short gasps.

"The attack has already begun, and you know that. You've known all along. Now tell me what's going to happen next." Blaine's fist caught Marchia in the chin sending his head ricocheting off Ziegelhofer's chest with a snap.

"There is nothing. You're doomed. . . ." Marchia whispered. Ziegelhofer gave him a sharp squeeze for good measure and Marchia heard another rib crack. The pain didn't matter anymore; he had won.

Blaine turned away from his captive and paced to the door and back again. "Okay, here's how it is. Because we don't have the intel we need to stop your little buddies, we're going to go straight to the top and pave over your entire, insignificant little corner of the globe. Make one huge parking lot—that's all it's good for, anyway."

Marchia assumed the man was joking. The United States was notoriously afraid of its own strength, and the Americans' version of strategic bombings would merely damage Allah's land but not desecrate it. That would require nuclear detonation.

Blaine thought he saw a light of realization in Marchia's ruined eyes. "Ah, so now you're getting it, huh, bastard? You're thinking we don't have the guts to detonate a nuclear explosion; but you're wrong, asshole. You've gone too far now—you've killed our kids. So we took the loss of a few soldiers on the chin, but you've killed our kids and unlike you, Mr. Marchia, we do not allow anyone to touch our children." Blaine was so close his lips brushed Marchia's nose. His tone was deadlier than any Marchia had heard in his life. And until that moment, the only man who ever inspired fear in him with his voice had been Osama bin Laden.

Marchia sagged in Ziegelhofer's arms, unable to hold himself upright any longer.

"Now, you tell me you stinking sand nigger—who's

behind this? Is it bin Laden? Saddam? Who? Who?" Blaine was nearly screaming now. Marchia felt something in his brain shift, snap, and suddenly nothing mattered anymore; he only wanted to die.

"You cannot win, you fucking pig," Marchia spat at Blaine tapping into the last of his reserves. "Osama bin Laden? Yes! Saddam? Yes! They will see you suffer in the hellfires of your own arrogance! Your children, your women, your country is dead and you don't even know it! You never could have done anything to stop it! Nothing you could have done would have made the slightest difference! Ha! You don't even recognize the traitors from within, your own people are willing to see you burn!"

Blaine's mind raced. It was bin Laden, and the attacks would have happened no matter what. He should have killed this slime right off the bat. Bleeding-heart liberal politicians be damned. Blaine wrapped his bloodied fingers around Marchia's neck and squeezed slightly.

"Okay, songbird, how about a tune about what happens next?"

Marchia laughed and blood sputtered through his teeth. "Why not? You cannot stop Allah's army now! The attacks will continue from all sides. And be assured, General Blaine," he managed to make the honorific into profanity, "our soldiers have Allah as their leader and they will succeed. They will succeed and use your own strength to send you to hell!"

Blaine's hands suddenly clenched on Marchia's neck and with a clean jerk he broke the man's spine, the body slumping lifeless to the floor as Ziegelhofer stepped back.

Blaine straightened up. "I want the bastard's family shipped back to Khartoum. I'm sure he had some male relatives around there you can leave them with and make sure they understand the horrible things that those bitches have been through." Blaine knew they would most likely die unimaginable deaths at the hands of outraged male relatives, who would see them as nothing more than soiled property.

Forty-Three

Georgetown Park Mall
Washington, D.C.

It was a typical day in the trendy neighborhood of Georgetown. Shoppers clogged the sidewalks in spite of the nip in the air. No one was particularly aware of the dozen or so casually dressed men who roamed the street vigilant to anything out of the ordinary. Roger Johnson and Michael Freedman, longtime partners and senior agents with the CIA, entered Georgetown Park Mall and moved through the crowd toward a coffee bar near the center of the mall.

The crowd was the typical yuppie mix of well-dressed men and women and self-confident teenagers, sprinkled with members of Washington's foreign population. Accents from across the globe could be heard in almost every corner of the high-class collection of expensive boutiques and fashionable eateries. This didn't make the job any easier for the CIA agents and National Guard officers who made up the patrol. They were relatively certain that their targets would be dark-skinned, dark-eyed Arabs, but they couldn't afford not to pay close attention to everyone.

Johnson and Freedman took their coffees and strolled down the row of shops, ostensibly window-shopping. At one end of the mall sat a high-end toy store, crowded with young parents and screaming children. Stopping under a potted tree, the two watched the shoppers milling in and out of the store when suddenly two men, one a slender, dark man with a bushy mustache, the other heavier and bearded, stopped directly in front of them and eyed the store. The agents exchanged quick glances before dropping their coffee cups in a trash bin and following the men as they moved closer to the toy store.

Outside the store a large box full of stuffed animals, robot toys and other discontinued items enticed passing children to stop. The two men approached the box; one of them poked at a few of the items, then reached into his jacket pocket and removed a small glass vial that appeared to be full of a powdered substance. Johnson stepped up behind the bearded man while Freedman moved beside his companion. The agents poked the barrels of their small automatics in each man's back.

"Okay, hold it right there, don't move." Freedman growled under his breath, praying the suspects understood at least a little English. Unexpectedly, the bearded man suddenly bolted sending Freedman sprawling into the box of toys. His companion, only a step behind him, followed through the crowd toward a back exit. Johnson left his partner to disentangle himself from the toys and pounded after the suspects while yelling instructions into the small radio pinned under his lapel.

The two men charged through the doors and out into the afternoon sunlight on a winding bike path that paralleled a shallow canal. The terrorists, desperate now, shoved bicyclists and walkers off the path and headed toward Wisconsin Avenue. Crossing over the bridge, they raced toward K Street with Johnson close on their heels. Startled pedestrians watched as a half dozen other similarly dressed men barreled down M Street to Wisconsin to take up the chase. The suspects ran across K

Street leaving startled motorists slamming on their brakes and at least one dented fender. Johnson and the other agents fanned out to surround the men as they headed into a parking lot on the other side of an overpass and straight toward the Potomac River. The bearded man suddenly turned, pulled a small automatic machine gun from beneath his trench coat, and fired on the pursuing agents. The agents answered with return fire but not before the bullets slammed through the chest of an agent Johnson had known since he first entered the CIA. Johnson could only watch as the man, dead on his feet, tumbled to the ground. Galvanized by the attack, the agents returned fire hitting the bearded terrorist repeatedly and forcing him back against a car, the gun flying from his grip before he finally crumpled. The second terrorist came to a stop on the bank of the river and stared into the murky water before turning to confront his pursuers.

Agent Johnson skidded to a halt a hundred feet from the man, his weapon drawn. "On the ground!" he bellowed. "Get down on the ground."

The man, his eyes hard and sparkling, glared at the agents surrounding him, his jaw set in grim determination. Johnson could see that he still clutched the vial in one hand.

"I said on the ground!" Johnson screamed again. The agents all knew what might be in that vial and they could each feel their own panic beginning to rise as they realized they would not be able to predict the man's next move. Agent Freedman pelted across the gravel parking lot just as the man turned back toward the river. A single shot rang out and the fabric of the man's jacket between his shoulder blades erupted. With a last rush of strength the terrorist slammed the vial to the riverbank where it shattered against a rock scattering the powdery substance into the water. The terrorist was dead before he hit the ground, facedown in the sluggish water.

The agents stood in shocked silence, struggling with the sudden realization of what might have just happened.

"Shit," Freedman muttered, "shit, shit, shit, shit!"

Forty–Four

Bethesda, Maryland

On a quiet residential street in Bethesda, the residents watched curiously as their new neighbors came and went. The women's head-to-toe robes and the men's dark, swarthy coloring weren't unusual in this suburb of Washington, D.C. What was unusual were the late-night comings and goings, and the packages and boxes that moved into the house, but never showed up as trash on the curb on pickup day. It appeared to be an extended family that purchased the medium-sized house on the corner, but no one noticed that there were no children.

Inside, the house was bare of furniture except for a folding table and chairs in the living room. The blinds were shut against the light and prying eyes. The heady smells of spicy foods came from the kitchen where women prepared meals. On the upper floors of the house, the bedrooms were stacked with boxes and crates. One room had been transformed into an armory—rifles and machine guns propped against the walls, and boxes of ammunition overflowing the closet.

But the biggest secret lay behind the locked door of the master bedroom. Inside the room, carefully stacked in short piles, were unlabeled boxes containing plastique, C-4, and other high-grade explosives. In the center of this room, carefully packed in a plain blue overnight bag, were a hundred small glass vials each half full of powdery dust contaminated with a virus. Enough virus to kill every man, woman, and child on the East Coast of the United States.

Downstairs in the living room seven grim men sat around the folding table talking softly. Their leader, a balding stocky man, smoothed a street map of Washington onto the table's surface.

"We have successfully managed to shock the American pigs with our gift to the schoolchildren. The news coverage has not mentioned the threat of the virus, but it is not likely that their doctors have missed the diagnosis." He looked at each man around the table. "The two men we sent to Georgetown gave their lives to infect even more of the infidels. If the reports we have received are correct they managed to get the virus into the river and the infidels know this. Now they will begin to panic and try to retaliate. We must continue our efforts in earnest."

The leader of the terrorists indicated points marked on the map, each one moving in a spiral toward the center, the White House. "We will move through these points one at a time until we have contaminated each sector of the city, the final infection taking place here at a point upwind of the White House. We will allow Allah to spread the virus to the infidel president on his blessed winds."

The men around the table nodded and murmured. "We have secured a helicopter, purchased for us by our American benefactor, which we will use to strike here tonight." He indicated a black circle on the map labeled Andrews Air Force Base. "It is the major base for the military in this area and the place where they store *Air Force One*. We will incapacitate the base, contaminate their aircraft and strand Mr. David Walsh in the city for the duration of our attack. We cannot fail; we are the army of Allah!"

* * *

On the other side of the street, from behind lacy dining room curtains, an elderly woman peered at the darkened house. Her husband, a former civilian employee at the Pentagon, rustled his newspaper from his chair behind her.

"Grace, come away from that window," he said, feeling like a broken record. "There's nothing to see."

"Herbert, I'm telling you, something's not right about the goings-on in that house."

"We've had a hundred neighbors over the years and a third of them have been foreigners. You know they always behave differently. This is probably just a family whose daddy works at an embassy." Herbert refolded his newspaper before beginning the crossword puzzle.

"No, this is different. What about those boxes they bring in late at night? Explain that to me." The old woman glanced back at her husband, annoyed.

"For the hundredth time, Grace, the man works all day and the only time he has to move is at night."

"And they packed their belongings in oblong boxes that look just like that artillery box you have in the basement."

"Maybe, Grace, but where are you going with this?"

"I'll bet you they're terrorists! Herbert! What if they're terrorists?"

"They are not terrorists! My God, woman; terrorists in the suburbs? Be sensible, would you?"

"And no children, Herbert; there are no children."

"Maybe they don't have any children."

Grace was working herself into a frenzy, egged on by her husband's disbelief. "All those men, all those women, and no children. I'm telling you, Herbert, there must be two dozen of them over there."

"I wouldn't know. They all look alike to me." Herbert turned his attention back to his puzzle with a sigh.

Grace grew quiet, intent on watching the sudden developments on the other side of the street. Three men had pulled up in a van and were unloading cases from the back. Grace squinted trying to read what was written on the boxes, but all she could make out was the logo printed neatly on each one.

"Herbert, come here. They're bringing in more boxes. Come look at this. I know that picture from somewhere, but I can't remember where."

Herbert sighed again and stood up deciding to humor the old girl for a moment before taking a nap. He peered out the window beside her and gasped.

"That little symbol means explosives, Gracie. I guess we better call someone."

Forty-Five

The Oval Office
The White House
Washington, D. C.

David Walsh could only stare, dumbfounded, at his press secretary while the news seeped into his brain. Asa Roberts fidgeted from one foot to the other, uncomfortable with the silence and wishing the president would take decisive action.

"In the river?" Walsh asked incredulous. "Are they sure it went into the water?"

"Yes, sir, the report is very specific. They're testing samples from points downstream now." Jim Sercu shook his head gravely. "They got us good this time. We can't contain the river."

"Shit," Walsh muttered. "And there's no way to clean this up?"

"No, it has to run its course and die out. It'll take a long time."

"And these terrorists, have they been questioned? Get Blaine on it."

"No, sir, dead, both of them, and they took one of our National Guard officers with them." Sercu stood stock-still and watched Walsh.

David didn't like how the death toll was beginning to climb. Already twenty-four of the students and teachers from Janey Elementary had perished. A marine and the guardsman brought the total to twenty-six. And how many more would there be now that the plague had an unstoppable conduit?

Ned Seiffert came into the Oval Office quietly and slipped beside Sercu. "It's been confirmed, sir; the river is contaminated."

Walsh could feel the blood draining away from his face, disliking the lightheaded feeling it left him with. "Okay, according to our emergency plan, what's the next step?" he asked, knowing what the answer would be but needing someone else to articulate it.

"Martial law," Seiffert said softly. "We have to close down the city and declare martial law to keep the people from panicking and making the situation worse. We'll have to deal with protests, possibly riots and looting. We can't afford to assume this will be smooth."

"No, no, we can't." Walsh turned to his press secretary, who stood mute, frightened by the ramifications of what he had just heard. "Asa, we're going to have to alert the press to an announcement I will make later this evening. Make sure the television networks, and I mean all of them, preempt their programming; get it on the radio, in the newspapers, the whole shebang."

"Sir," Seiffert interrupted, "if we declare martial law, you will have to do this as a statement to the country, no press can be allowed in the White House from this moment forward. Those presently here will have to be asked to leave."

"We'll wait until after the announcement to ask them to go. I don't want any hint of this leaking out beforehand." David drew a deep breath and let it out slowly. He felt more galvanized now that they could take some action. Any action. He turned to Sercu, "Jim, get everybody together again in the Situation Room. We'll announce it there first. And make sure the warrant officer is there. And get on the phone to Barbara Howe in Jordan. I'm going to have to fill her in on the situation before she goes any further."

"Yes, sir." Sercu ushered Seiffert and Roberts out of the Oval Office to give the president a few minutes to collect himself. When they were gone, Walsh stood by the window and looked out over his adopted city. Logically he couldn't grasp that any of this was happening. How could it? Things like this didn't even happen to presidents who held office for years.

Behind him he heard the door open and close softly. Feminine footsteps approached the window.

"David," Sarah said quietly, "I passed Jim in the hall. He looked terrible and refused to talk to me. Is something going on?" She put her hand on her husband's shoulder and turned him to face her. Tears tumbled down his cheeks and his eyes squeezed shut as he tried to hold them back. Sarah wrapped her arms around him and held him for a moment while he let the emotion pass.

"Presidents aren't allowed to cry," he said, fumbling for a handkerchief to dry his face. "You won't tell anyone will you?"

Sarah smiled indulgently. "Of course not, silly, and I'll bet you that every single president has cried," she laughed.

David wanted to laugh; more than anything in the world he wanted to laugh, but the laughter was gone. Laughter didn't exist in his world anymore.

"Now tell me what's going on." Sarah's voice switched into her forceful attorney tone.

"Those kids at that school?" Walsh found it difficult to put the words together. "They died from anthrax. Planted on the playground by the terrorists who have been threatening to bring this country to its knees."

Sarah could only stare, eyes wide in disbelief.

"Earlier today our agents—we've had patrols in some of the heavily populated areas, shopping malls, and tourist attractions—caught two terrorists at Georgetown Park Mall trying to plant more of the virus. They chased them down to the river. Both terrorists were killed along with one of our men, but not before they managed to infect the Potomac River with the virus." There. He'd said it, but that didn't make it any easier.

"Oh my God!" Sarah gasped. "Are you sure? Anthrax?"

"Yes, Ned just confirmed it."

"What do we do now?"

"We have to implement an emergency plan, declare martial law. They want us to move the government out to Greenbrier. The bunkers there will protect us from almost anything. You've already been vaccinated. . . ."

"You mean that shot the doctor said was a flu shot?"

"Yes, that was an anthrax vaccination. You'll have to have another in a week. I want you to go now, get whatever you want packed and get ready to fly out to Greenbrier as soon as possible. I . . ."

"The birds?" Sarah interrupted him. "The canaries, like in coal mines. That's why there're canaries all over the White House all of a sudden, isn't it?"

"Yes, Sarah, the birds should succumb to the virus before a human and give us a chance to do something about it."

Sarah looked at the cage on the coffee table where the two bright yellow little birds flitted about, not singing, possibly quieted by the atmosphere that surrounded them.

"The poor things," Sarah whispered.

"The birds can't be our concern, Sarah, not with the hundreds of thousands of people who may die if this continues. Now, as I said, I want you to get your things packed. As soon as my address is over tonight, I want you on the helicopter and out to Greenbrier." Walsh kissed her softly on the cheek.

Sarah's eyes grew wide. "No, no, David. I can't leave you, not during this."

"You're not leaving me, Sarah." He pulled her closer to his chest. "You're going where you won't be in harm's way. You'll be safe so I don't have to worry about you and I can concentrate on other things."

"But what about you, David? You're not going to be safe!" The tears were welling up in her eyes again.

Walsh smiled, "Don't worry about that. Jim and Ned and the rest will be hustling me out of here shortly after I get you off, believe me. They aren't going to let me do anything stupid."

The squawk of the intercom interrupted the couple's momentary solitude. "I'm sorry to interrupt, sir," Colleen announced, ever efficiently, "but they're ready for you."

Walsh cupped his wife's face in both hands and kissed her long and deep. He could feel her melt into his kiss like she hadn't in many, many years. He could feel the passion rising up in himself and regretted allowing them to grow so far apart for so long. There wasn't any time anymore. He kissed her again.

"I have to go." He crushed her to him. "Please, Sarah, please go and be safe. I'll be with you again before you know it."

Sarah was sobbing loudly now. She swiped at her face with clenched fists and stepped away from him. "Okay, David, but if you don't make it, I'm going to find you and make you suffer for it." She smiled at him weakly.

Walsh swallowed back the tears and dabbed at her face with his handkerchief. "You got it, lady."

* * *

Once again in the Situation Room, Walsh looked around at his staff and cabinet: "Are we in agreement that the emergency plan has to be implemented now?"

A chorus of yeses was accompanied by nodding heads. No one was comfortable with the decision, but they all knew that there was no other choice. The greater good had to be the ultimate concern from now on. Vice President Harry Dent had been out keeping his regular engagements and trying to maintain an air of normalcy. He had been recalled and now sat to David's right, paler than ever, but back held straight, chin high. "He's going to be all right," Walsh thought with relief.

"Okay, then, we need to get Barbara Howe back here now. Jim, see to that, please."

"Yes, sir. We've begun work on your address, sir, and the stations have been alerted for 7 P.M." Sercu interjected. "We need to cover the emergency procedures before we continue with anything else." Walsh nodded and Ned Seiffert rose, gesturing to a tall, slender officer who stood to one side. The man approached the conference table and David glanced at the large black leather case in his left hand. The case was handcuffed to the man's left arm with a shackle that looked like it weighed several pounds.

"Mr. President," the chief warrant officer saluted Walsh with his right hand.

"Martin," David nodded at the officer. He had made a point of knowing the warrant officers responsible for the football. He had been amused when he was first introduced to the concept of the football, the code name for the case the chief warrant officer always wore shackled to his arm. The case contained all of the access codes and documentation that the president would need should a nuclear war be declared. A warrant officer was never more than fifty feet from the president. Warrant officers were provided with a small office beside the Oval Office and a suite of rooms directly adjacent to the president's quarters.

Walsh was suddenly aware of the key, suspended from a heavy stainless steel chain he wore tucked into his shirt. The warrant officer would have a similar key on a similar chain around his neck. It required both keys, used simultaneously, to open the case. A duplicate football was stored somewhere deep in the bowels of the White House in the unfortunate event something happened to the warrant officer in charge. Should anyone attempt to open the case without both keys, the internal explosives would ensure that no trace of the documentation would be left. Unfortunately, neither would the assailant or the warrant officer.

"You all have been briefed about the nature of the football and the contents therein. It has been decided that the safety zone will be decreased to twenty-five feet for the duration of the emergency." Seiffert paused for a moment. "I have ordered both *Air Force One* and *Two* to be prepped and on standby. Should events escalate faster than we anticipate, I recommend that the president and the vice president be flown immediately to Andrews and be put into the air. The duplicate football will accompany Vice President Dent on *Air Force Two* should there be a need for a transfer of power."

Walsh thought he could feel Dent tense, but was distracted by a question from Bill Cassidy.

"Ned, I understand that keeping the president airborne is the best way to keep him out of the way of the virus, but what about the threat of aerial attack?"

"Our defense grid is now fully activated and both *Air Force One* and *Two* will have a full escort squadron of F-15s. It's highly unlikely any attacking planes could get close enough to be a threat. There will be a complete staff aboard each plane. Refueling will be provided by the Air Support Wing of the Air National Guard out of Niagara Falls." Seiffert paused, and drank deeply from his glass of water before continuing. "All cabinet members and their essential staff members should prepare for, at minimum, a one-week stay at Greenbrier, which is outfitted with all the equipment and communications facilities you will need. For the moment, we would ask that Mr. Tuttle remain with the rest of the staff here at the White House. Mr. Sercu, Mr. Cassidy and I will be aboard *Air Force One* with the president. Our seconds will be aboard *Air Force Two*. The First Lady and Mrs. Dent will be flown out to Greenbrier immediately following the address this evening. The rest of you must be ready no later than 5:00 A.M. tomorrow."

Seiffert looked around the table waiting for any further questions. When none came, he turned back to Walsh. "I know you would prefer to be here where you can oversee our defense, but I assure you, sir, we must keep you safe."

David smiled. Ned had expected a protest. "I understand completely, Ned, and it's the only logical way to proceed. Thank you." Seiffert returned to his seat and the warrant officer stepped back to his position.

Walsh stood and took a moment to look at each and every person seated at the table. He saw a sea of expectant and worried faces that all looked to him for leadership and a way out of this mess. "I appreciate everyone's hard work over the past few days. But it's not over yet by any means. If we can just hold our country together, we can beat this thing." He was having trouble finding the right words, which worried him. He had another, bigger speech to give in just a couple of hours. "Thank you. All of you. Now let's put this thing into motion and show those bastards just who they're dealing with."

FORTY-SIX

Andrews Air Force Base
Maryland

FIVE MINUTES AFTER GENERAL SEIFFERT'S ORDERS CAME THROUGH, THE base was swarming with activity. All leaves had been canceled, security tightened, and nonessential civilian personnel sent home. That was the part Airman Bobby Williams liked the least. The women in the military were okay, but Williams had a soft spot for the pretty secretaries with their short skirts and soft sweaters.

Williams sat in the darkened radar bunker, eyes fixed on a blank screen. Nothing was happening overhead, that was obvious. Commercial flights had been rerouted around the base to keep the airspace open. The commander had said specifically there was no present threat of air attack, so why did he have to watch empty airspace? Williams let his mind wander back to the absent secretaries. It would be spring soon and the dresses would get scantier. He could hardly wait.

A blaring alarm snapped Williams out of his daydream, and he stared dumbly at the small blip crossing his screen. The man behind him bellowed for the commander, and the small radar room exploded with noise and madly shouting voices.

"What the hell is it?

"I can't see anything, but the blip is there!"

"It's coming in low and really fast!"

"What the hell?"

"It's one of those little traffic 'copters!"

Williams heard orders shouted for defensive air cover and spun about in his seat to glance at the closed-circuit screen. The camera outside the bunker showed the airfield in a panic, crewmen ducking for cover and pilots scrambling to their fighters as fast as they could. The little helicopter buzzed across the airfield headed for the hangars where *Air Force One* and *Two* were being prepped for the next mission. Suddenly a fine spray of liquid was discharged from the two tanks suspended below the helicopter's bubble, saturating the planes, the men, and the ground. The wind carried the spray directly into the hangars and the open hatches on both planes.

Williams's mind froze. He had heard scuttlebutt about anthrax, and that attack on the school. Anthrax! That's why they all had been vaccinated. Suddenly an F-15 boomed over head and the little helicopter burst into a ball of flames and plummeted into a bird sanctuary that abutted the airfield. Williams and the others in the radar facility stood dumbly staring at the screen, sharing the same thought and the same panic.

* * *

David paced around the Oval Office, running through his speech again and again. As always, James Sercu had managed to orchestrate a speech that both summed up the situation and would make Walsh look like he was in complete control. Hopefully, the public would believe it and give him their confidence.

"Everyone is handling the current crisis very well," he thought. He was thankful for the team he had assembled, which brought his thoughts back to Ian. He didn't like the fact that General Seiffert had announced, openly at their last meeting, that

Tuttle would be left behind in the White House to handle any emergencies that might come up. That had a been a tactical decision, a way to keep Tuttle under watch while keeping him out of the decision making that would be so critical over the next few days.

But David saw the look in Ian's eyes when the announcement was made. A cross between abject terror and dawning realization. He probably knew they had caught on to him. It was the terror that made Walsh uneasy. Was he afraid of the consequences, or afraid of what the terrorists might do once their plan was exposed? And where was Warren Dunn during all this?

He was still mulling over the possibilities, his speech temporarily forgotten, when the door to the Oval Office burst open, Jim Sercu tapping on it as he opened it. Walsh stared as Sercu stomped across the room with Ned Seiffert and Ian Tuttle close on his heels. He must not have been able to shake Tuttle, which could only mean the news was bad.

"I'm sorry, sir, but we've just had a report from Andrews Air Force Base," Sercu dropped a few sheets of paper on Walsh's desk but kept talking. "Not ten minutes ago, the base was strafed by what appeared to be a small traffic helicopter that sprayed the entire base with a liquid substance that has tested positive for the anthrax virus."

Walsh felt his mouth drop open involuntarily. The bastards had dared attack a U.S. military installation with a traffic helicopter?

Ned Seiffert was more than a little agitated and cut Sercu off. "That's four hundred men and women infected with the virus, sir!" His voice snapped and popped with fury. "Fourteen have died so far, and both *Air Force One* and *Two* have been infected. There's no way to get them cleaned up enough to make it safe for you to take off, sir!"

"I thought we had the base inoculated," Walsh said, trying to stall while he scanned the report.

"The inoculations were begun, sir, but as you know, there has to be a booster shot two weeks after the initial inoculation to make the antivirus one hundred percent effective. Some of the men had already had the second shot. Some don't seem to be having any trouble shaking off the virus without it, but fourteen weren't so lucky. Medical staff are distributing the booster shot as we speak."

"And civilians?" Walsh surprised himself by remaining cool and logical when this should have sent him over the edge.

"We had dismissed all civilian employees and the virus was dropped on the base itself. It will, of course, spread if we can't stop it."

"And if we can't stop it?" He already knew the answer, but prayed someone would have a different one this time.

"There is no way to stop it, David," Jim Sercu said almost in a whisper.

FORTY-SEVEN

President's Private Study
The White House
Washington, D.C.

PRESIDENT DAVID WALSH STOOD IN HIS PRIVATE STUDY OFF THE OVAL Office, with sweaty palms and a stomach full of wrought-iron butterflies, waiting to be called to make a speech that would change history. He wanted to pace, but didn't want to give anyone the idea that he was the least bit nervous. He wanted to be alone, but understood the need for the cadre of Secret Service agents posted around the room. He wanted—desperately wanted—to wake up from this nightmare and find himself back at his first day in office with nothing but the promise of the next four years ahead of him.

He couldn't stand still anymore, and marched briskly into the Oval Office followed by his Secret Service agents. In the Oval Office, the White House television crew bustled around setting up lights and cameras, stringing cables and rearranging the pictures and knickknacks on the credenza behind the high leather chair. Sercu and the speechwriters were huddled to one side making last-minute tweaks to the speech. Ian Tuttle, Walsh noticed, was obvious in his absence from the tableau. But he couldn't be concerned about Tuttle now.

Barbara Howe had called a half hour earlier to report a

crushing lack of success with her mission. The leaders who agreed to meet with her basically laughed when they heard what she had to propose, but the majority of them refused even to see her. Perhaps in their small minds, the U.S. emissary being a woman was reason enough to turn their backs on her. But Walsh could not resign himself to their appalling lack of concern for the events that were about to escalate into a war. He had studied Middle Eastern politics and sociology and understood there were fundamental differences in cultural attitudes and biases. But he didn't understand the wholesale lack of value placed on human life.

A soft touch on his arm brought Walsh out of his thoughts, and he turned to find Sarah standing beside him. She wore a simple black pantsuit with a strand of pearls draped around her elegant neck. Her hair had been brushed to a shimmer and fell over her shoulders in a coppery cascade. She was beautiful and David was ever grateful for her grace and presence.

"Jim told me what happened at Andrews . . ." she began in a whisper.

"I'm sorry I didn't tell you myself."

"You've been busy, David. Don't worry about that. You've got a country to worry about."

Walsh smiled down at her. "That doesn't change the fact that I still want you off to Greenbrier as soon as this is over."

"No, David, we're not going anywhere. You need all of us around you and if you're going to be cut off from a safe escape, I'm not going anywhere."

Walsh was momentarily overcome by a wave of gratitude but reality soon replaced that. "No, Sarah, you're not safe here. I want you away from here as fast as possible."

Now it was her turn to smile. "No, Mr. President, I'm afraid you've been vetoed."

Sercu chose that moment to announce, "Mr. President, it's time."

Walsh turned and kissed his wife, holding her as though he would never see her again. When he stepped away, tears glistened in her eyes. The Secret Service agents had turned away politely, but a couple of the cameramen grinned broadly.

* * *

David sat stiffly in his desk chair waiting for his cue. The prepared speech waited on the TelePrompTer. As the director counted down the last seconds, David took a deep breath and forced himself to relax. "Ladies and gentlemen, the President of the United States," he heard the television announcer's voice and the director pointed at him. The red lights on the cameras snapped on, and he knew his time had run out. The moment had come.

"Good evening. I am coming to you tonight to talk about some events that have occurred here in Washington, D.C., over the past few days that are of serious consequence to the security of this nation."

As he talked, Sarah dropped into an armchair at the back of the room. She had never been so proud of her husband or so afraid in her entire life. Like so many other Americans, she had lived secure in the safety provided by living within the borders of the last great superpower on the planet. Now she understood how the Brits must have felt as they watched the Nazis drop bomb after bomb on their homes. She had an overwhelming urge to run and hide, to find that bunker in Greenbrier and never come out of it. But her place was here beside her husband.

"I am sure you all have heard the disturbing news about a mysterious outbreak at Janey Elementary School. At first it was believed that the illness was caused by alleged toxic chemicals leeching into the water table from closed military facilities around

Spring Valley. But we have discovered that the deaths and illnesses are the result of an attack by terrorists who infected the playground with biochemical agents designed just for this purpose." Sercu had removed the direct reference to anthrax, feeling that it would be too much information too fast. Walsh agreed.

* * *

Herbert and Grace Daniels sat in their darkened living room, eyes glued to their television set. Grace's usual running chatter about whatever Henry chose to watch was silenced.

"There have been other incidents, the president continued. Attacks on the general population by this as-yet-unidentified terrorist organization."

"I knew it," Grace whispered. "They are terrorists."

"We don't know that yet, Grace. I only reported it a couple of hours ago, and there's been nothing happening over there to indicate they're even being investigated."

"Don't be naïve, Henry. It's written all over the president's face."

Henry waved a silencing hand at his wife. He was terrified that she might be right.

". . . therefore, I have made the difficult but necessary decision to declare a state of martial law in the city of Washington extending as far north as Baltimore, Maryland, and as far south as Quantico, Virginia. Under this state of emergency, there will be a 9:00 P.M. curfew imposed. Anyone not on essential or life-and-death business shall be escorted home. Businesses will be asked to close early to accommodate this curfew. Public schools are now on temporary recess until further notice. Parents are encouraged to keep their children in their own yards closely supervised during the day and indoors come nightfall. Employers are hereby required to grant leaves of absence to any employees needing time to care for children."

* * *

Throughout the halls of the Executive Office Building the silence was broken by curses and shouts.

"Damn it, they can't do that!"

"Why wasn't Congress notified of this plan?"

"I don't care if it is martial law, Walsh can't just shut down the city at his whim!"

Congressmen and senators grabbed telephones and frantically dialed their fellow senators and congressmen mobilizing to fight what they perceived as the president's grab for total power. James Sercu had predicted this, and had dispatched pages who raced through the halls distributing packets of information detailing the situation and begging the representatives to maintain strict security when discussing the information, most of all begging them to stay calm and be patient until the president could address them personally.

"Citizens of Washington and the surrounding area will notice the placement of armed forces in all public areas. Please cooperate with them whenever and wherever possible. Follow their instructions to the letter. They are stationed there for your protection. I realize this is a shock to most of you, especially those of you in other parts of this great nation. The threat of outside forces invading our homes and our workplaces has never been so real as it is tonight. I ask only for your cooperation and continued patriotism as we fight to defeat those who have targeted our children."

Walsh stared into the camera for a moment, concentrating on sending a message of hope and trust with his entire being.

"We will keep you informed of events as they occur; tune to your local newscasts for more information. If you have any concerns or questions, contact your local legislators and representatives. Thank you, and good night."

Forty-Eight

The Oval Office
The White House
Washington, D.C.

The cameras were off, the lights extinguished, and the technicians were rolling up the yards of cables strung throughout the Oval Office. David Walsh still sat, motionless, in the big leather chair behind a desk that had seen countless presidents face countless crises. Those present continued with their business, occasionally stealing secret glances at their president. Sarah Walsh, too, sat still in her chair regarding her husband and allowing his words to echo through her mind, trying to adjust to the idea of living in a siege state.

Sarah had resolved finally to go to him and draw him out of his reverie when Ned Seiffert pushed his way into the room and, grabbing Jim Sercu, approached the desk. Sarah rose and followed behind them quietly, lest they ask her to leave the room.

"Mr. President," Seiffert said as though waving his hand before David's unseeing eyes. "We've had a report that just might lead us to the location of the terrorists' hideout."

Sercu snapped his head around to stare at the general, but Walsh merely raised his eyes slowly.

"Please tell me this won't be a wild goose chase," Walsh said quietly.

"I don't think so, sir. The report comes from a Dr. Herbert Daniels, a former civilian employee of the Pentagon, retired. He and his wife live in Bethesda, a residential neighborhood often favored by embassy employees, so they're used to foreigners moving in and out. But in this case the house seems to be occupied by at least a dozen adult men and women, no children. The Daniels thought something was amiss when they spotted what looked like artillery boxes labeled with an explosives symbol being moved in and out of the house."

Walsh felt the blood returning to his brain. Could this mean the threat would soon be over? Dared he hope so?

"Okay, Ned, get on it. I want it thoroughly investigated, and no mistakes."

"Begging your pardon, sir, but I've already sent out a team."

* * *

It was barely thirty minutes after the president's address to the nation when General Louis Blaine led his team through the quiet streets of suburban Bethesda, Maryland. They had to be careful and quiet—get in, get what they came for, and get out without causing too much fuss. Nosy neighbors could be hazardous to his men in an operation like this. He had already driven by the house identified by Dr. Daniels and his wife. Lights burned in almost every window and three cars sat in the driveway. They should be able to get most, if not all, of the terrorists in one raid.

When Seiffert had received the report from Dr. Daniels, the tax rolls were checked immediately to identify the owner of the house. A minor real-estate trader claimed to have leased the home to a local company to be used as transient employee housing. The rent was paid a year in advance, and he had received no complaints. But when they had checked into the local company, it was found that the organization never existed. The money-hungry landlord apparently dispensed with a background check when he saw the number of zeros on the rent check.

Blaine watched as a black panel truck pulled to the curb two blocks from the house and his men slipped out the back and vanished into the hedges and gardens of the neighborhood. They would move in on the home unseen and, dropping a flash grenade to blind the residents, take them all prisoner without gunfire or bloodshed. At least that was the plan. But in case the plan didn't quite work out, their weapons had been outfitted with silencers and bayonets should there be a need for hands-on action.

One by one the squad leaders checked in. Everyone was in place and ready to go. Blaine hesitated for a minute, allowing the atmosphere in the neighborhood to settle before he ordered them in.

Hawley Sheppard was first through the rear patio door where he surprised a woman alone in the kitchen. When she saw the huge man, she dropped to her knees and pleaded with him in Arabic. He gestured for the rest of his men to move into the house. A pop and sizzle followed the igniting of a flash grenade in the front room and his men paused for a moment to let the flash fade before they burst in to meet up with their teammates in the empty dining room. After a quick glance at the empty folding table and scattered chairs, the soldiers fanned out through the house overturning furniture and searching every closet and cranny they could find. It seemed the only person left there was the woman, now handcuffed in the kitchen.

Hawley Sheppard stepped carefully through the house watching the men work at their search. He had just mounted the stairs to the second floor when a bang echoed down the stairwell from the third floor followed by the hollow thumps of automatic weapons fire through silencers. Sheppard pounded up the stairs two at a time followed by half of his squad.

On the empty third floor he found three of his men huddled around the unmoving form of Major Bruce Giaccobbi. A bullet had caught him in the side of the jaw, shattering his helmet on the other side as it exited his skull.

In a far corner lay the man responsible, his chest riddled with the soldier's return fire.

Blaine pulled his car up to the curb outside the house just as the report of the shooting crackled over his radio.

"God damned son of a bitch fucking bastards!" he muttered under his breath, slamming the car door behind him and charging into the house. Two of Sheppard's men were carrying Giacobbi's body down the staircase as he burst through the door. Blaine stopped short and stared for a moment, his fury turning the scene a hazy blood red.

"Are there any survivors?" he bellowed at no one in particular.

"Yes, sir!" one of the men snapped off a salute. "There's only one, a woman, in the kitchen, sir!"

Hawley Sheppard clomped down the stairs in time to see Blaine race off for the kitchen, his fury like a ticking bomb behind his eyes.

Sheppard raced after him.

In the kitchen, the woman still knelt on the floor, her forehead bowed to the tiles, praying and keening and sobbing.

Blaine grabbed her by the back of the neck and hauled her to her feet. The fear in her eyes was suddenly replaced by revulsion, which only fueled Blaine's anger.

"Where the fuck are they, bitch!" Blaine bellowed at her.

"Sir," Sheppard tried to distract his superior officer before he throttled the woman, "I don't think she understands English."

Blaine shot Sheppard a look that made the big man's blood go cold.

"I don't really give a shit, Sheppard! The lives of our children mean nothing to them, so why should I care anything about one of their women?!"

Sheppard knew enough to see he'd crossed a line he might not ever recover from. He stepped back and turned away from Blaine.

"Now," Blaine turned back to his captive, "where the fuck are the rest of them?!" He shook her violently, hoisting her feet off the floor and squeezing until she started to choke. He eased up enough so she could catch a breath, but when she did she hurled a string of Arabic at him that could not be mistaken for anything but insults and curses. She punctuated her litany by spitting in Blaine's face.

Sheppard heard the whoosh and crash as the woman was heaved across the kitchen into the open door. Her body crumpled to the floor as the glass from the window pelted down around her.

"Get her out of here. Get the bodies out of here. I want the entire place scoured. Call in a forensics team. When we get every scrap of information we possibly can out of this place, I want it sterilized. Then I want that fucking landlord brought up on charges."

"Charges, sir?" Sheppard asked, regretting the question but needing to know what he had to do next.

"Treason, Sheppard. Let's start with treason!"

* * *

The streets of Adams Morgan were still crowded with people making the best of the last half hour before the president's new curfew took effect. A few made their way quickly to the neighborhood markets and take-out restaurants to stock up for the night. Others were on their way back home after leisurely dinners, or quick drinks, or late nights at work.

The news of the president's speech had spread quickly.

Heated arguments broke out from time to time in the bars, restaurants and even on the street corners. Public opinion was widely divided and many people didn't believe that President Walsh had been entirely up-front with the American people.

Hysteria and paranoia had yet to settle on the residents of Washington, D.C., so no one paid any attention to the large van that rolled slowly up 18th Street in the tight traffic. It then pulled into the alley alongside a rug store that claimed to specialize in authentic Persian carpets and antique rugs from Turkey. In the dark shadows of the alleyway, the van's occupants were able to unload the final boxes of explosives into the storage room of the rug store.

The move from the suburbs of Maryland to the trendy Adams Morgan neighborhood had been part of their plan from the beginning. They had no idea how narrowly they had escaped capture by the Americans. The man and woman left at the house had been instructed to finish emptying it out and closing it up before joining their comrades at the new headquarters. The loss of the two, especially the woman, would be of little consequence to the plan. Not now that the second stage had been set in motion.

Forty-Nine

President's Private Study
The White House
Washington, D.C.

The President's small private study was suddenly crowded with people. His valet had brought in a dinner tray, which lay spread out on the desk. Sarah hovered over her husband, directing the meal and picking at it herself when he didn't eat fast enough. All he really wanted was a cup of coffee, but he was content to make his wife happy and to eat a little.

Ian Tuttle had managed to find his way into the study and stood against the far wall, saying nothing. James Sercu sat across from David, running through the immediate results of the president's address.

"The White House switchboard was flooded with calls after the first five minutes of the speech, roughly by the time you said martial law," Sercu said, glancing at pages of notes in his lap. "As we predicted, the Senate and House offices were in an uproar."

"Did you send around that briefing packet?" Walsh asked.

"Yes, sir, we managed to time it so that the packet went out just about the time you began discussing the emergency measures."

"Have things quieted down?"

"Barely. I think members are taking up sides in preparation for your presentation tomorrow."

"And what about Harry? Did he get out of that embassy reception before the shit hit the fan?"

Sarah reached over his shoulder and grabbed a dinner roll.

"Yes, sir. He and Mrs. Dent are due to arrive here in about two minutes."

"What about their girls?" Sarah asked.

"We discussed it, and it was decided that they were better off at school. They're far enough away from D.C. to be fairly safe for now. I've increased their Secret Service protection, and we'll be keeping a close eye on them from here." Walsh patted her hand reassuringly.

The intercom chirped, startling everyone—but no one so much as Tuttle, who appeared to jump a foot in the air.

"How do you stand that thing?" Sarah asked, eyeing it suspiciously.

"Excuse me, ma'am?" Colleen sounded confused.

"It's okay," Walsh laughed, slapping his wife's hand. "What's up, Colleen?"

"General Seiffert and General Blaine are here. They say it's important."

"Everything's important right now, Colleen. Send them in." David grimaced at Sercu as the door opened and the two military men marched into the study.

"Sorry for the interruption, Mr. President," Seiffert snapped in his usual efficient manner, "but I thought that a report on the mission to the terrorist headquarters was necessary."

"Of course, Ned." The small sense of control Walsh had been able to take away from his time in front of the camera melted under the serious set of the generals' faces.

"General." Seiffert passed the floor to Blaine, who snapped off a salute before beginning.

"We were able to secure the house in question, but it appeared that the terrorists might have had advance warning. The house was essentially empty except for two individuals. . . ."

"Wait a minute, general," Walsh interrupted. "How could they have had any warning? Correct me if I'm wrong, but General Seiffert ordered the raid almost the minute he received the report." David was angry and didn't try to hide it. This game playing with the terrorists was becoming annoying. Sarah, still standing behind her husband, stole a glance at Tuttle and wasn't surprised to see that the color had drained out of the man's face and his hands were trembling.

"Excuse me, sir," Seiffert answered before Blaine could open his mouth. "The initial report came in through Dr. Daniels's contacts at the Pentagon. It did take some time for the report to reach the White House."

Walsh glared at Seiffert. "Is there any chance at all that it was just bad luck and not a leak?"

"I suppose there's always that chance, sir," Seiffert said brusquely.

Sarah watched Tuttle, who squirmed like a rat caught in a trap. His eyes darted from one man to another. The man made a horrible mole.

"Okay, okay, I'm sorry, gentlemen. General Blaine, please continue."

"Yes, sir. We found two individuals at the house. One male and one female. The male was successful in bringing down one of my officers before he was dispatched. The woman is in custody."

"Bringing down?" Sarah said. "You mean he killed one of our men?"

"Yes, ma'am." Blaine hesitated a moment before continuing. "We found chemical traces of weapons in several rooms and in the vehicles left in the driveway. There were also several empty diplomatic pouches. But nothing of any consequence beyond that."

"So, in other words, no real clues." Walsh shook his head.

"That would be correct, sir."

Walsh stared at the surface of his desk, thinking hard. As far as he knew, Tuttle had been under close watch and hadn't even known about the raid on the house until Blaine and his men were on their way to Bethesda. There was no way he could have alerted anyone in time. So at least this wasn't Tuttle's doing. Without thinking, Walsh glanced over where Tuttle stood against the wall. The man's eyes were the size of dinner plates and his skin the color of school paste. "One hell of a spy," Walsh thought. He considered asking Blaine to give his chief of staff a dirty look. The man would probably spill the beans on the whole plot right there. The thought made him smile.

"Sir?" Sercu asked, noting the change in expression.

"Oh, nothing, Jim, just reminded of something. Okay, so what we need to do is interrogate the woman, find out where the terrorists have moved, and get on that as fast as we can."

"I can have the prisoner removed to the safe house and ready for interrogation in two hours." Blaine snapped back to attention.

"No, general, no time for that. It'll have to happen here." Walsh eyed the military man waiting for an argument; he wasn't disappointed.

"But, sir, our interrogation facilities . . ."

"General," Walsh cut him off sharply and rose to his feet, "I understand our facilities here aren't the same as yours, but as I said, there's no time, so you'll just have to resort to the old fashioned way."

"The old fashioned way, sir?"

"Yes, talk to her."

* * *

In the back room of the rug store in Adams Morgan, four men had just finished sorting through the boxes and crates they had spent the day moving from Bethesda when the rear door slammed shut and a fifth man rushed in.

"Ahmad, where is Daulah?"

"I am afraid the heathens found the house. Daulah is dead and they took Nathifa Durah prisoner."

"She is dead to us now, so we must accelerate our plans. The infidels cannot be allowed to interfere with our mission. Siraj, did you find suitable water transport for our needs?"

One of the men pulled a tightly folded map from his pocket and passed it to his leader. "Yes, there is a marina here," he indicated a small blue area on the map. "We can borrow one of the yachts moored there, and it is only a short way to the Aberdeen Proving Grounds, our objective."

"Very good. After evening prayer we will go to this marina, and prepare for our next glorious victory."

The men, all members of the Hezbollah and all willing to give their lives for their beliefs, smiled at one another. Victory was sure to be theirs, and with it the eternal glory of Allah.

Several small groups of their brothers had already set off for locations around Washington where they would detonate carefully placed explosives and release the cleansing virus. There was no way they could fail.

FIFTY

The White House Situation Room
Washington, D.C.

PRESIDENT WALSH'S CONCERN OVER IAN TUTTLE'S INVOLVEMENT WITH the terrorist crisis had reached a point where it was interfering with his concentration on other problems. The man had to be dealt with—and soon. He had called together a few select members of his staff, including Jim Marshall and Dennis Murphy, heads of the FBI and CIA, respectively.

"Gentlemen," Walsh addressed the small group, "we have to decide on a course of action for dealing with Tuttle, and I believe we have to do it now before any more damage can be done to our battle against these terrorists."

Walsh looked around at the faces of his most trusted friends. Harry Dent sat to his right. The man had held up well during the recent crisis and David had come to depend on him to keep the outside appointments—the speeches, tours of schools, and other public relations events that he no longer had time for. But now that the city had been locked down, Harry's role would have to change, and David could see the stress on his vice president's face.

Ned Seiffert held his eyes glued to the far wall. Treason was a very serious charge and required that they be absolutely sure before they acted. Jim Sercu watched Walsh in return, taking in and assessing the situation moment by moment. Bill Cassidy fidgeted, something he did whenever a situation became uncomfortable, and this was more than uncomfortable for all of them. Jim Marshall sat, a stack of reports on the table before him, jaw clenched. And Dennis Murphy, normally jovial with bright dancing eyes, now looking drawn and tense, caught David's eye and nodded solemnly.

"So it's agreed that the time for action is now?" Walsh asked. The men all nodded.

"Jim, have your investigations turned up anything else?" David dropped into his chair and spun slightly to face Jim Marshall.

"I'm afraid so, sir. It seems that Ian Tuttle had an ongoing communication with Warren Dunn prior to your election. We have uncovered travel and phone records indicating numerous trips to Oklahoma, the headquarters of OILCO, and frankly hundreds of phone calls over the past two years."

"So we're pretty sure that Dunn must be involved in this?"

"Given Dunn's track record, there's almost no doubt," Dennis Murphy chimed in, "and we've found something even more disturbing." Murphy looked to Marshall to continue.

"There's an organization, a club—very elite, very secretive , and very powerful. They call themselves the Bohemian Club, although we're not sure if that's really the name or just a code name of some sort." Marshall swallowed hard, a sheen of sweat sparkled on his forehead. Walsh didn't think he'd ever seen Marshall quite so disturbed. They had known each other since David had been governor of Oklahoma and he counted Jim among his friends.

"What's so remarkable about this club, and what does it have to do with Dunn?" Walsh was trying to keep the discussion moving forward.

"Membership in the club is a highly guarded secret. But from what we've been able to uncover, some of the most powerful men in Washington are part of the inner elite."

David chuckled, "I'm not a member. They can't be that good!"

"Me either," Harry chimed in, elbowing the president lightly.

Walsh wanted Marshall to relax and get on with it, but the humor didn't seem to help.

"No, sir, neither of you are, and neither are any of the people in this room. But that's not to say that there aren't members in the White House right now. And there certainly are in the Senate, and the House, and the UN, and the military, and every other branch of government, commission, and Fortune 500 corporation." Marshall paused and drew a deep breath. "From the looks of the little bit of information we've been able to gather, they control just about everything. And Warren Dunn is a member."

Walsh knew that the implications of this information were far-reaching and, if these men were somehow involved in this crisis, there might not be a way out. But what good could it do them?

"Why?" he asked.

"Why would they be involved in this? I don't know." Marshall shook his head.

"Sir," Jim Sercu suddenly spoke up; Walsh turned to look at him, hoping that in his own brilliant way he would be able to connect the dots and put the situation into a recognizable perspective, "if it's accurate that Tuttle is involved with Dunn, then the reasons behind Dunn's involvement have to be the oil connection." Sercu paused to let it sink in for a moment.

"And if it is the oil connection, then Dunn must think that this could be used to control you, to force you into perhaps abandoning OPEC, opening up supply lines individually with the nations involved, or perhaps abolishing trade limits. It could mean billions to Dunn if he was there first."

"So he bought Tuttle to influence me, and made a deal with the terrorists. But why would Dunn want to cause that much damage here? Does he want me booted out of office? Why not fight the battle on Middle Eastern soil?" David felt the questions coming faster than he could put them into words.

Bill Cassidy suddenly stopped fidgeting, "We know that any deals with Middle Eastern countries, especially the oil barons, are tenuous. They don't see agreements as binding in every sense as we do. And terrorists—we know negotiations don't work with terrorists. Perhaps this has gotten out of hand for Dunn, too."

"That makes sense. He's obviously lost control over Tuttle. The man is ready to snap if you say 'boo.' So what do we do about this?" The president's voice grew strong with the confidence derived from positive action. But they still had a lot of work to do.

* * *

Warren Dunn left Washington on the heels of the president's speech declaring martial law. But instead of going back to Oklahoma, which simply felt too far away from the action, he flew to New York City. Dunn settled himself into a suite at the Plaza Hotel where he could watch the events unfold.

He was mildly concerned by the attacks the terrorists had been leveling at the people in Washington. He wasn't thrilled by the attack on the grammar school, but they felt it was needed, so who was he to argue? He was more disturbed by the actions of the esteemed President Walsh. Dunn knew it would be a challenge to turn Walsh's actions to meet his own ends, but he had had more faith in Ian Tuttle than the man apparently deserved. However, the Bohemian Club had stepped in and they were beginning their own carefully orchestrated manipulations. All Dunn had to do was sit back and wait. He was good at waiting. Besides, the pay-off would be worth it.

* * *

Ian Tuttle had his own demons to deal with. At that moment he could not locate President Walsh or Jim Sercu, two men on whom he had to keep a close eye, for his own safety. But he was the chief of staff. Nobody could question his search for the president.

There was no response to his knock at the door of the president's private study, so Tuttle went to the formal entrance to the Oval Office.

"Hi, Colleen. Can I see President Walsh, please?"

Colleen looked at Tuttle, a hint of suspicion in her eyes. She wasn't stupid and had noticed his deliberate exclusion from meetings in the last couple of days, which made her wonder what he was up to.

"No, Mr. Tuttle. I'm sorry, the president cannot be disturbed right now." She flashed him a tight smile and wished he'd just go back to his own office. The man's shifting eyes and trembling hands made her uneasy, as if there wasn't enough to be uneasy about right now.

"But I really do need to see him, Colleen. Just for a moment." He fought to keep the desperation from his voice. The other secretaries and aides in the anteoffice looked up at him wonderingly.

"As I said, Mr. Tuttle, the president cannot be disturbed right now. I will tell him you need to talk with him as soon as I can." Colleen set her voice as though she were speaking to a misbehaving child, a technique she found often worked with overeager staff.

Tuttle stared at her. "The bitch is hiding something," he thought, but he spun about on his heel and marched out of the room. He could feel the eyes of every person on his back as he left.

Back in his own office, Ian felt the walls closing in on him. Dunn had given him specific instructions. He found himself unable, or rather stopped, from carrying out those instructions, which could mean only one thing. Someone, somewhere had become suspicious and had warned Walsh, who in his paranoid state of mind, probably believed them. It was probably Walsh's wife. That bitch never had any respect for Tuttle, or for his place in the administration. It was she, he was sure of it. Sarah Walsh had probably made up some far-fetched story just to turn her husband against him. There was no way she could have been smart enough to figure out or even to guess at the truth.

Tuttle fumbled his cell phone out of a jacket pocket and clicked it on. He had to update Dunn on what was happening. The dial tone buzzed, then clicked twice and buzzed again. Ian looked at the phone. Could they have tapped it? He shut off the phone and picked up the desk phone. He asked the operator for an outside line and listened as the phone clicked before giving him a dial tone. It had never done that before. They did have his phone bugged. Now what was he going to do?

Fifty-One

Lafayette Park
Washington, D.C.

A squad of fully armed marines, dressed in battle fatigues, moved systematically across the park. One man carried a large box with a telescoping arm fitted with a large flat plate that looked vaguely like a metal detector. He waved the sensor dish across the grass and kept his eyes glued to the digital readout. When he indicated certain areas, another man bent down to take a sample of the grass or soil or gravel.

So far, the prototype "sniffer" developed to detect the presence of biological weapons seemed to be working well. When any hint of contamination was found, a sample was taken and cataloged to be checked at a lab, just to be sure. The one hundred prototype sniffers were in use across the city, and worked spectacularly well when contaminants were identified.

A similar team worked along the walkways surrounding the Tidal Basin. The stark skeletons of the Japanese cherry trees, readying themselves for their annual show in the spring, gave a somber backdrop to the gray day. The city seemed deserted. Remaining tourists stayed indoors, away from the attractions, most of which were closed under the lockdown.

A few visitors still insisted on touring the sights, and were punctuated by the inevitable joggers who were forced around the squad of marines. Two of the men held their weapons at the ready, their eyes sweeping the scattered people for signs of anything unusual.

Asif al Ahmad stood with his back to the marines, leaning on the railing and staring down into the water of the Tidal Basin. He clasped the small vial of infected material in one hand and the dead man's switch that was linked to the ten pounds of C4 explosive strapped around his waist in the other. He didn't want to open the vial to dump the contents in the water until the marines were well past. He didn't know how well their device might detect the virus before he was able to get it into the water.

The marines moved slowly and steadily around the basin, careful not to become complacent since they had yet to find anything. Lieutenant Robert Ryan glanced at Asif al Ahmad briefly before moving on. But something about the way the man glanced at him out of the corner of his eye caught the officer's attention. He stepped up next to the man and leaned over the railing to glance into the water, feigning interest, in an attempt to get a look at the man's face.

Asif glanced at the marine, noting the gun at the ready, and decided that he could not risk allowing this heathen to interfere with his mission. With one fluid motion, Asif slammed the glass vial against the railing and allowed the shards of glass and infected dust to fall to the water. As he turned to face the barrel of Ryan's automatic, Asif pulled his coat open to reveal the C4 strapped to his waist. He waved the dead man's switch at Ryan, who stepped back several feet and shouted to his squad.

With an audible click of safeties, the terrorist found himself surrounded by the armed marines. He laughed out loud as two of the men herded the few people there out of the way.

"You will fail, infidels!" Asif screamed. "Your people are doomed!"

"Careful! He's wired!" Ryan snapped to the others. They all could see the dead man's switch clenched in the terrorist's grip. If they took him out now, his thumb would release its pressure on the detonator, and the C4 would blast a hole in the park the size of a tennis court. Ryan could see no way out unless they could force him over the edge and into the water, which would cushion some of the blast. He shot a glance at another man in the unit who began circling around Asif to the other side.

"Okay, buddy," Ryan said in a conciliatory tone. "We don't want anybody hurt here, okay?" Ryan wanted nothing more than to blow the guy away. Someone else had already alerted the other units in the area, which were probably converging on the Tidal Basin at that moment. A lot of good that would do. There was no way to stop this. Ryan lowered his weapon and took a step forward.

"If you just disconnect the switch, I'll see that nothing happens to you. You have my word," Ryan lied. He had no problem lying now, not after these bastards killed all those little kids.

"Ha! I am no fool, Mr. American Soldier!" Asif waved the switch at all of them. "I will die for the glory of Allah! You, too, will die for the glory of Allah—and in Allah's heaven you will be punished for your crimes against us!"

The man was working himself into a religious fervor. Ryan kept an eye on the man moving up behind the terrorist. They had to time it just right.

"So what difference does it make if we die now or later? I mean if Allah will get his revenge in the end, what difference if the end is now or later?" Ryan searched for something to say, something to stall the man for just another moment.

"Stay back, swine!" Asif waved his arms, which gave the marine coming up behind him just enough opportunity. The man charged, catching Asif in the back and sending him hurtling over the railing into the Tidal Basin. The marines hit the ground screaming for the few gawkers to take cover.

Asif al Ahmad had only a second to mutter a prayer to Allah as his thumb slipped off the detonator and he hit the water. The C4 ignited, sending a plume of water and debris 100 feet into the air, high enough to be seen from the windows of the Oval Office. The ground around the Tidal Basin shook violently, toppling two weakened cherry trees and sending pedestrians for blocks around stumbling into one another. The sound of the explosion set off car alarms for miles and shattered windows in neighboring buildings.

When the noise had died away and the ground settled down, the marines climbed shakily to their feet. The spray from the plume of water soaked everything. Lieutenant Ryan shook the water from his clothes and then stopped dead, the color drained from this face.

"Daniels, where's that sniffer?" he yelled to a younger man.

"Right here, sir." Daniels trotted over with the device, quickly running through a check to make sure it was working all right.

"Scan the water," Ryan ordered, his voice dropping to keep the onlookers from hearing.

Daniels ran the meter over Ryan's wet clothing and the saturated grass at their feet.

"It's hot, sir," the young man choked, realizing what had happened. "Everything is really hot."

* * *

David Walsh thought the whole Capitol building was coming down around his ears, and he grabbed for the podium to keep from getting knocked off his feet. In the huge room, the members of Congress held tight to the arms of their chairs, a few of them scrambling to get under the long rows of desks. Secret Service and armed guards stationed around the room raced for the exits to assess the situation. But the rumbling stopped as quickly as it had begun, and the shaken legislators gathered themselves up and returned to their seats with an all clear from the chief security officer.

Walsh ordered one of his Secret Service agents to get a report on what had happened before turning back to face Congress. The blast had come at a moment when David feared that the meeting would degenerate into an angry mob. Protocol forgotten in the midst of a flurry of overwhelming emotions, the members fought one another for the floor to hurl their accusations and demands at the president. Walsh wiped his face with a handkerchief and gratefully accepted a glass of water that was pressed into his hand.

"Everybody all right, no injuries?" he said into the microphone.

A chorus of grunts and mumbles met his question, and one person near the back called out, "No casualties, sir!"

"Okay then, where were we? Oh yes, Senator Blake, you were saying?"

Archibald Blake, twenty-year senator from Missouri stood, rearranged his jacket and cleared his throat. "I was saying, Mr. President, that I find it difficult to believe that with all the new security technology in place our military allowed terrorists to set foot on American soil. I have heard talk that leads me to believe that one was actually brought into the White House. A terrorist in the White House? Can such a thing be true?"

Archibald Blake had not hidden his feelings about the new president from the beginning. A staunch, old-school conservative, he felt that Walsh's own conservative approach was too far to the left to be tolerated. He was a dignified gentleman; always impeccably tailored and reputed to have more power than any other single member of the Senate or the House—power garnered, some said, through his involvement in a very secret club. David knew Blake's name appeared on Jim Marshall's list of suspected members of the Bohemian Club.

"Senator Blake, I understand your concern, and I assure you that any actions taken by this administration regarding the terrorists were taken with the safety of this nation and its people as the only motivation." He glanced to the side where Jim Sercu stood. Sercu dipped his head once, almost imperceptibly, and David continued. "Yes, Mr. Blake, there was a terrorist in the White House."

A murmur swept through the room and several senators leapt to their feet hoping Blake would relinquish the floor, which he did not.

"Would you care to explain that to the worthy assembly, Mr. President?" Blake said slowly, with an undertone of menace.

"Of course, Mr. Blake. When we learned of the terrorist plot, a mission was deployed to stop it from going any further. The mastermind of the plot was captured and brought to the United States for questioning. He refused to cooperate unless he spoke with me personally."

The murmur rose to an audible whisper. Many senators were shaking their heads—whether in disbelief or protest wasn't clear.

"My security advisers did not want me meeting with this man outside of their control, so it was decided to bring the man to a secure area within the complex for an interview." He paused, waiting for Blake to interrupt. He didn't.

"I spoke with the terrorist and was given some information, which has aided us in determining some of the attacks that would take place and, therefore, to prevent them. I believe that that information alone made the meeting necessary."

"But you could not prevent an attack on schoolchildren, could you, Mr. President?" Blake accused.

"No, sir, I could not and I regret that more deeply than you know."

"What is it these terrorists want from the United States, Mr. President?" Blake continued.

"I was told outright that they wanted us to end all aid to Israel, cut all diplomatic ties with them. It was implied that they wanted us to put an end to OPEC; also, to end restrictions on oil trade, what restrictions there are, and open the industry to their control." Walsh glanced at Sercu, who hadn't been expecting that. Sercu smiled a small tight smile.

"So you're saying that all we have to do is cut Israel loose and step out of the oil industry and all this is for naught?" Blake's voice rose to an evangelical pitch, something he was famous for.

"Basically, yes, I guess that is what I am saying, Mr. Blake."

"Then why don't you just do it, Mr. President? It seems a small price to pay for the safety of our children, doesn't it, Mr. President?"

David paused for a moment. Was that an admission? Was it safe even to read anything into it, or was it merely a logical question to ask?

"Mr. Blake, it has been the policy of this administration and many administrations before this one not to negotiate with terrorists. If we betray that policy now, we only open ourselves up to more terrorist attacks in the future."

The noise level began to rise again, and Sercu took the opportunity to approach the podium.

"Sir, we have a report that a terrorist was found near the Tidal Basin. The man was wired with plastic explosives, which detonated when the marines managed to push him into the water," Sercu whispered.

"So that was the shaking?" Walsh quietly asked, glancing around the room.

"Yes, sir. But the bad news is that the water was infected. The explosion sent the spray up to a mile away from the river and with it, the virus."

"Shit. Can we do anything?"

"We're trying to round up anyone who came in direct contact with the water and get them into hospitals before it goes any farther." Walsh could hear the distant drone of sirens over the raised voices. He straightened and signaled to the Speaker of the House, who called order with a few bangs of his gavel.

"Ladies and gentlemen," Walsh said to the assembly. " We've just had a report of another terrorist attack. That was the explosion that rocked this building a few moments ago. No one was injured in the explosion, although there was some damage done to the Tidal Basin." David decided it best to end the meeting. He could hardly wait to escape.

"Sir!" It was Blake again. "I understand your attentions are now needed elsewhere. But we need to know what you plan to do about this threat."

"In the short term, we are tracking down the terrorists here at home and dispatching the threat," Walsh said with more confidence than he was feeling.

"And in the long term, sir?" Blake asked. The room grew quiet; the moment of truth was upon him.

"In the long term, if we cannot raise the support we need from the members of the United Arab Emirates, we will have no choice but tactical nuclear strikes."

Surprisingly, the room remained deadly quiet while each member of the Senate digested the reality of what their president had just said.

"It requires an act of Congress to declare war, Mr. President," Blake said, maneuvering him into position as though he were a piece on a giant chessboard. But Walsh was tired of being used as a pawn—it was time to throw down the gauntlet and damn the consequences.

"I understand that, Mr. Blake, but I don't intend to start a war, merely eliminate the threat to this country."

Fifty-Two

Private Quarters of the President and First Lady
The White House
Washington, D. C.

"Just go ahead and say it, Jim. You don't have to dance around the subject," Walsh said from his closet. He had insisted on getting cleaned up as soon as they returned to the White House. Something about his encounter with Archibald Blake on the floor of the Senate had left him feeling tainted, almost dirty.

"I'm not mincing words with you, David," Sercu replied. He sat in a deep armchair, a small scotch balanced on the arm.

"Then just tell me you don't agree with what I did out there." Walsh stepped out of the closet buttoning a fresh white shirt. "Thank God somebody else does the laundry," he thought, "or I'd be a mess by now."

"Oh, I don't disagree with it, David. I think it was marvelous!" Sercu grinned. "I don't think anyone has ever stopped Blake in his tracks like that before. He didn't know how to react."

Walsh returned the grin. "Good, I know it was a risk, but I wanted it to be clear that I wasn't going to allow a bunch of congressmen to get in the way of what I believe to be the right course of action."

"Oh, I think you delivered that message loud and clear!" Sercu raised his glass in a toast before draining the mouthful of amber liquid.

Walsh glanced around the room. "Any idea where Sarah's gotten to?"

"George Washington Hospital. She insisted on going to visit the victims of the attack on the grammar school. It's a good PR move in any case."

"You taking care of her, Jim?" Walsh asked, knowing the answer but concerned nonetheless.

"Of course, double security detail, aides, armored limo, the works. I wouldn't let anything happen to her now that you two have found some common ground again."

"Yeah, it seems we have, doesn't it?" Walsh let himself feel the happiness for just a moment before turning his attention back to the problems at hand. "So, what's happening here and what do we need to do now?"

"Well," Sercu flipped open a notebook on his lap, "General Blaine is interrogating the female prisoner from the terrorist headquarters."

Walsh shook his head. "I wonder how much of her will be left by the time he's finished."

* * *

General Louis Blaine stood over the woman who lay sobbing at his feet, her hands shackled before her. The confidential interpreter, a small weaselly man with big round glasses, stood to one side holding a handkerchief over his mouth. He refused to look at either Blaine or the prisoner.

"Now let me get this straight—you're just a cook and you don't know anything at all about terrorist plots?" Blaine snarled. The interpreter repeated him in rapid-fire Arabic.

The woman looked up at her captor pleadingly and cried out a few words which the interpreter repeated back. "She says all she did was prepare meals and didn't know anything about any plot. She thought the men she worked for were diplomats."

"And the firearms, the explosives, meant nothing to you?" Blaine dragged the woman to her feet by her hair, which had fallen loose when he had pulled off her *khimar*.

"She says that she was told that was how Americans practiced diplomacy."

Blaine glared at the little man before throwing the woman into a chair that sat at the center of the room. "Ask her where they went."

After a moment's babbling, the interpreter said, "She says she knew they were moving, but the only thing that they told her was Tariq-Al."

"Yeah, what does that mean in English?"

"It's a name; it doesn't really mean anything," the interpreter's suit coat was now soaked in sweat. It was clear that Blaine terrified him, but what terrified him even more was Blaine's lack of respect for the woman's human rights. He didn't believe the woman knew anything more than she was telling them.

"Is she educated?" Blaine snapped.

"What? Oh, uh, no, not by the way she speaks. Her dialect suggests rural Saudi Arabia and the pronunciation indicates a lack of education." The interpreter could not take his eyes off her bruised face. She was beautiful in a careworn way that he found appealing.

"All right, I don't think she knows anything either," Blaine muttered, banging on the secure door. A watch officer opened the door and the interpreter followed him out of the cell.

"What will happen to her now?" he asked nonchalantly.

Blaine favored him with an iron glare. "She's a prisoner of the United States and will be treated as such."

In the meantime, the watch officer had collected the prisoner and was pushing her out of the cell before him. In a flash the woman shot forward and grabbed a pair of office scissors that had been left lying on a table. She turned to face her captors with the weapon held out.

Blaine and the watch officer had their weapons drawn. Blaine shoved the interpreter out of the way. "Put it down!" he bellowed.

The interpreter shouted Blaine's order at the woman and pleaded with her in Arabic not to do anything, that she would be all right. The woman babbled back at him, then turning the scissors toward herself plunged them deep into her own heart. She was dead before her body hit the floor.

"Jesus!" the watch officer screamed, dropping his weapon to his side.

"Damn it! Who the hell . . . damn it!" Blaine was furious. This was no place for an interrogation—security was too lax and this was the result.

He turned on the interpreter, fire in his eyes. "What was she saying?" he screamed. "What?"

The man could not take his eyes off the woman's body, a moment ago so alive. "I, uh, she, she, she asked Allah to forgive her," he stammered.

* * *

David had no sooner tucked in to a big roast beef sandwich than he was summoned to the Situation Room. Eyeing the food longingly, he grabbed his coat and headed for the elevators.

When he arrived, General Seiffert was standing and watching General Blaine, who paced about like a caged animal.

"I don't know who was responsible for leaving them out, but heads are going to . . ." Blaine stopped dead and snapped to attention when the president entered the room.

"Gentlemen, what's happened to pull me away from my lunch?" He gestured for everyone to be seated.

"Sir, we have completed interrogation of the prisoner, but there has been a problem," General Seiffert began. Walsh noted his distressed expression.

"So what did she tell us? Anything?"

Seiffert gestured to Blaine. "Sir, she claimed to be nothing more than a cook for a detail of diplomats," Blaine said simply.

"Do you believe that to be the truth, general?" the president asked, watching the big military man keep his temper under control.

"I believed it at the time she said it, sir. She was obviously uneducated; therefore, probably not an operative of any kind. It made sense at the time." Blaine was uncomfortable and Walsh didn't want to wait for the punch line.

"So did she give us anything to work with?"

"Just a name, sir. Tariq-Al. Other than that, nothing, sir."

"Okay, at least it's something." David glanced at Seiffert. "So what aren't you telling me?"

"The prisoner was being moved to a secure holding cell," Seiffert said, "when she grabbed a pair of scissors that were carelessly left on a table. She killed herself, sir."

"With a pair of scissors?" Walsh asked incredulous.

"Yes, sir. That's why General Blaine now feels that she might have had more to tell. An uneducated cook shouldn't have the wherewithal to commit suicide with a pair of office shears."

"I see your point," Walsh swallowed hard. How did anyone deal with a people whose least important members were capable of something like that? "Does this name she gave us mean anything to you?"

"No, sir, I've got my people working on it, but nothing yet," Seiffert answered. "All right, get on it and get me anything you can as soon as possible." Walsh rose and headed for the door. He stopped to let two of the agents in his security detail enter the hallway before him. He smiled at Martin Briggs, chief warrant officer, and current star forward to carry the football. He placed a friendly hand on the man's shoulder.

"Hangin' in there, Marty?" David smiled.

"Yes, sir, hangin' in there." Briggs returned the smile, hiding his growing unease from the president.

* * *

David was headed back toward the bank of elevators when James Sercu rounded a corner and stopped there to wait.

"Did they get anything out of that woman?" he asked, falling into step with the president.

"No, not much. She killed herself with a pair of office scissors."

"I heard." Sercu shook his head. "Amazing commitment."

"You're not kidding!" The two men rode the elevator in silence, both lost in thought. When the elevator doors slid open, Walsh stepped out and stopped.

"Does the name or word "Tariq-Al" mean anything to you?"

"Oh, hello, Mrs. Walsh," Sercu greeted Sarah as she walked up behind them.

"Jim." Sarah took her husband's hand and squeezed it hard.

"How are the kids doing?" David asked her. She frowned.

"They're sick, David. Some are really sick. It's horrible."

He kissed her on the cheek. "Why don't you go and get some rest; try to let it go for awhile."

"You're right, I probably should," Sarah smiled weakly before turning away. "Oh, Tariq-Al is that rug store in Adams Morgan, on 18th. You remember; we went in there once when we were here about five years ago. I'm surprised it's still open."

Walsh's jaw dropped as the realization hit him. That's why it sounded so familiar! Sercu looked at him questioningly. "Have Seiffert and Blaine get up here. I think we just found our terrorists."

Fifty-Three

Piney Narrows Yacht Haven
Kent Island, Maryland

It was just a few hours before dawn when a black van pulled into the Piney Narrows marina, just a few miles from the Aberdeen Proving Grounds. Inside the van three men prepared for their mission, a mission from which none expected to return alive.

Earlier, a scout had pinpointed the yacht they would steal for the trip down the coast to the proving grounds. At the end of the pier, the *Bitter End* swayed like a ghost in the darkness. Quietly, the trio carried crates containing 300 pounds of plastique explosives to the yacht, where they carefully loaded the cargo in the bow of the boat and wired impact detonators to the decking before returning to their truck for their prize. Only the night before, a small team of terrorists had made a daring raid against an armory in Washington, D.C., and escaped with three Brunswick Rifleman's assault weapons, known to the soldiers who used them as B-RAWs. The device, a five-and-one-half-inch diameter spin-stabilized elongated boll, bolted to the underside of a soldier's personal weapon, and fired ammunition equivalent to a 105-mm Howitzer. Using tungsten balls for ammunition, each could launch three thousand a minute in a

150-square-meter arc, cutting through anything that happened to be in its path. The terrorists were counting on them ripping through the fencing and the mustard gas cylinders with ease, as well as being deadly against any chase boats or helicopters that tried to stop them.

As the first rays of sunlight warmed the farthest horizon, the terrorists swung the yacht into the shipping lane and headed south for the short trip to their target.

The craft moved rapidly through the quiet waters aimed directly for the Edgewood area of the proving grounds. Armed patrols randomly cruised the entire perimeter of Aberdeen, so the terrorists had to keep a close watch for military boats. The guards would shoot to kill on sight.

At Edgewood, 1,800 keg-shaped containers were stacked three high right beside the water and surrounded by a double perimeter of chain-link fence, the only protection for the 1,600 tons of mustard gas stored in the containers. From more than a mile's distance, the men could see the glare of the high-powered spotlights that illuminated the storage facility twenty-four hours a day.

They shut down the engines on the yacht and stopped their preparations for a moment to face the east. They each softly recited prayers for the success of their mission before returning to their tasks. They quickly and quietly readied the detonators and loaded their B-RAWs.

One man watched through binoculars as a patrol sped past in the distance playing its searchlights over the water. Once the boat was out of sight, the yacht's engines kicked to life and the bow pointed directly toward the storage facility. They intended to ram the boat into the stockpile of mustard gas, provided they could avoid the patrol boats.

As the yacht gained speed, the sun reared up over the horizon, effectively blinding anyone who might have been looking out over the water. They were well on the way to their meeting with the shoreline before any of the guards spotted the yacht and raised the alarm. Five patrol boats spun about and throttled toward the yacht at full speed, alarms blaring. On the shore, a general alarm was raised and the man on the yacht with the binoculars could see soldiers racing toward the ground-mounted artillery to try and blow the boat out of the water. He glanced at his companions who raised their weapons to target the approaching patrol boats. The third man targeted the piles of cylinders on the shore, his ammunition ripping gashes in the sides of the containers and sending mustard gas spewing into the environment. Several of the shore patrol succumbed to the gas before they could get upwind of it.

The terrorists managed to blow holes through two of the patrol boats before artillery shells, dropped into the water around them, sent up huge founts of water as they detonated, each shell falling well shy of its mark.

The shoreline was only a hundred yards away when the terrorists put down their weapons and knelt together near the bow of the boat. They had succeeded. The infidels would soon be brought to their knees.

The yacht grounded with a rip of wood and crunch of struts. It was only a split second before the blast of 300 pounds of detonated plastique filled the sky and sent a mini-tidal wave racing back from shore. The remaining patrol boats spun about and attempted to escape the fireball and rain of debris that followed the wave into the bay.

Onshore, a thousand pounds of mustard gas boiled in the heat of the explosion and hissed out of ruptured containers. The westerly wind caught the vapor and dispersed it slowly over the Maryland coast from Kent Island up to Baltimore before a prevailing wind swept it south toward Washington, D.C.

Within half an hour, little-used air-raid sirens suddenly found their voices and bellowed out the emergency across the state. Children were hustled into the interiors of schools as windows were sealed and ventilation systems shut down. Haz-Mat units sprang into action, although no one was sure what they could do. An hour later, hospital emergency rooms were overflowing with people who were caught in the open when the cloud spread.

The governor of Maryland declared a state of emergency in and around the city of Baltimore, resulting in clogged highways as people tried to escape the cloud. Baltimore/Washington International Airport was closed down and the Baltimore/Washington Parkway was little more than a giant parking lot halfway to Washington. By dinnertime that day, the mayor of Baltimore had appeared on television begging people to just stay in their homes with the windows shut tight until it could be determined that the threat had dissipated.

* * *

In the meantime, some twenty remaining terrorists began a full assault on carefully chosen targets around the District of Columbia, successfully contaminating the reservoir that fed fresh-water to the city, shutting down the naval hospital, the Library of Congress, and the Treasury Building. The city's hospitals overflowed with victims in the first stages of anthrax infection. Washington's homeless population was the hardest hit. Unable to find medical attention, the street people suffered and died in the parks and alleyways of the nation's capital.

The television broadcasts were filled with the protests of local activists, undeterred by the danger, who picketed the Capitol and the White House and demanded immediate action by the government.

National Guard units, medical teams, and paramedics were

imported from across the country in a vain attempt to keep the peace and to help as many victims as possible.

As a stunned nation watched, their capital city crumbled under the onslaught of a terrorist campaign that few believed could actually happen in the United States.

FIFTY-FOUR

The White House Situation Room
Washington, D.C.

"I FEEL LIKE I'VE BEEN ASLEEP AT THE WHEEL!" SAID PRESIDENT DAVID Walsh as he paced the floor of the Situation Room, his frustration finding expression in the waving of his arms and his raised voice. "How could it have gotten out of control this fast? How?"

The members of his cabinet and a few key staffers sat around the long conference table watching him silently. Walsh looked at their faces, the fear and apprehension in their eyes frustrating him even more.

"Okay, okay, I'm sorry," he said, shaking his head sadly before resuming his seat at the head of the table. "Bill, what's the word on Aberdeen?"

Bill Cassidy flipped open a file folder that sat before him. He rustled the papers, a frown creasing his face. "Well, sir, preliminary reports suggest that the terrorists stole a yacht from a small marina at Piney Narrows, loaded it up with plastique, and wired the thing for impact detonation before driving it straight into the shoreline at Edgewood."

"And no one tried to stop it?" Walsh snapped, regretting his tone as soon as the words left his lips.

"Yes, sir. The patrol boats that guard that section of the shore did round on the yacht and try to intercept, but they were armed with grenade launchers. . . ."

"Rocket launchers." Ned Seiffert corrected him. "I'm sorry, sir."

"Rocket launchers." Cassidy gave Seiffert an obviously dirty look. "They were able to take out two of the patrol boats before they could reach ramming speed."

"Fatalities?" Walsh asked.

"The crews of both patrol boats as well as about a dozen personnel onshore when it exploded. Twenty-three in all." Cassidy kept his eyes lowered to the folder in front of him. Walsh had finally allowed his temper to show, and no one at the table wanted to be in the line of fire when he erupted.

"And the other attacks?"

Walsh waited for someone to answer, and when no one did, Jim Sercu cleared his throat. "Separate attacks on the reservoir, the naval hospital and the Treasury Building. Another terrorist was stopped on Pennsylvania Avenue approaching the White House."

"Did they take even one of them alive?" Walsh glared at General Seiffert, then looked to Bill Cassidy.

"No, sir," Cassidy answered. "In every instance when military personnel attempted to apprehend the terrorists they either detonated explosives hidden on themselves or engaged the patrols in a firefight that ended in their death."

"Okay, then no one is left to give us any answers." Walsh glanced at Seiffert again. The general sat eyes forward, no expression on his face. "What about the mustard gas? What's the word on that?"

Again, Jim Sercu stepped up to the plate with the information the president was looking for. "The vapor dispersed over a wide area of the Maryland countryside. Baltimore was hit hard and has been declared a disaster area. The hospitals are overflowing and the Baltimore/Washington Parkway is useless. Local government has to bring personnel and supplies in by helicopter."

"Why was something like this even stored in an open area in the first place?" Walsh demanded, smacking the table with his open hand. "I thought the EPA had been on us to get rid of the stuff."

"They were, sir, and have been for a long time," Cassidy spoke up, "but the whole process has been bogged down in military red tape and fell through the cracks."

"Not good enough!" Walsh snapped. "What kind of environmental problem are we looking at here? How far can this gas spread?"

Harry Dent, sitting to Walsh's right, sat forward. "I thought mustard gas wasn't technically a gas but a liquid. Why is it even spreading that far?"

"It isn't a gas," Seiffert spoke up. "It's a liquid, but when brought to a high enough temperature the liquid boils and turns to a vapor. The vapor can then be carried by winds across miles."

"Can it be cleaned up somehow?" Dent asked.

"No, but eventually it disperses to the point where it becomes inert and then just fades."

"And how long does that take?" Walsh asked.

"It depends on the weather conditions. The hotter it is, the farther it spreads but the effective life is shorter. In colder weather it disperses much more slowly, but it lasts four times as long. Given the current conditions, I would imagine it's going to be around for another day or so."

"Well, it could be a lot worse," Harry Dent tried to sound optimistic, but the words were hollow.

"Yes, I guess it could. But in the meantime, we've got hospitals full of people who will probably have permanent problems from the burning and damage to their respiratory systems."

Seiffert shook his head sadly. "Why the damned stuff was ever invented, I'll never know."

"Unfortunately, that's the least of our problems now. We've still got an unstoppable plague ravaging Washington. People, I think the time has come for us to take some definitive action." Walsh stood suddenly. He noted the panicked expression take hold of Tuttle's face. He couldn't discuss attack plans with that liability in the room. "I have a couple of phone calls to make, then I want everyone back here in an hour."

* * *

James Sercu hurried to catch up with the president as he charged down the hallway.

"Jim, I want Marshall and Murphy in my office yesterday." Walsh turned to the head of his security unit. "John, for the next fifteen minutes, I want a detailed report of everywhere Ian Tuttle goes, what he does, who he talks to, everything. If he uses the men's room, I want to know if it was onesies or twosies. Got it?" The burly Secret Service agent swallowed a smile and headed off to carry out his orders. Jim Sercu, in the meantime, had dispatched aides to find Murphy and Marshall. By the time the president threw open the door to the Oval Office, the two men were on his heels.

* * *

Ian Tuttle was in a panic. If Walsh called a nuclear strike against any of the oil powers, it would mean the end of the deals and plans Warren Dunn had carefully set into place. And it would probably mean the end of Tuttle as well.

He was worked into such a frenzy by the time he headed out of the Situation Room for the guest quarters that he didn't notice the new Secret Service agent who had relieved one of his usual guards.

Tuttle's mind raced. He had to contact Dunn, but he couldn't even use his own phone. There were phones provided in the staff rooms on the lower level; he'd have to go down there and find a way to let Dunn know what was happening without being overheard. Tuttle pounded down a short flight of service stairs with his Secret Service escort close behind him. In the staff area he found a lounge where a small television played some soap opera or other and three women in cleaning uniforms sat around the set, cups of coffee cradled in their worn hands. Tuttle headed straight for the phone and demanded an outside line. In his haste and fear, he didn't bother to pay attention to any stray noises on the line.

* * *

Warren Dunn, in his posh suite at the Plaza Hotel, was marveling at the speed with which CNN was able to get reports on the scene of any major, life-threatening event almost before the smoke cleared when his cell phone trilled.

"Dunn," he said simply, lowering the volume on the set.

Tuttle's tension-wracked voice whispered down the line, "It's Tuttle. No control. They're going to do it. I can't stop him."

"What are you babbling about now, Tuttle?"

"Bombing . . . they're going to bomb," Tuttle whispered. "My phone, bugged, can't talk."

"Tuttle, you moron! Why the hell aren't you in there fixing this?" Dunn was enraged. With one simple sentence, Tuttle had sent years of careful planning tumbling around his ears.

"Can't . . . on to me . . . have no control anymore . . . don't know what to do." Tuttle was desperate and Dunn could hear his resolve giving way in every word he whispered.

"All right, I'm coming down there. Don't let Walsh out of your sight, got it?"

"But . . ." Dunn clicked off before Tuttle could protest. The little weasel had certainly fucked up things this time.

* * *

Tuttle listened to the dead line until the dial tone clicked in and the White House operator picked up. "Can I help you, sir?"

Tuttle slammed the receiver down and charged out of the lounge, oblivious to the burly new Secret Service agent, who pulled out a cell phone and relayed orders in a whisper.

Fifty-Five

The Oval Office
The White House
Washington, D.C.

WALSH SAT AT THE BIG DESK STARING AT THE EMERGENCY PHONE THAT he would use to contact Eli Mordachi in Israel. He mustn't, in all good conscience, discuss the next step with the prime minister. They needed full Israeli support if the bombing was to be carried out—not only for the safety of their men, but also the safety of the countries that chose to remain allies of the United States.

David had just laid his hand on the receiver when the intercom buzzed. He released his breath in a rush.

"Yes, Colleen?"

"Mr. Marshall is here, sir. He says it's very important."

"Send him in." Walsh adjusted his suit coat and smoothed his already immaculate hair as the door swung open and James Marshall hurried into the room.

"I'm sorry to interrupt, sir, but we've had a report from John Brandt about Mr. Tuttle." Marshall paused.

"Go ahead, Jim, nothing could be be any worse than the news of the past few days."

"Tuttle headed for one of the staff lounges and used a phone there to contact Warren Dunn."

"Oh he did, did he? What was said?"

"Mr. Tuttle informed Dunn that you were planning a nuclear strike. Dunn instructed him to keep you from proceeding until he could get here. He's on his way from New York City right now."

Walsh couldn't hide the disappointment in his expression. Somewhere inside he had hoped beyond hope that in the end Tuttle would manage to redeem himself somehow. But his gut told him otherwise, and that had been confirmed repeatedly.

"Okay, keep an eye on Mr. Tuttle and get someone on Dunn. We're going to have to move fast once he gets here."

Marshall, taking the cue, nodded and left the room. Walsh watched the door close. He had to come to grips with the repercussions of every move he made from now on.

With renewed resolve he reached for the phone and asked the secure operator to get him the Israeli prime minister.

* * *

On the other side of the world Israeli prime minister Eli Mordachi had kept a close watch on the news reports coming out of the United States. The situation didn't look good for the Americans, and if one listened to the Iraqi news, they had already lost the battle. Mordachi knew better, and waited patiently to hear from his friend, David Walsh.

When the operator buzzed through to inform him that President Walsh was on the secure line, Mordachi dismissed his secretary and reached for the phone with a measure of trepidation.

"David, how are you doing?"

"Well, I've certainly been better!" Walsh laughed. "Eli, am I interrupting anything?"

"Never, my friend, I am always available for you."

"Well, I suppose you've seen the reports and know how delicate our situation has become."

"Yes, I have. I will spare you the conclusions of the Iraqi press for the moment. What can I do to help?"

"I'll get right to the point. The terrorist incursion here is much worse than we were led to believe. Much worse than even we had guessed. Too many innocent lives are at stake now, and I feel that I have only one choice left."

There was nothing but a heavy silence on the line for a moment.

"I assume you mean a nuclear strike?" Mordachi said softly.

"Unfortunately, yes. We haven't found any other acceptable recourse. Secretary Howe has had no luck communicating the tenuousness of the situation to the emirates. I just don't know that there's anything else to do, Eli."

Mordachi could tell by the sound of David's voice that this decision weighed heavily on the man. Trading the innocent lives of his own people for the innocent lives of another people, a faraway people, was not an easy thing for any westerner. But this was a time of war, and sacrifices had to be made. Better they be someone else's than your own.

"David, I have already told you that I am behind you one hundred percent and the Israeli military stands ready for whatever support you need."

"I appreciate that, Eli, but you have your own war to deal with," Walsh said.

"I don't think that our conflict with the Palestinians will turn against us if we support our allies in this."

"I appreciate that, Eli. We can use all the help we can get. I have to meet with my cabinet shortly to finalize plans. I'll make sure that everything is coordinated with your government before I give the order." He was trying to sound more firm and decisive than he felt since he was rapidly approaching the point of no return.

Now David had to make a similar call to John Laughton in London.

* * *

Warren Dunn was in no mood for the condemning looks that greeted him as he entered the Bohemian Club's chapter house. He knew the whole plan hung by a thread, and didn't need these well-heeled fops giving him any grief over it. What did they know? They hid behind the cover of the organization and let people like him do their dirty work for them. They had no idea how difficult it was to control an operation of this magnitude—no idea at all.

Dunn's Italian loafers made small slaps on the marble floor as he walked purposefully down the wide hallway. They knew he was here and he knew they knew it. His every move was shadowed by the glinting eyes of closed-circuit cameras mounted inconspicuously around the manor. He glared up at one, imagining the fawning pawn watching from some security station hidden deep in the chapter house. He was simply in no mood for the games.

At the end of the hall, a butler, in full and very old-fashioned livery, swung the large oak door open and ushered him into one of the many private offices scattered about the place. Like all the other rooms, this one was darkly paneled and outfitted in comfortable, overstuffed leather furniture. A single tusk of an African elephant, about eight feet long and slightly curved, hung over the mantle—a million dollars worth of ivory and very illegal.

The high-backed leather desk chair spun about slowly as Dunn entered to allow the senator to turn and face him. His expression was not one of pleasure; anger burned in his pale gray eyes.

"Warren," the senator said simply.

"Senator, I assume you have been briefed on our current hitch." Dunn, not wanting to give the senator any more control than he had to, remained standing, drawn up to his full height, arms loose at his sides.

"Yes, I have been apprised of the 'hitch', as you call it." The senator's tone remained even, though the fire in his eyes blazed.

"It is nothing more than a hitch, I assure you. Once I can get Tuttle in a face-to-face meeting, I will again have total control of the situation."

"Is that what you believe, Warren?" Dunn hesitated for a moment, taken aback by the question. It was not what he had been anticipating.

"Yes, of course. We always assumed Tuttle would need to be closely controlled; this is just one instance of that."

"Have you considered the possibility, however remote, that someone may suspect your Mr. Tuttle's dealings are less than in the president's best interests?"

"Of course, but there has been no sign of it. Tuttle isn't that much of a fool." Dunn wondered if he believed his own words. Tuttle was a fool, but not so much of a fool as to turn over on them.

"Well, I'm afraid we don't agree with you, Warren." The senator slowly picked up a lighter and a cigar and worked at it until it was evenly lit and burning brightly.

Dunn waited until the ritual was concluded. "Why is that, sir?"

"Because of things that we have heard and seen. Because of things Walsh said when he addressed the House yesterday. We think you may have overestimated your control of the situation. We think your plan for regaining control will not work."

Dunn couldn't begin to guess what the senator was implying, why he was playing yet another game. "Do you have some other course of action in mind, sir?" Dunn chose to placate rather than engage the senator in an argument—wait it out, see what came of the senator's implications.

"Oh, yes. Yes, we do. You are to contact the White House. Inform President Walsh that you have just flown into town and you would like to do what you can to assist in this crisis. Then do whatever it is he asks of you. Put all your resources at his disposal. When you have sufficiently lulled him into reliance upon you, then you can sway our glorious leader in the direction we need for him to go. But you must work fast, Warren. There is no longer time to spare."

"But, sir, with all due respect, that would place me in the jaws of the beast, so to speak. If there is some indication that Tuttle is involved with me, then I would be walking right up to the firing squad." Dunn hid his alarm, his mind racing to find an alternative that the senator would accept.

"Yes, I suppose that's true. In which case, you had better be very careful. You definitely won't like the consequences should you expose any involvement with this organization. Do you understand what I'm talking about, Dunn?"

Dunn understood completely. There was once a highly placed and powerful U.S. attorney general who was discovered to have some unsavory dealings with militant guerrillas in South America. When he was questioned before Congress, he attempted to implicate the Bohemian Club in the operation. Shortly thereafter, he was found hanging from the chandelier in his living room, a note of confession pinned to his pajamas. The investigation never proceeded further.

As Dunn struggled to find his voice to respond, the senator slowly turned his chair back toward the fireplace, ending the interview. Dunn left the office and charged back down the hall, his mind racing. How could he limit his exposure and still carry out the orders he had just been given? There didn't seem to be any way out of it.

FIFTY-SIX

The White House Situation Room
The Washington, D. C.

"GENTLEMEN," DAVID WALSH STOOD BEFORE THE ASSEMBLED CABINET members and others necessary for the next step of the American defense against the terrorist attacks. "We've reached the point where certain decisions must be made and may never be doubted. From here on, there will be no going back. The position of the United States on the political map of the world has forever been altered, and our actions over the next few days will determine whether we survive this or lose all of the fruits of the hard and unending toil of the past two hundred years."

Walsh wasn't sure where he wanted to go with this address, but he knew he had to have the complete support and trust of these people or he would never keep the trust of the American people.

"I have contacted the Israeli prime minister and been assured of the complete cooperation of his government in whatever decision we reach here today. Secretary Howe, who was trying to gain the cooperation of the oil emirates in the Middle East, is on her way back right now. I don't think I need to say more than that she was unsuccessful in her mission."

The grim faces around the table watched him steadily. In

some ways, this small gathering was more nerve-racking than his address on the Senate floor the day before.

"We have attempted negotiation. We have tried to battle the terrorists here at home. Now we must look farther afield. These terrorists have shown that nothing is off-limits for their attacks. They have targeted our children, our hospitals, our military, and our resources. The water supplies of Washington have been contaminated. Thousands of people are now ill with the anthrax virus, and thousands more have been affected by the mustard gas that was released in the attack on Aberdeen.

"We can no longer afford to waste time fighting a few individuals here at home. I believe the time has come to target the source. I believe the time has come to mobilize our artillery and strike the terrorists in their homelands, as they have attacked us."

David allowed himself to regard the faces looking back at him. Harry Dent sat perfectly still. The reality was finally hitting home with his vice president, and the implications of their decisions were weighing heavily on him. General Seiffert also sat, looking straight ahead, his mind clicking through the details of possible plans while General Blaine watched Walsh with a knowing expression, almost pleased.

President Walsh slowly moved to his seat at the long table. He sat down, leaned his elbows on the table and braced himself for argument, conjecture and the pros and cons of their next step.

"Therefore," he said authoritatively, "I am ordering a nuclear assault on the countries that have supported these terrorists and refused to put an end to the violence and destruction that have placed us in this unsavory position."

The room erupted into conversation.

* * *

Soon the White House was buzzing with activity as the necessary preparations were made preceding the ordered assault. Allies of the United States had to be informed of the impending strikes, and reactions were mixed. The majority of countries agreed with the American position on retaliation. However, a few, like Russia and China, always suspicious of any move the United States made, expressed concern that the repercussions would wash up on their own shores.

In the Oval Office, the president fielded a few phone calls from foreign leaders, but for the most part he needed the time alone to be sure he was making the correct decision for his country. He sat watching the canaries in their cage, flitting about, oblivious to the threat around them. Walsh wished he could experience their innocence for a few minutes, just a short respite from the worries that pounded his every thought.

What if this was the wrong decision? What if it resulted in an all-out war? The responsibility was overwhelming, but he was the only individual entrusted to make that decision for the rest of the country. It was part and parcel of the job.

The phone rang and Colleen's voice spoke out from the small speaker. She was doing an admirable job of maintaining her usual efficiency and businesslike manner, which impressed Walsh.

"Sir? Mr. Dunn is on the phone. You did say you wanted to speak to him should he call?"

"That's correct, Colleen. Put him through." Walsh drew a deep breath. "Well, Dunn didn't waste any time," he thought. When the phone beeped he slowly raised the receiver to his ear. "Warren! What can I do for you."

"Hello, Mr. President. I think the question is more, what can I do for you? I've been following the news reports and it seems that you've got your hands full right now. I was wondering if there was any way I could help, given my connections in the Middle East."

David was amazed. The man was a master. "How could I ever have trusted him," Walsh asked himself? "Just between you and me, Warren, we can use all the help we can get. Your contacts might, indeed, be useful."

"Just tell me what you need, Mr. President. Just name it."

"Could you come to the White House? I'd like you to sit down with some of the cabinet and discuss a few things."

"Of course, I'm in Washington right now. In fact, I could be there in a few minutes."

"Wonderful, Warren. Just show your ID at the guardhouse. I'll let them know to expect you."

The line clicked and went dead. Before he got the receiver back to the cradle, there was a knock on the door to his private study and Jim Marshall stepped into the room, a grim expression shadowing his face.

"Jim, he's on his way."

"We know, sir. Colleen alerted us when he called and we tapped the line. The whole call is recorded. The question now is how to trap him?"

"What do you think the chances are that Tuttle will roll over on him?" Walsh felt the iron band tightening around his chest again.

"My guess is pretty good. Tuttle seems to be running scared, if we can just scare him a little more, he might sing quite willingly."

Walsh regarded Marshall for a moment. The two men hadn't known each other long, but they had become fast friends with a large measure of mutual respect. Marshall was obviously disturbed by something he wasn't saying.

"What's wrong, Jim? Do you see a problem with this?"

"Well, Mr. President," Marshall was torn. It was his job to think of all the possible permutations of a situation, but he did not know how to voice this one. "If you'll pardon me for saying so, but, uh . . . wasn't Warren Dunn a supporter of your campaign for this office? I seem to recall some rather large campaign contributions."

The same thought had been lurking in the back of Walsh's mind since Dunn's name was first mentioned. Certain members of Congress would love to get their hands on that information. He could easily be implicated in the same plot as Dunn and Tuttle.

"I can't worry about that right now, Jim. We've got to end this crisis and then I'll worry about it. If, when it's all over, I'm accused of any wrongdoing, I'll deal with it then."

"Yes, sir. I'm sorry, sir." Marshall was clearly embarrassed.

David rose and stepped around the desk. Placing his hand on Marshall's shoulder he said warmly, "For what? For doing your job? I would expect you to do nothing less." Marshall nodded. "Now, I want you and some of your agents present when Mr. Dunn arrives. I'm going to ask Dennis to sit in on our meeting. While that's taking place, why don't you have a little talk with Mr. Tuttle?"

FIFTY-SEVEN

Washington, D.C.

ACROSS WASHINGTON, D.C., ARMED TROOPS WERE POSITIONED AT EVERY public utility, subway station, public building, tourist attraction, hospital, shopping mall—anywhere the people gathered. Washingtonians were still not accustomed to the sight of so much force, and ushered their children away from the soldiers, giving them a wide berth.

Under the declaration of martial law, public schools had taken an indefinite break, but businesses and local government carried on as best they could. Some business owners used the local media to voice their displeasure with the early curfew times, claiming lost business. The lack of tourist business was going to hit the economy hard. Even the locals chose to stay at home rather than risk being in the wrong place at the wrong time.

Scattered protests still broke out across the city for everything from equal rights for Third World countries to the damage done to Maryland's wildlife refuges by the release of the mustard gas cloud. Most of these were peaceful demonstrations that broke up as soon as the National Guard arrived.

But the latest terrorist attack at the Dalecarlia Reservoir in northwest Washington had the troops themselves skittish. A single terrorist, loaded with plastique and a dead man's switch, had managed to kill fourteen armed guardsmen and nine civilians in the worst attack so far. Soldiers from one end of the city to the other now watched every person with suspicion, unsure about where the next danger would occur.

Outside the vice president's mansion on the grounds of the Naval Observatory, about a dozen protesters had decided to demonstrate on a number of issues mostly centering around what they perceived as unfair and undemocratic trade agreements, taxes on fossil fuels, and what little was left of nuclear proliferation. They were a quiet bunch who mostly waved their placards and shouted at passing cars.

General Louis Blaine, touring some of the postings around the city to check on security, stood just inside the entrance to the grounds watching the protesters. He would have preferred that all demonstrations be outlawed, and not just for the duration of the emergency. He found the constant intrusion of civilians in government business a nuisance. If they simply went about their lives, they would be told what they needed to know.

As Blaine watched, a man who was dressed simply in a windbreaker and khaki slacks, approached one of the men on duty and appeared to be asking questions. As Blaine watched, the man's questions seemed to grow in intensity until the trooper swung his automatic rifle around toward the man. Then Blaine noticed the extra bulge around the man's waist and a small wire that ran from his right hand up under the cuff of the windbreaker. Drawing his sidearm, Blaine moved quickly toward the man. Coming up behind him, Blaine pressed the barrel of his gun into the man's neck and grabbed his right hand, pressing the fingers down into the palm to hold the dead man's switch in place. Without hesitation he squeezed the trigger once. The terrorist slumped to the ground, the hair on the back of his head smoldering.

Blaine looked up into the astonished face of the trooper, the terrorist's right hand still clenched in his own. "Get the bomb squad over here immediately!"

Later that evening, Blaine's face would be broadcast repeatedly on every local and national news show spurring further demonstrations against military brutality.

Fifty-Eight

The White House
Washington, D.C.

"You just have to make it clear to the press that the man was loaded with plastic explosives and probably would have killed the guards as well as the demonstrators had the stuff gone off." James Sercu's tone was gruff, sending the president's press secretary, Asa Roberts, hurrying to relay the message to the mob of reporters waiting in the press room. David Walsh motioned to Sercu, who fell into step with him.

"Trouble?" Walsh asked.

"Not five minutes after Blaine killed that last terrorist, we were overrun with reporters demanding to know why we are practicing wholesale slaughter. I don't really blame Blaine, but it would have been so much better if there hadn't been news crews everywhere." Sercu fished a worn handkerchief out of his pocket and mopped his forehead. Tempers were growing thin and sometimes it was all he could do to keep his own in check.

"Pull yourself together, Jim. I've just had word that Dunn's limo has pulled onto the grounds. I've sent someone down to meet him and bring him up." David straightened his tie and buttoned his jacket.

"I hope we're doing the right thing with this, Mr. President." Sercu stuffed the handkerchief back in his pocket.

"We'll soon find out."

"Right this way, Mr. Dunn." Walsh and Sercu were warned of the approach before Dunn turned the corner. At that moment, Ian Tuttle appeared in a doorway across the hall. In the moment it took for him to register Dunn's presence, his face blanched and his hands began to tremble. Tuttle scampered across the hallway, nearly tripping over his own feet.

"Mr. President, nice to see you again," Dunn said in a hearty voice.

Walsh took his hand and pumped it vigorously. "You, too, Warren. It's been a long time. We appreciate you giving us a hand with this. You remember Jim Sercu?"

Dunn and Sercu exchanged handshakes; then Dunn turned to Tuttle. In a voice that remarkably betrayed nothing of his hidden agenda, Dunn said, "And, Mr. Tuttle, nice to see you again." Dunn grasped Tuttle's hand tight enough to cause pain, a subtle warning.

"We should get right to it," the president said, placing a hand on Dunn's back and guiding him down the hall toward the Oval Office. "We haven't got a lot of time anymore."

"Quite right," Dunn replied, allowing himself to be led away from where Tuttle still stood, sweat gleaming on his face. As they passed, Walsh dared a look at Jim Marshall, who stepped away from a secretary's desk and made a beeline for Tuttle.

* * *

Inside the Oval Office, David Walsh, Warren Dunn and Jim Sercu were joined by Bill Cassidy and Dennis Murphy. Dunn eyed Murphy wondering at the CIA director's presence for this type of meeting, but shrugged it off. The CIA was probably involved in whatever covert missions the president had up his sleeves.

Walsh and Sercu had discussed how to handle this meeting,

and the whole thing was being tape-recorded by a technician stationed in the next room. They needed some proof, any proof that Dunn had ulterior motives for offering his help, and that, at best, he'd had an agenda for all the help he had provided to Walsh since the beginning of his candidacy. And if that failed, at least they could keep Dunn sequestered in the White House until after they had carried out their nuclear strike.

As planned, Walsh jumped right in. "I suppose I should run down briefly what we're up against here and what we've done so far. What we believed to be a small terrorist threat has become a full-fledged attack on the United States. We've approached the oil emirates and asked for their cooperation in putting a stop to this, but have gotten no positive responses at all. All of our efforts to stop the terrorists have failed. We have only one option left, and that's a carefully planned nuclear strike."

David watched Dunn's face for a reaction, but the man's expression remained impassive. "I didn't realize the problem had escalated to that degree," Warren said, glancing at the other men in the room. "Have you considered the implications of such a plan? This could damage our trade relationships with other countries, not to mention the oil industry in this country."

"And the loss of innocent life," Bill Cassidy added, not hiding his dislike of consulting a man with personal interests to defend.

"I believe the military refers to it as collateral damage," Dunn said simply. "This is a big decision. No wonder you are taking your time with it, Mr. President."

"Actually we aren't taking any time with it. It's been decided. When you called and offered your help, I thought you might be able to get through to some of these countries through your contacts without, of course, letting on that we plan to blow them off the planet."

Sercu looked at Walsh, fighting to hide his stunned expression.

They hadn't discussed putting such a fine point on the situation. David hoped his gamble would pay off.

* * *

James Marshall followed Ian Tuttle into Tuttle's office and pushed the door closed. "I'm just worried about you, Ian. You don't look well. You did get the vaccine, didn't you?" Marshall didn't sound concerned, but in Ian's excited state he paid no attention.

"No, I'm fine, just a little stressed-out is all." Tuttle dropped into his chair and began fidgeting with the papers strewn across the desk. Marshall sat down slowly across from him.

"It just seems like you're taking this harder than any of the rest of us."

"I have a lot riding . . ." he caught himself, and regarded Marshall for a second before continuing. "President Walsh has a lot riding on the outcome of this crisis and, as you know, my career rides on his at the moment."

"Oh, of course, Ian, I know. But surely you have faith that he will pull this off, don't you?"

"Yes, yes, I'm just not sure that this plan to bomb half of the Middle East is a wise one."

"Have you expressed these concerns to the president?"

"Of course, countless times, but he seems set on taking the advice of the military instead of his own staff." The thought of Walsh blatantly ignoring the advice of his chief of staff, his campaign adviser, angered Ian. The color began to return to his face. The more he thought about it, the angrier he became.

"What other choice do we have?" Marshall asked. This was ridiculously easy, Marshall thought—too easy. He had to be careful not to have his trap backfire on him.

"Well, it's not like the terrorists' request was really off the mark. What harm would it do, really, to back off from trade relations with Israel? It's a small country; not a real power in any event." Tuttle paused again and caught his breath. "And, besides that, imagine what a little cooperation would do for the crude oil situation."

"I don't understand." Marshall leaned toward the desk eagerly; he wanted to make Tuttle feel like he had a willing audience. It worked.

"If we cooperated with the emirates, gave in a little bit more, not only would they call off their terrorists, but it would certainly improve the state of oil production here at home. Imagine the money that could come from that sort of arrangement. It's obvious that the whole oil problem would be solved if it could be consolidated under one government, one controlling body." Tuttle had done exactly what Marshall had predicted; get him started expounding on this peculiar ideology and he would spill everything. The pieces began to fit into place.

"So, why do you think Warren Dunn is here?" Marshall asked.

"Dunn? Well, ah, he controls a large part of the foreign oil trade through OILCO. Maybe the president is finally looking at the situation from another point of view." Tuttle was getting worked up again. His eyes were wide and darted about the room frantically. He chewed on a thumbnail and stared into space.

"Ian? Are you okay, buddy?" Marshall asked quietly, trying to draw Tuttle back into the conversation, but not break the momentum of the man's raving. Marshall had to wonder if they were dealing with more than greed. Perhaps there was a bit of mental instability at work in the chief of staff.

"Maybe," Tuttle said, a crazed glint in his eye, "maybe Dunn will be able to make a deal to stop the bombing. . . ." Tuttle's voice dropped away into nothing. Marshall waited, playing his hand out slowly, not wanting to scare him into clamming up. "Maybe

Dunn will be able to convince the president not to ruin our plans!"

"What plans, Ian?" Marshall asked.

* * *

Tuttle had given Marshall just enough information that he took the risk of putting the chief of staff into custody. Once surrounded by FBI agents and powerless to stop the course of events, he confessed only to working with Dunn to influence the president in the current situation. But it was enough to bring a treason charge on both of them and certainly enough to end Tuttle's career in government.

Tuttle seemed almost relieved as Marshall escorted him to a suite of guest rooms in the east wing of the White House where he would be put under house arrest until they could determine what to do with him.

Now Marshall had to get word to the president so a decision could be made about Dunn. He asked the president's secretary, Colleen, to call Jim Sercu out of the meeting on a pretense.

"I think we've got enough to press charges," Marshall quietly said to Sercu once the adviser had joined him in the hallway.

Sercu nodded. "Okay, call in the U.S. Marshals. We'll have Dunn and Tuttle taken into custody and see what we can get out of them."

Sercu returned to the Oval Office and delivered a subtle hand signal that told the president that they had enough information to question Dunn under more official procedures. Walsh acknowledged the message with a nod.

"So, what you're saying is that we have a better chance of ending this siege through negotiations rather than through direct force?" Walsh tried to pin down Dunn, but without much success.

"No, Mr. President, I'm merely throwing out alternative scenarios, if you will. In business you cannot make a firm decision without first considering all the options and all the possible outcomes. I thought you wanted a fresh perspective on the situation."

"What I wanted, Warren, was your cooperation in contacting the leaders of these countries and delivering an ultimatum."

"Ultimatums don't work with the Muslims, sir. You must be aware of that." Dunn was getting annoyed and his anger slipped through his defenses occasionally, though he forced himself to remain calm.

Walsh knew he was pushing buttons that might set off the man and wished he could push him over the edge before the Marshals arrived. They needed all the evidence they could get. "So, you don't have that kind of influence then?"

Dunn's eyes flashed, and Walsh couldn't help but smile. Something might finally be going right.

* * *

All activity in the corridors of the White House came to a halt when twelve brawny U.S. Marshals marched through the rear entrance and split into two groups. One group headed for the guest quarters in the east wing. The other headed directly for the Oval Office. Asa Roberts had managed to keep the reporters confined to the press room. The rest of the White House staff knew better than to ask questions.

When the president's secretary buzzed the intercom, David Walsh knew that he could relax just slightly with one potential catastrophe averted.

The six marshals entered the office and approached Warren Dunn. The senior officer announced, "Mr. Warren Dunn, you are under arrest for suspicion of treasonous activities against the United States."

The look on Dunn's face said it all. The marshals quickly put him into handcuffs and marched him out of the Oval Office, each man saluting the president as he left.

In the east wing, a similar scene played out for Ian Tuttle, who handed himself over to the marshals' care with a sense of relief. At least Dunn would no longer be able to reach him.

* * *

Walsh looked at the faces standing around the Oval Office. Dennis Murphy had a self-satisfied expression in his eyes and gave the president a small smile. Jim Sercu pulled out his ever-present handkerchief and mopped his forehead. Bill Cassidy only sighed.

"Well, gentlemen, we still have some other fish to fry. We better get to it."

Fifty-Nine

50,000 Feet Over the Mediterranean Sea

Four specially outfitted B-52 bombers flew in an attack formation over the quiet waters of the Mediterranean Sea. From so high up the world looked deceptively peaceful.

Colonel Daniel Landis watched the horizon from the cockpit of the lead bomber. The crew of each plane had been through rigorous training and knew the drill inside out and backward. If they met no opposition, the mission would be a cakewalk. It was the guys on the ground shooting back at them that they had to worry about. The bombers ran under radio silence until they met up with their Israeli and British escorts. Landis would feel a lot better when they were flanked by F-15s.

Landis thought about the cargo the plane carried in its huge bombbay. Five minutes earlier, he had made final check-in with the chairman of the joint chiefs. At that time he and his copilot, and the pilots and co-pilots of the other three planes, had opened the code safe mounted beneath the control console in the cockpit. Inside were the arming codes that matched the same codes the president had sent to NORAD earlier in the day. With those codes, the chief bombardier on each plane would arm the nuclear missile and prepare for the final run to its assigned target.

At the same time a coded signal crackled over Landis's headset, he caught sight of the British escort that would accompany his plane to its target in Iraq. A similar squadron fell into position around a second bomber that headed for Afghanistan. An Israeli squad would join the third bomber for its run on Yemen. The fourth bomber would maintain altitude, prepared to back up any strike that failed.

Landis drew a deep breath of the canned air being pumped into the cockpit; it tasted stale. He nodded to his copilot, and the huge plane banked away from the formation tailed by its escort and headed for its assigned target.

"Good luck, guys," Landis thought, praying he would see them all again in a few hours, none the worse for the wear.

Sixty

The White House Situation Room
Washington, D.C.

The preparations were complete, and President Walsh's staff gathered in the Situation Room to witness the final order. Most of the staff of the White House had been sent home. The more critical workers were moved to the bunkers at White Súlfur Springs where they would carry on the work of the government until the crisis had passed. Congress had called a special session and was busily making its plans for coping with the potential war.

Asa Roberts addressed the press corps telling them only that the president would be making an address. Their interest piqued, the reporters raced to the bank of phones in the press room to alert their offices.

David Walsh managed to find a half hour to take a quick shower and change into some fresh clothes. Sarah had hovered over him during the entire time, asking him general questions about what would happen next and what he needed her to do. When he was again clean shaven and dressed, he took his wife in his arms and kissed her long and passionately.

* * *

The Situation Room was totally silent. The usual mumblings and murmurings were hushed and those assembled waited for the president's arrival. When the door swung open, all eyes turned to watch the president enter the room.

"Sit down everyone, please." When they were all seated, Walsh turned and gestured to his chief warrant officer, who approached the long conference table and carefully laid the big leather briefcase on its surface.

Taking the silver key from its chain around his neck, the officer turned to the president. Walsh fished the key out from under his shirt and both men slid their keys smoothly into the locks of the briefcase, clicked them open, and raised the lid.

Walsh took a deep breath before he looked into the case. The lid of the briefcase held several plain file folders containing necessary documentation. The body of the case was filled with the electronics that would send the final order to NORAD headquarters. Walsh stared at the two red lights, unblinking like silent eyes staring out at him.

He was suddenly overwhelmed by the responsibility of this decision. There were so many lives at stake, both in the United States and on the other side of the world. Walsh looked around at the faces looking back at him from around the room.

To his right, vice president Harry Dent appeared cool and composed, having fully come to grips with the situation and the necessity of this course of action. Dent nodded once, as if to say, "I'm with you."

Ned Seiffert regarded his president, his face set in an indifferent expression that was betrayed by the emotion in his eyes.

Jim Sercu, Bill Cassidy, James Marshall and Dennis Murphy watched Walsh closely. The others displayed a mix of fear and sadness that David didn't remember ever seeing on their faces before.

"Mr. President," Jim Sercu spoke from Walsh's left. "It's time. The British and Israelis are waiting."

David smiled weakly at his friend and adviser and looked back into the case. It was time. There was no going back now. He looked to the warrant officer and both men inserted their keys in the transmission locks below the glowing red lights. At precisely the same moment, they both turned their keys to the right and the red lights began to blink green. If the transmission was not made within thirty seconds, the system would reset and the locks would have to be activated again before the order could be sent.

With a final deep breath, Walsh pressed the button sending the order to NORAD and activating the first retaliatory strike launched from American shores.

Deep inside a mountain in the Rocky Mountains of Colorado, the order was received and relayed through the chain of command. The outer doors to the mountain complex were sealed, all life-support systems switched to self-supporting, and all communication systems went into a rotating encryption designed to keep spy planes and satellites from picking up the transmissions.

In Fort Knox, Kentucky, similar events were taking place at the National Depository. All military bases across the country were placed on full alert and reserve forces were activated.

In Washington, D.C., the staff of the Smithsonian Institution hurried to move the nation's treasures into secure vaults and storage facilities in subbasements below the museums. The Constitution, Declaration of Independence, and Bill of Rights were moved into specially designed vaults a hundred feet below the city streets where they would be preserved no matter what the outcome of the conflict.

* * *

President David Walsh stepped up to the podium in the press conference room of the White House to make an announcement that no American had heard since 1945. This room too grew silent in anticipation, but unlike those assembled in the Situation Room, these people had no idea what the president was about to say to them.

"Good evening, everyone. Thank you for coming." David looked up to see Sarah standing at the side of the room looking at him with soft, wet eyes. She understood how hard this was for him, and having one person there who really knew him gave him the strength he needed to carry on.

"As you know, this country has been the target of several savage attacks from an unidentified terrorist organization seeking to force the United States to turn its back on its allies in the Mideast. Our efforts to thwart these attacks have not always been successful." Walsh paused and glanced around the room. No one moved. No one even blinked.

He cleared his throat. "I've been forced to make a decision that I never thought I would make while in this office. It has been a difficult decision and I want it to be clear that I believe it is the best course of action to protect the American people."

President Walsh suddenly felt as though he would never be able to utter the words.

"In approximately five minutes, U.S. aircraft will be joined by the Israeli Air Force and the British Royal Air Force in a strategic attack on specific targets in Iraq, Yemen and Afghanistan. Nuclear warheads will be dropped on these targets. We will keep you apprised of the situation as events progress."

He turned away from the podium and moved toward the door as Asa Roberts stepped up behind him and announced there would be no questions taken.

The reporters were in an uproar. Questions flew at Walsh's retreating back. He ignored them, his mind filled with the enormity of what was happening on the other side of the world.

Sarah stepped up beside him and snaked her hand through

his arm. He looked extremely pale to her, and she was worried that the stress had finally become too much for him. At the door to the Oval Office, he turned and looked at her. She nodded and allowed him to go in alone.

* * *

President David Walsh felt as if he were looking over the edge of an abyss and there was nowhere else to go. He had been advised that he still had ten minutes or so to recall the bombers and end the attack, but he also knew that he had to prove to the terrorists and the rest of the world that America could still take care of herself, and was still the world power she had always been.

He sank slowly into his desk chair, his eyes unfocused and unseeing. The room was as quiet as a tomb. When the intercom beeped, he flinched, the noise like a rasp on his already frayed nerves.

"Yes," his voice sounded like a croak.

"It's prime minister Laughton, sir, on the secure line."

"Thank you, Colleen." Walsh laid a hand on the receiver, but didn't pick up the phone. He imagined the bombers cruising high above the clouds, zeroing in on their unsuspecting targets thousands of miles away.

Walsh slowly raised the phone to his ear. "David Walsh," he mumbled.

"David? You don't sound so good, old son." Laughton's voice could have been coming from the next room.

Walsh imagined he could hear the soft rustle of the man's immaculately tailored suits, and the tea cooling in a china cup on his desk. "I've been better, John. I understand our planes are on their way."

"Yes, I've had that confirmed on this end also. It's only a matter of time now."

"Yeah." Walsh couldn't concentrate on what Laughton was saying. The world seemed very far away.

"Well, you've earned a rest. I suggest you get it while you can." Laughton obviously didn't know what to say or do.

"Thank you, John, for everything."

"If there's anything else, please don't hesitate to let me know."

"I will, John. Thank you again." Walsh let the receiver slip back into the cradle. He glanced at the clock on his desk. His chance to recall the flight had passed.

SIXTY-ONE

The Air Over Baghdad, Iraq

COLONEL DANIEL LANDIS LOOKED DOWN ON THE SPARSE CLOUD COVER that shadowed the countryside below the B-52. The bombardier's countdown echoed in Landis's headset, ticking off the last few seconds. With twenty seconds to release, a flight of Russian built MIGs appeared through the clouds and headed directly for the B-52. Just before they entered targeting range, the British F-15s barreled around the huge bomber on a direct intercept course. Within seconds, the British fighters had downed all three MIGs, clearing the way for the bomber to complete its mission.

Landis felt the shudder as the bomb bay doors dropped open and the missile fell away from the plane on its own course toward the target below. Landis banked the plane sharply and opened the throttle to move the plane out of the blast range as fast as it would go. It wasn't until they were well away that he remembered to breathe.

Then the flash illuminated one side of the plane. If Landis pushed his face against his window he could just see the swelling mushroom cloud behind them. A few minutes later, the shock wave gently rocked the plane, mute confirmation that their mission was complete. Within a few minutes, the same scene played out over Yemen and Afghanistan as the other bombers delivered their cargoes. The fourth plane, unnecessary, turned and made its way back to Malta where the four teams would refuel before heading back to the United States.

Sixty-Two

The United States

Across the United States, every local and national television station broadcast the president's announcement again and again to a shocked populace. Radical groups wasted no time planning demonstrations and firing off E-mails and letters of protest.

The nation came to a halt as everyone held their breath waiting to hear what would happen next.

All over the world, attention was turned to America. Reactions were mixed. Allies supported President Walsh's decision. Those who weren't allies opposed it. Only one thing was absolute: The world had to sit up and pay attention.

Sixty-Three

The Oval Office
The White House
Washington, D.C.

David Walsh was joined in the Oval Office by Harry Dent, Sarah, and his closest advisers, Jim Sercu, Bill Cassidy and General Ned Seiffert. They were silent as cups of coffee were passed around the little group. They had come together to wait, to have the support of people who shared the same apprehensions, to be together when the final reports started to come in.

David simply was numb. There was nothing left to feel, as he'd already felt the whole gamut of emotions. Now, he just wanted it to end. He wanted life to return to normal. Sarah sat on the arm of his chair and gently laid a hand on his shoulder. The warmth of her touch soothed him a little and he was grateful for it.

"How long before we know, Ned?" David asked.

Seiffert snapped out of his own thoughts with a start. "Anytime now, sir. They should be leaving the target zones now."

The room fell silent again.

* * *

Louis Blaine paced about the Situation Room waiting for the reports to be relayed from the U.S. battleships posted in the Arabian Sea.

One of his men had filled him in on the events of the day and Blaine wondered what the U.S. Marshals had wanted with Ian Tuttle. He'd never liked the man personally, a bit of a pussy as far as he was concerned, but to have the president's chief of staff escorted out by U.S. Marshals was a bad sign.

"Sir!" the major handling the radio snapped to attention. "Incoming from General Leland."

Blaine picked up the handset on the secure phone and listened closely. "Thank you, general."

* * *

The knock at the door to the Oval Office was rapid and purposeful. Everyone knew who it would be.

"Come in," the president called out.

General Blaine marched into the room, came to attention, and snapped off a salute.

"Sir! We have reports from the front."

The front? Walsh didn't like the term—it was too close to war, the one thing he was trying to avoid at all costs.

"Yes?"

"All targets have been attained and destroyed, sir. Our bombers are returning to Malta."

"No defensive attacks?"

"Yes, sir, but they were dispatched by the British and Israeli fighters. Seven MIGs downed, sir."

David let the news sink in. The attack was successful. That was something, anyway. But what would happen now?

"With your permission, Mr. President, I'll check on the status of damage reports." Walsh looked up at Sercu's drawn face. They all needed rest.

"Of course, Jim, go ahead."

"Now what?" Sarah whispered, half to herself.

"We clean up Washington," Walsh tried to sound matter-of-fact about it, but the enormity of the job made it impossible to be completely convincing.

"We still have to deal with the reactions from the Mideast," Bill Cassidy said.

"Yeah, that, too." David stared into his coffee, now cold. "But we've got a couple of hours before that becomes a problem."

There was a soft rap on the door, and Jim Sercu slipped in without waiting for an answer. The look on his face warned them all that something was wrong.

"What is it, Jim?" Walsh asked, dreading the answer.

"Well . . . sir . . ." Sercu struggled to find the best way to deliver his news. "It seems that at the time of the bombing, the head of the Afghan military was on the line to discuss a compromise with the United States on the subject of terrorists harbored within Afghanistan's borders. The general was calling from Kabul when the bomb hit." Kabul was the target city in Afghanistan. Sercu didn't need to say more.

"Have we heard anything from the Afghan government?"

"No, but Kabul was the center of government. I would imagine it will be a while before they can pull another one together."

Walsh didn't think he could be any more stunned, but this was a kick in the ass.

"Sir," Ned Seiffert said, "you had no way of knowing."

Walsh looked at the aging general sadly. "I know, but it does not make it any better does it?"

No one answered.

* * *

Reluctantly, Sarah and David Walsh retired to their private quarters to try and get some rest before the statistics started coming in. There would be diplomats to deal with, official protests and Congress. And then there would be the massive job of cleaning up Washington.

Sarah was already in bed when David got out of the shower and climbed in next to her. She wrapped her arms around him and pulled his head onto her shoulder.

"You did what you had to do to protect this country, David. You have to stop beating yourself up for that," she said quietly.

"I know, but I was the one who ordered the deaths of all those people, just me and no one else." The tears began to well up in his eyes. Now that it was just the two of them, he let his guard drop and the emotions rushed through him in waves.

"Those terrorists thought nothing of murdering schoolchildren. They felt no remorse. You do. That makes you more human and a better man than any of them."

David knew she was trying to help, but he could hear the tears in her voice. Nothing would make the pain easier to bear for either of them. He pulled her to him and they held each other tighter than they ever had before.

Sixty-Four

The White House Situation Room
Washington, D.C.

Morning brought no relief for David Walsh. He spent a fitful night dozing and dreaming of firestorms and destruction. More than once he had been jerked awake by his own screams, the bedsheets drenched in sweat. The exhaustion showed in his hollow-eyed expression as he joined his cabinet in the Situation Room.

"Good morning, Mr. President," they said in unison, the words echoing around the table.

"Good morning." Walsh dropped into his chair and gratefully accepted the cup of hot coffee that was placed before him. After a moment he caught Jim Sercu's eye. "So, what have you got for me this morning?"

Sercu cleared his throat and coughed. He looked no better than Walsh. None of them did. "Sir, so far we only have damage estimates, no verified figures as yet. It's too soon."

"Well, then give me a ballpark of the bad news."

"A rough estimate of the combined deaths in all three countries, both at ground zero and from the radiation cloud and the blast wave, is 9,345,000 dead, of which about 2,500,000 are estimated to be wounded or exposed to lethal doses of radiation. The property damage is in the billions."

David forgot to breathe. None of this should have been a surprise, but the numbers themselves were shocking. "How about here at home?"

"Our best estimates are about 140,000 dead in Washington, another 125,000 in Baltimore, and 100,000 in the surrounding areas. There are about 2,000,000 in all who have been infected by the virus and have yet to show symptoms or are hanging on in area hospitals. Most of those are expected to die." Sercu's voice dropped.

The numbers were staggering. So many wasted lives. So much lost because of the religious zeal and megalomania of a couple of charismatic leaders. The world had learned so little from Hitler and the Nazis.

Walsh looked around the table at the careworn faces of his cabinet and staff. They had been through a lot together and the crisis still wasn't over. His gaze settled on his press secretary.

"Asa, what kind of a statement have we released to the press?"

"Very little, sir, mostly that you are waiting for damage results from the air raids before releasing a formal statement."

"Okay, and what about Congress?"

"It's in an uproar, sir," Sercu spoke up. "It's almost equally divided, and not down party lines. Blake is leading the opponents. There've been some rumblings about calling for an impeachment. But the supporters seem to be screaming just as loudly. They will, of course, expect you to address them about everything."

"Of course," Walsh echoed sarcastically. "And the cleanup here at home?"

"Progressing, sir, as best as we can," Neil Underwood, secretary of interior, chimed in. "We've shut down public water systems, except sewage, and we've got teams working on bacterial filters to be installed in the waste processing plants. We're trucking in water supplies. But there's still a serious shortage of hospital beds and medical facilities. We can't ship patients out to other hospitals because of the contamination threat."

"Can we get volunteer doctors to come and handle the overflow? Maybe set up some of the government buildings as field hospitals?" Walsh asked, starting to feel more confident now that he had a proactive role to play.

"Some doctors are already being flown in. We're still looking for more, and I'll look into the field hospital idea, sir." Underwood began scribbling notes.

"Okay, what else?" Walsh threw the question out to the table.

Bill Cassidy was first to speak. "Mr. President, we're going to have to deal with negative reactions from the surrounding countries—Saudi Arabia, Yemen, Turkey. There are already rumblings about the oil supplies to this country being cut off."

"That's to be expected. We'll just have to cope with it. If we can't convince them otherwise or influence OPEC, then we'll start looking at alternative fuel sources, something that should have happened long ago."

An aide moved silently around the table and handed a slip of paper to General Ned Seiffert, who had been keeping his own counsel throughout the meeting. He scanned it briefly, then looked to the president.

"Go ahead, Ned. What is it?"

"Mr. President, we have early reports—and these aren't confirmed yet—but reconnaissance missions are reporting the destruction of the suspected hideouts of both Saddam Hussein and Osama bin Laden, and the complete destruction of Saddam's compound outside Baghdad. According to sources within the countries themselves, it is beginning to look like both men were killed in the bombing."

A hush fell over the table. David blinked at Seiffert, hardly believing what he had just heard. Could they actually have hit the real targets of the retaliation? It hardly seemed possible.

"You mean?" Walsh choked out.

"Yes, sir, we may well have eliminated further threats at the source."

Sixty-Five

One Week Later

The world was a different place. Places long known as Baghdad, Basra and Kabul no longer existed. Shortly after the bombing raids, the Arab oil powers met and determined to make America pay for the attack by shutting down all supply lines to the United States and her allies. With Jordan's support and backed by the threat of further retaliation by the United States, the United Nations was about to step in and take control of OPEC.

Suddenly, events were moving very fast.

In the United Staes, the cleanup of Washington, D.C., and the surrounding area progressed at a slow but steady rate. Death rates had finally begun to lessen and the first survivors of the virus were being sent home from hospitals.

President David Walsh found himself unable to duck the spotlight for long. Once General Blaine and his team had rooted out the remaining terrorists and destroyed the stockpiles of weapons and contaminated material, life in Washington could begin to return to normal.

It was a hazy sort of Washington morning, the promise of spring just around the corner in the warming breezes blowing in off the coast. President Walsh had been convinced to spend a few hours away from the White House making personal appearances at hospitals and shelters. As Jim Sercu had reminded him, the game of politics never took a break, not even for a national disaster. Sarah sat with him in the back of the armored presidential limousine, talking about the children they had visited in a special isolation ward at George Washington University Hospital. Some were still struggling with complications from the anthrax infection. Some, on life support, were not expected to celebrate their next birthdays. While Sarah dabbed at her red eyes with a handkerchief, David was repeatedly drawn to the scene outside the limo's bulletproof windows. Almost no traffic competed for space on the wide avenues around Washington's central mall—the existing traffic was mostly military or trucks carrying in supplies. There were few passenger cars or taxis. The national monuments, once bustling with tourists, were eerily empty, the mall itself abandoned, and the Smithsonian museums locked tight. He had never seen Washington so deserted, not even in the off-season when the tourists headed for sunnier climates.

Sarah had grown quiet, her gaze matching her husband's, locked on the barren city around them.

"I'll be happy when the tourists come back," she said softly.

"Even the White House tours?" Walsh took her hand and smiled. She hated the intrusion of the regular guided tours of the White House and used to hide in her office when they were scheduled.

"If there was just one guided tour, I'd personally go down and say hello to each and every one of them!" she laughed. Walsh grinned at the sound. It was so good to hear happiness in his wife's voice again. It had been far too long. He resolved that no matter what challenges might face him in the future, he was not going to risk losing her again.

"Are the cherry blossoms due soon?" Sarah asked, her face open and childlike.

"I don't know for sure. Hey, Martin, when are the cherry blossoms due?"

The burly Secret Service agent who sat with them glanced at the date on his watch. "Another couple of weeks I'd say, sir." He smiled warmly at the First Lady. Everyone was starting to relax and be thankful they had survived, so David decided to let the man's slip of decorum go. He grinned back.

The car rolled to a stop at a red light. Sarah, momentarily lost in the comfort of the moment, reached over and touched the control that rolled down her side window halfway.

"Mrs. Walsh!" the Secret Service agent threw himself across the car, between Sarah and the window, but not before David caught a glimpse of a man, dressed simply and wrapped in a light coat, running toward their car. As he approached he reached inside his coat and screamed, "Death to American scum!" The words were barely off his lips before a volley of gunfire erupted from the lead car and the car directly behind the limousine. The man hit the ground in a shower of blood, skidded several feet, and came to rest against the side of the limo. Gunshots continued to pluck at his body for a few seconds, then silence flooded the street.

President Walsh grabbed Sarah and crushed her to his chest; she shook violently but not a sound left her lips. Their Secret Service agent peered out of the open window while the body was dragged away from the car. Several agents kept their guns trained on the corpse, while the rest fanned out around the street and directed the attendant police officers in a search of the area.

Martin took a deep breath, looked back at the First Couple and said, "Stay here, please, sir." He raised the window and climbed quickly out of the car, shutting the door behind him. The driver clicked the automatic locks back in place. Walsh could hear someone giving Martin hell about the window.

Sarah finally began to relax and sagged into her husband's arms, and he realized she was sobbing softly. "I'm sorry, David. Oh my God, I'm so sorry," she gasped.

"It's all right. We were all feeling too comfortable. Nobody got hurt, that's the main thing."

"But that man . . ."

"You don't have to worry about that man, Sarah. He can't hurt us anymore."

There was a tap on the window and the lock clicked allowing a different agent to slide into the seat across from the president.

"With your permission, sir, we're going to postpone the rest of your schedule and return to the White House."

Walsh suddenly felt the prison walls closing in on him again and would have insisted they continue, but he knew Sarah wouldn't be able to go on.

"That's a good idea. Take us home."

Sixty-Six

The Oval Office
The White House
Washington, D.C.

President Walsh was in his favorite place in the Oval Office, at the window overlooking the Rose Garden. The silence outside the window disturbed him. It was midday and he knew the sky over Washington should have been filled with commercial air traffic. The streets he could see in the distance should have been filled with traffic, and the sidewalks with the first of the early spring tourists. But Washington remained silent while her people worked to clean up their neighborhoods and get their sick back home. The cemeteries were the busiest places in town. And that thought greatly saddened him as he recalled the faces of the children he and Sarah had visited at local hospitals. They could clean up the city, and slowly things would start to look normal again, but the grief and the fear that from now on would be part and parcel of their lives would never go away.

The United States, for so long separate and apart from the battles that ravaged other parts of the world, was now just as much a battlefield as Gaza, Beirut, Bosnia and India. The troubles of the world had finally come home.

David knew he was wasting valuable time just staring out the window, but on a deeper level he also knew that he needed it. For the first time since he took office, there was nothing that could not wait for five minutes.

The peace was shattered by a sharp rap at the door. He ignored it, letting his attention drift back out into the city. Another knock and he glanced at the closed door, annoyed. When the intercom buzzed and Colleen's voice called out to him from the outer office, David knew he would be unable to ignore it any longer.

"Yes, Colleen, what is it?" He knew the annoyance rang in his voice, but didn't bother to try and hide it.

"I'm sorry to disturb you, sir. Mr. Sercu and Mr. Cassidy are here and they are anxious to speak with you."

The carefully chosen word, anxious, told Walsh that Colleen would be willing to turn them away if he wanted her to. But the past months had taught him not to put anything off. The consequences could be too dire.

"It's all right, Colleen. Tell them to come on in." Walsh sat up, smoothed the wrinkles in his jacket and adjusted his tie, feeling the mantle of presidency settling back onto his shoulders like a familiar sweater.

Jim Sercu, flanked by secretary of defense Bill Cassidy, burst through the door and approached the president's desk. Walsh noticed that both men were finally beginning to look rested again, although he imagined the extra lines in their faces and gray in their hair would be there to remind them for the rest of their lives.

"Jim. Bill." He nodded to each of them before rising and coming around the desk to join them in the conversation area in front of the fireplace. "What's up?" He indicated they each take a seat, and noted they hesitated until he had settled himself in his usual spot.

"We just heard from Barbara Howe in New York," Sercu said,

dropping into a seat across from the president. "The UN has put the proposal up to vote."

"How does it look?" Walsh asked, secretly crossing his fingers.

"As much as she has been able to tell, it's going to go in our favor, but it may just slip by," Cassidy said. "The Europeans are behind us, Japan, most of Africa, Canada and about three-quarters of South America. But China and Russia are wild cards, and of course we know how Iraq, Afghanistan and Yemen are going to vote."

"Why are their votes being counted at all?" David knew the representatives of their target nations were still at the UN, ostensibly to look out for the welfare of what was left of their countries. But he didn't know they would be voting on the custodianship of their countries.

"The votes are being weighted by population and economic interest," Sercu said. "They're being allowed to vote only as a courtesy. The weighting makes their votes basically meaningless."

"Politics," Walsh thought, "we're playing politics to the end. "

"And the plan, did it go to the vote as we presented it?" Walsh asked.

Sercu sat back and seemed to relax a little. "For the most part, sir. There was a great deal of debate about giving only three countries control of the oil fields in Iraq, Yemen and Afghanistan, mostly Middle Eastern countries. But I understand that Jordan and Israel have suggested that they may want to keep quiet about it, considering their neighbors' current situation."

"I want to avoid threatening any more countries, Jim. Let's not go that far unless it's absolutely necessary." David still struggled with the reality of what he had done, and the thought of having to do it again was terrifying. "Any further threats?"

"No, sir, not since it was announced that bin Laden had been killed in the attack. Intelligence suggests that the threat came from a rogue cell that escaped our notice previously. They're probably too small to be of concern right now." Cassidy answered with a casualness that angered Walsh.

"We cannot afford to be blasé about any possible terrorist cell right now. So, make sure it is found and taken care of. Get Israel involved if you have to." The only good thing that had come from all this, David decided, was that now he could order the rooting out of terrorist cells and not have to justify his actions to anyone.

"All right, so if the vote goes in our favor, what happens next?" Walsh had been over the scenario so many times, he knew it by heart. But he had to be sure that everyone else understood it the same way he did.

"If the plan is implemented, the United States, Israel and Britain will be made provisional governors of Iraq, Yemen and Afghanistan, respectively. A governing body will be installed in each country to oversee the drilling and distribution of crude from the oil fields, prices will be mandated by the UN and profits will be used to rehabilitate the countries." Sercu glanced at Walsh, waiting for his reaction.

"That's new," David said, catching Sercu's eye.

"Yes, sir, the UN insisted on it. And I believe there is some logic in it. Without the redirection of profits, there isn't any money to begin rebuilding the countries. If we're seen as a benevolent governor, the people will be more open to a democratic government in the future."

"Which of course is the long-term goal of the governorship."

"Yes, sir."

"Has Egypt had anything to say about all this?" Walsh asked. He had been thinking about previous attempts to find a peaceful solution to the constant battling over land in the Mideast, and wondered what Begin and Sadat would say about his methods.

"No, sir, they seem to be taking a sit-back-and-watch approach," Cassidy said.

"Do we have any idea how they will vote?"

"Probably with the United States, if history is any indicator."

The president knew Cassidy was right. It wouldn't benefit Egypt to turn its back on an old ally. That was at least one more place he could turn to for support.

"When will we know the outcome of the vote?" Walsh asked after a few moments of silence.

"Probably late today," Sercu answered. "We've already had word from the Hill. Congress is putting together their oversight team."

"Well, we knew that would happen. Who's helming it?" Congress had already been vocal in criticizing the plan's stewardship of the Middle Eastern countries devastated by the bombing. They had insisted that a committee be appointed to oversee American involvement in the plan.

Sercu's expression hardened and he hesitated, letting David know that he wasn't going to like the answer. "Blake."

Walsh held Sercu's gaze for a long moment while the answer sunk in. Archibald Blake, the man whose conservative approach put the right wing to shame. Blake had been there to publicly and loudly denounce every step President Walsh had made since entering office. Walsh expected to have Blake's choice of socks or breakfast cereal brought into play someday soon.

"Well, we probably should have seen that coming, too," David said, shaking his head. "So we just have to make absolutely certain that there's nothing, nothing at all, for Mr. Blake to complain about."

"That won't stop him," Cassidy muttered under his breath.

Walsh smiled in spite of himself. He had good people around him and that's all he needed. Why should he let a petty little senator from Missouri with a Napoleonic complex intimidate him?

"What about the Warren Dunn connection?" Sercu asked, chasing the smile from David's lips.

"Well, there's always that," the president thought.

"Did the FBI or CIA manage to dig up anything on that?" David asked.

"No, all we've got is what Tuttle said in the interrogation. He may be right, but given the state he's in right now, Ian's not a reliable witness."

Tuttle had suffered a severe nervous breakdown when he had finally realized the seriousness of his situation, and now occupied a softly padded room in a high-security psychiatric facility in Virginia.

"Well, without something to connect Blake to Dunn, there's not much we can do." And now the man was going to have his nose and his spies in the Middle East.

The intercom on Walsh's desk buzzed. "Yes, Colleen," Walsh called out, not bothering to get up.

"Secretary Howe is on the phone from New York, sir."

"Put her through to the conference phone, Colleen."

The phone on the low coffee table rang and Walsh hit the speaker button. "Barbara, I was just discussing the vote with Bill and Jim. How are things going?"

"The vote is in, sir. The plan was passed in its entirety."

"That's it, gentlemen. We've got our work cut out for us."

Sixty-Seven

Federal Correctional Institution
Cumberland, Maryland

WARREN DUNN WAITED PATIENTLY FOR SOME WORD FROM THE OUTSIDE world. But as the days dragged by, it began to look more and more like his sponsor had forsaken him. Dunn's attorney had promised to carry a message to the senator, but Dunn could understand the senator wanting to distance himself from the situation.

He was shocked the morning the guard had banged on his cell door and announced that he had a visitor. Dunn assumed that his lawyer had come to discuss some aspect of the legal proceedings, and was surprised when the guard took him past the legal conference rooms to the main visitors area, and seated him behind a thick sheet of glass. A woman strode purposefully up to the window and sank gracefully into the chair. Dunn took in her short skirt, tailored jacket, and silk blouse before looking into her face. She was dark with a mane of thick black hair cascading around her high cheekbones and down over her slim shoulders. It wasn't until he had been caught in her huge dark eyes that he realized he was looking at what had been hidden beneath the robes the day Najla had come to his private office.

"Najla?" he said in a whisper into the telephone receiver. She smiled, blinking languidly at him through the shield.

"How are you, Warren?" Her voice was smooth and richer than he remembered.

"I've been better. May I ask what you're doing here?"

"I merely wanted to see how my dear, dear brother was getting along during his stay in this facility," she purred.

"Oh, I see. Sister." He tried the word on for size. He would not have been allowed any visitors except for family and he did have a sister, although one he hadn't spoken to in twenty years. "This is a different look for you, isn't it?"

"Well, sometimes one must change one's wardrobe when one changes employers."

"A change of employers? Weren't they paying you enough?"

"Let's just say they are no longer capable of paying anyone. I have brought a message for you." She looked slowly from side to side assessing the people sitting around her.

"I'll bite," Dunn laughed. "Who is this message from?"

"My new employer," Najla returned his smile. "Your sponsor."

Sixty-Eight

Private Quarters of the President and First Lady
The White House
Washington, D.C.

The lack of formal functions at the White House during the crisis prompted some underutilized protocol officer to suggest a commemorative dinner to celebrate the appointment of the governing body of Iraq. President Walsh had to admit it was probably a good idea. Time to get back to the required pomp and circumstance of the affairs of state.

A formal summit had been planned to be held in Ottawa, Canada, to begin organizing the rebuilding of the Middle East. Walsh had been impressed with the choice. Several important summits had taken place in Ottawa over the past seventy-five years. Churchill and Truman had met there secretly to plan defense during the Second World War. Ronald Reagan, Jimmy Carter and George Bush had met there with various world leaders during their administrations. David felt this history might bring their mission some extra luck.

The night of the White House dinner found President David Walsh at the mirror in his private quarters struggling with a bow tie.

"Sarah!" he called out, putting a whiny pitch to his voice, which made his wife giggle from her dressing room.

"I'm going to buy you a clip-on," she called out, still laughing.

"Oh great, CNN can carry a special report, 'President of United States can't tie bow tie.' Are you trying to ruin my career?" He turned away from the mirror just as his wife floated out of her dressing room. Walsh drew in a breath and stared at her, tears threatening to well up in his eyes. There was the woman he had married. She wore a floor-length sleeveless gown of beaded, deep purple flowing fabric, a matching shawl tucked over her shoulders.

"You are the most beautiful thing in the world," he whispered, staring at her.

* * *

When the president and First Lady entered the dining room accompanied by the Marine Corps band belting out "Ruffles and Flourishes" as though they would never play the tune again, David Walsh finally felt that he had proven himself worthy of the Oval Office.

The gathered diplomats, cabinet members, congressmen, and a dozen other VIPs all turned to face the president and applauded raucously. David grinned and Sarah blushed charmingly. Walsh believed there hadn't been a more poised First Lady since Jackie Kennedy. He led her across the great hall to their places at the head table, shaking hands and smiling broadly.

After he had seated Sarah, Walsh turned to face the room. "I want to break with tradition for a minute and propose a toast." He picked up a wineglass and saluted the gathering. "I want to propose a toast to everyone who worked day and night to help bring this country through the terrorist crisis." The dinner guests cheered and clinked their glasses together. All but one. Walsh noticed the new head of the Congressional Committee to Oversee Operations in Iraq, Archibald Blake, standing quietly to one side of the room, regarding him coldly. Walsh shook off the feeling that the man would rather have seen him dead and called for quiet.

"I would also like to propose a toast to all the men, women, and children, here and in the Mideast, who lost their lives during the crisis and the resolution. We should never forget them." The crowd murmured their agreement quietly and touched their glasses together with a somber reserve. Walsh took his seat, signaling the beginning of the formal program.

"That was wonderful, David," Sarah said turning to him, tears glistened in her eyes like tiny diamonds. "I love you."

"And I love you," he said, suddenly forgetting the icy stare that continued to bore into him from across the room.

* * *

Dinner that night was the best food David Walsh had tasted in a long time. Or rather it was the first food he had actually taken the time to taste in a long time. He allowed himself the luxury of reveling in every bite, and anticipated the arrival of the next course like a small boy in an ice cream shop. Sarah kept pace beside him, her normally birdlike appetite as lusty as his own, and they grinned at each other like teenagers. David was torn between wanting the dinner to last all night and wanting the band to strike up the dance music so he could whisk his wife across the floor and grab a few moments of solitude with her in the middle of the crowded room.

When the dessert dishes had finally been cleared away and coffee and brandy offered around the room, couples began to drift into the White House ballroom, where the Marine Corps band was tuning up. The president pushed away from the table and offered his arm to his wife.

"I'm just going to slip away and powder my nose." She grinned at him.

"Your nose is beautiful just the way it is." He smiled at her and kissed her cheek. "I'll just wander around and be a politician for a couple of minutes. I'll see you in the ballroom."

Walsh worked his way across the room, shaking hands and clapping backs as he went. He had forgotten just how good he was capable of feeling, and found himself thankful to the official who suggested this dinner. He was brought up short when he turned to find Archibald Blake stepping up to him and extending his hand, the expression on his face unchanged.

"Senator Blake." He pumped the man's hand with as much sincerity as he could muster. "I'm glad you could attend. Congratulations on your appointment to the committee."

"Thank you, sir." Blake was civil, but still cold, almost menacing.

"You will be coming with us to Ottawa tomorrow, won't you?" Walsh asked, already knowing the answer. Of course Blake would be there.

"Yes, sir, I am, in my capacity as head of the committee, of course."

"Good, thank you again for coming." Walsh tried to move on to the next smiling face waiting for his attention, but Blake placed a long, almost skeletal hand on his sleeve, then pulled it away.

"If I may, sir, I suggest that you shouldn't allow recent successes to make you careless. I suggest that you be very careful." Blake dipped his head once and spun around sharply to stride across the room where the Secret Service manned the exit. David was frozen to the spot, stunned, until he realized that Jim Sercu stood at his elbow.

"Did you hear that, Jim?" he asked in a whisper.

"Yes, sir, I did," Sercu said stepping in front of Walsh. "We may have an even larger problem than we anticipated."

Walsh continued to watch Blake's back until he vanished through the door. He looked at Sercu, suppressing the urge to shake off the chill the man had left with his touch.

The two men looked at one another for a moment before Jim broke the spell, "Perhaps you should consider an early night tonight, sir."

"Yeah, maybe you're right."

Sixty-Nine

Andrews Air Force Base
Maryland

The President's helicopter circled the airfield once before dropping to a gentle landing next to two gleaming, new Boeing 747s. The planes were draped in bunting and a huge red bow hung across the bottom of one gangway. A crowd lined the red carpet leading to the planes.

Sarah grabbed David's hand and smiled. "It's like the launching of a ship," she said.

"Yup, you know they're going to ask you to break the champagne on her." He hadn't told Sarah about that part of the morning's ceremony, knowing she'd probably be both flattered and reluctant.

"Really?" she stared out the window, eyes bright and child like. David could only laugh.

On the tarmac, the president was greeted by Vice President Harry Dent and Mrs. Dent, and the two couples walked up the red carpet to the new planes where the president and CEO of Boeing waited to make the formal presentation.

"Mr. President," Dan Landro, the man in charge of the aircraft company, greeted them. "We at Boeing and everyone in this country are grateful for your diligence and protection during the recent crisis. Since your air transportation was unfortunately contaminated during the terrorist attacks, Boeing decided that we had to do something to ensure that you would be able to continue functioning as president of this glorious nation. Therefore, on behalf of Boeing, its five thousand employees, and every citizen of the United States, I would like to present you with VC-26A, tail number 30000 and VC-26B, tail number 31000, the new *Air Force One* and *Two*."

The crowd let out a cheer, forcing Mr. Landro to wait until things quieted down before continuing.

"Boeing is pleased to present you and the American government with these aircraft at no charge as a thank-you for the fine work you all have done protecting this country." Landro shook each of their hands, a little too enthusiastically for Walsh's taste, then snapped his fingers. A mousy-looking girl scurried up carrying a magnum of champagne, which Landro snatched out of her hands before waving her away. He turned to the First Lady.

"Mrs. Walsh, if you would be so kind." He handed her the bottle and guided her toward the gangway with a flourish.

Sarah hesitated for a moment before turning to grab Lynn Dent by the arm. The two women clattered to the top of the gangway and together hoisted the bottle in a batter's swing aimed at the presidential insignia on the side of the plane. It took three tries and a lot of giggles before the bottle finally shattered, spraying the president and vice president with champagne. The crowd roared, Walsh thanked Landro, and the president headed up the gangway to join his wife. The Dents would be staying in Washington.

David and Sarah turned one last time to wave at the onlookers before stepping into the plane. Walsh was greeted by two new pilots he didn't recognize.

"Welcome aboard, sir." The young man barely looked old

enough to have a driver's license, but sported a major's rank on his uniform.

"Major," Walsh greeted him, "I was expecting to see Jeff Scott."

"I'm sorry, sir," the major said, dropping his salute, but staying at formal attention.

"Sorry, major?"

"Colonel Scott didn't make it, sir."

"Didn't make it?"

"When the hangar was infected, Colonel Scott got too much of a lungful, sir. He was right there when it happened. He passed away two days later."

Walsh felt a hitch grab at his chest, knocking the wind right out of him. "He's dead?" he asked in disbelief.

"Yes, sir. I'm afraid so, sir."

Walsh drew a deep breath—there were no tears, just hollowness. So many dead, but until this moment he had not heard the name of a single person whom he had counted as a friend. He had known Jeff Scott for years. Their fathers had been friends, and when Scott had been given the command of *Air Force One* shortly before David took the oath of office, David had been thrilled. Now he was gone.

"Do his memory justice, major." Walsh turned away as the young man snapped another salute.

"I'll do my best, sir."

He walked down the small hallway to the door to his private office. Sarah was already there, waiting for him. "I'm sorry, David, I know how much Jeff meant to you."

"I did do the right thing, didn't I, Sarah?" he asked, forcing back the tears that threatened to ruin his composure.

"Yes, David, you did, and Jeff would have said the same thing." She wrapped her arms around him and held on until the pilot announced they would be taxiing to the runway for take-off.

When they were settled into the specially designed seats, belted in for takeoff, the pilot's voice crackled over the intercom. "Mr. President, ground control would like to speak with you for a moment."

"Certainly, major," Walsh answered, trying to get comfortable.

The intercom clicked and a slight whooshing on the speaker announced an outside connection. A deep baritone voice resonated through the speaker and filled the cabin.

"Mr. President, VC-26A, you are now *Air Force One*."

EPILOGUE

Joint Session of Congress
Capitol Hill
Washington, D.C.

PRESIDENT DAVID WALSH SAT IN THE SMALL ANTEROOM WAITING TO BE called to address the joint session of Congress regarding the Ottawa Summit and the future of the United States. His speech had been prepared while he flew back from Canada and he had been going over it for an entire day, but he still felt nervous.

The summit had gone well from a political standpoint. They had hammered out the logistics for governance of Iraq, Yemen and Afghanistan, and worked out plans for getting the oil fields up and running. They reviewed projections for oil output and profit margins, and began preliminary plans for returning the three countries to independence. He had even managed to convince them to appoint his old friend, Bill Derrick, to oversee the marketing of oil produced under the new plan. Derrick owned a home on Eleuthera, and David hoped to find the time to whisk Sarah away for a few days of warmth and sun.

From other points of view, the summit had been a mess. They were greeted in Ottawa by throngs of protesters clogging the streets. Radical groups from all over the world had managed to get to Ottawa. They were organized enough to ensure that every venue, every hotel, and every government office was besieged by screaming protesters berating the Americans for killing millions, the Canadians for supporting them, and everyone else for not joining the protest.

The demonstrations often became violent and resulted in a few terrifying moments for the president and First Lady as they traveled from the airport to meeting after meeting. But they were back on home soil now, safe and sound.

Overall, David was pleased with the work they had done and the things they would accomplish over the next few years. Only one vision stuck in his mind and kept creeping into his thoughts at unexpected moments. Archibald Blake had, as expected, attended every meeting he could get clearance for, but never once said anything, never asked a question, made a comment, or participated in a debate. By all accounts, Mr. Blake had never stayed out of a debate, but he kept silent for the five days of the summit.

Walsh shook his head sharply, physically trying to dislodge the image of Blake watching him coldly from across a conference table.

There was a knock at the door and Jim Sercu slipped in, keeping the door almost closed. "Are you ready, sir?"

"As ready as I'll ever be. Full house?" Walsh stood and straightened his jacket.

"Oh, yes, that is definitely a full house," Sercu said with uncharacteristic humor.

"Oh, great, make me nervous now, why don't you?" David laughed and clapped a hand warmly on his friend's shoulder. "Thank you, Jim, thank you."

"For what, sir?" Sercu looked puzzled.

"For all your hard work and loyalty, and for being a good friend."

Sercu smiled, the expression lighting his eyes in a way Walsh didn't think he had ever seen before. "Thank you, sir."

* * *

Sercu walked the president down the short corridor toward the door that would spill him into the chaos of a joint session of Congress. David ran through the list of special guests who would be in attendance for this pivotal address. Eli Mordachi, the prime minister of Israel, would be sitting with John Laughton, the prime minister of Great Britain. Their wives would be beside them with Sarah. And the king and queen of Jordan would be there.

As they approached the door, an aging man with twinkling eyes and a ready smile stepped forward.

"Good evening, Mr. President. May I say it's a pleasure to meet you."

Walsh took the man's hand and glanced at Sercu, who stepped up. "Sir, this is Jim Molloy, the last doorkeeper of the House."

"I thought I recognized you. How are you, Mr. Molloy?" Walsh recalled that many years back when the Republicans had wrested control of the House from the Democrats, one of the first things they had done was to eliminate Jim Molloy's position, turning the duties of introduction over to the House Speaker. "I was sorry to hear that the Republicans eliminated your role here, Mr. Molloy. For what it's worth, I think it was a grave mistake."

Molloy grinned. "Yes, sir, so do I."

"I think they're ready, sir," Sercu took the president's hand in a warm grasp. "Good luck, sir."

David could only nod as he watched Jim Molloy push open the double doors, step into the aisle leading to the floor and shout out, as if he had never left, "Mistah Speaka, the president of the United States!"